SHEN AND THE
TREASURE FLEET

Shen and the Treasure Fleet

RAY CONLOGUE

annick press
toronto + new york + vancouver

Annick Press Ltd.

Cataloguing in Publication

Conlogue, Ray
Shen and the treasure fleet / by Ray Conlogue.

ISBN 978-1-55451-104-4 (bound)
ISBN 978-1-55451-103-7 (pbk.)

1. Nan-ching shih (China)—History—Juvenile fiction.
2. China—Commerce—History—Juvenile fiction. 3. China—History—Ming dynasty, 1368–1644—Juvenile fiction. I. Title.
PS8605.O563S46 2007   jC813'.6   C2007-902458-0

Edited by Barbara Pulling
Copy edited and proofread by Heather Sangster
Cover design by Kong Njo
Cover illustration by He Qing
Interior design by Lisa Hemingway
Interior illustrations from a 17th-century woodcut of Zheng He's fleet

We acknowledge the support of the Canada Council for the Arts, the Ontario Arts Council, and the Government of Canada through the Book Publishing Industry Development Program (BPIDP) and the Ontario Book Publishing Tax Credit (OBPTC) for our publishing activities.

Printed and bound in Canada

Published in the U.S.A. by	**Distributed in Canada by**	**Distributed in the U.S.A. by**
Annick Press (U.S.) Ltd.	Firefly Books Ltd.	Firefly Books (U.S.) Inc.
	66 Leek Crescent	P.O. Box 1338
	Richmond Hill, ON	Ellicott Station
	L4B 1H1	Buffalo, NY 14205

Visit our website at **www.annickpress.com**

To Joanne, and the children.

"A rest from the road, and an end of journeying."

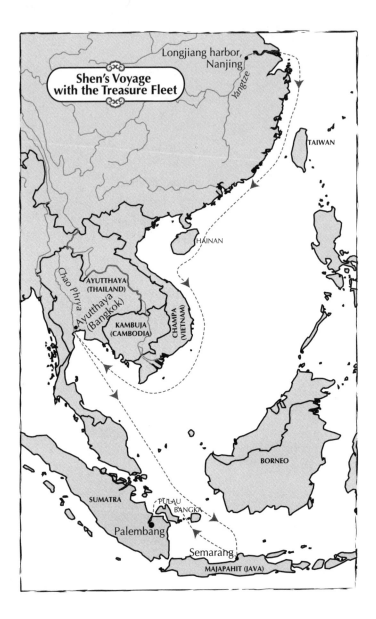

Shen's Voyage with the Treasure Fleet

Longjiang harbor, Nanjing

Yangtze

TAIWAN

HAINAN

AYUTTHAYA (THAILAND)

Chao Phrya

Ayutthaya (Bangkok)

KAMBUJA (CAMBODIA)

CHAMPA (VIETNAM)

BORNEO

SUMATRA

PULAU BANGKA

Palembang

Semarang

MAJAPAHIT (JAVA)

INTRODUCTION

OVER THE PAST FIFTY years, scholars have pieced together the tale of a forgotten—but epic—Chinese adventure that occurred 600 years ago. A fleet of advanced wooden ships, some 120 meters (400 feet) long, made seven journeys under an admiral named Zheng He. They traveled as far as Australia and the southern tip of Africa. A few people believe they sailed around the world a century before Europeans did.

The more I learned about this story, the more it seemed unreal—a romantic adventure. And like the best adventures, it ended in mystery. Sometime after the fleet's last voyage in 1433, the ships and all the maps and navigational logs were destroyed. For centuries the name of Zheng He—one of the greatest explorers of all time—was forgotten.

As bits and pieces of his story began to appear in the Western media, I shared them with my children. One day I told my son Jonathan about the colossal battle between the Treasure Fleet and the armada of the pirate king Chen Zuyi. Jonathan's judgment was firm: "You're making this up."

I wasn't, but it began to seem like a good idea. The story of Zheng He is far too rich with evil conspirators and pirate kings to be left in the hands of historians. It wants storytellers.

There is early proof of this. Zheng, who was a Muslim, longed to sail his ships to Mecca. When the red-painted behemoths entered the harbor city near Mecca, of course the Arabs wanted to know who was in command. Somehow they only remembered Zheng's nickname, which was Sanbao. And from this came the tales of Sinbad the Sailor.

In China, there were also stories about Zheng He, in which he is a villain. My favorite is a play written around 1590, where the murdered victims of Zheng He are pleading with the King of Hell to punish him for his crimes. As the King thinks it over, the gates of Hell are split open and in come Zheng He and his soldiers. Having run out of countries to pillage in the World Above, they have decided to ransack Hell as well.

We know today that Zheng He did not attack anybody (except the pirate king). By the standards of his time, he was open and curious about other religions and cultures. Why then were his ships destroyed? How did he become a villain?

It seems that it was because he was a eunuch, which means a man who is unable to have children. Eunuchs were outsiders because the family was the most important institution in China. This was the teaching of the ancient sage Confucius, and if you wanted to have an important job in the government you had to study Confucius. His teachings were part of the difficult exams that candidates had to pass in order to become high officials.

Confucius's ideas on good government helped to make China the most powerful country in the world. By 1405, when the Treasure Fleet was launched, it had a population of more than 75 million (at that time, England and France between them had no more than 3 million).

This huge population was ruled by an Emperor. But it was the Emperor's thousands of Confucian officials who ran the country. And over the centuries they had become very conservative. They had sealed off China from the rest of the world because they felt that there was nothing to learn from other peoples.

This changed with shocking abruptness in 1403, when an ambitious prince overthrew the Emperor Hui Di. The new Emperor called himself Zhu Di and declared that China must open itself to the rest of the world.

Because the Confucians would not cooperate, he put eunuchs such as Zheng He in charge of his projects. The first of these was the Treasure Fleet, which was, amazingly, built in two years.

The Treasure Fleet carried 28,000 people and could comfortably stay at sea for many months. When Christopher Columbus went to America nearly a century later, he had only three little ships manned by about 100 sailors.

But when Zhu Di died in 1424, the Confucians reasserted their power. The fleet was permitted one last voyage before it was ordered into port, where it was left to decay. Much later, a Confucian named Liu Daxia burned all evidence that the Treasure Fleet had ever existed.

But that's in the future. Our story takes place at that hopeful moment when the Treasure Fleet was launched. It had magnificent ambitions. But it also had a rather shameful job to do. The Emperor Zhu Di commanded the fleet to hunt down the deposed Emperor. It seemed that young Hui Di, who was little more than a teenager, had escaped Zhu Di's triumphant army.

It was said that Hui Di had fled to a foreign land. In reality, he was never found. But in this story—because it is a story—he is indeed found. And one of those who finds him is a young cabin boy named Fei Shen.

Since so many things in this story are real, you might wonder if Fei Shen was also real. Here is what I can tell you about that.

One of Zheng He's ships was captained by a man named Fei Xin, who wrote a book called *The Triumphant Tour of the Star Raft.* In it, he says that he visited eighteen countries with Zheng's fleet. I found myself wondering how Fei Xin became part of this adventure. Not much is known about him, but it seems likely he was a teenager when Nanjing was besieged in 1403 by the Prince of Yan. Upon completion of my book, I learned that Fei Xin's father (or grandfather, as the record isn't clear) was a criminal. Like my Fei Shen, he had good reason to join the Treasure Fleet.

In my story, Fei Xin becomes Fei Shen because my children had trouble pronouncing names beginning with X. And that is the least of the challenges in telling a story that is far away, in distance, culture, and time, from one's own world.

I spent many happy hours learning a thousand things about the extravagant and lost world in which a boy such as

Fei Shen might have lived. But, as a storyteller, I also changed many things for my own reasons. I put giraffes into this tale, though they didn't actually arrive in China until eleven years later. I have the fleet visiting Thailand (then called Ayutthaya) on its first voyage, when in fact it didn't get there until the last one. And Shen's sister is named Chang, a name rarely used for girls. Back then most Chinese girls had pretty names such as Chrysanthemum, Virtue, or Grace. Chang has many meanings, one of which is "assertive." I think this is the kind of name she would have chosen for herself.

And that's not the only thing about Chang that is imagined. Girls usually didn't learn to ride horses—or to read. Chang can read because her mother, as an actress, was one of a tiny minority of women permitted to be literate. And while it's true that some Chinese women even before Chang's time were famous for horseback riding, it's not very likely that Captain Fei would have taught his daughter to ride. Fortunately, he did, for reasons that will become obvious as you read on.

There is much controversy about whether Zheng He's flagships were really 400 feet long, as surviving Ming records indicate. Europeans never managed to build a wooden ship that big without using an iron frame. But I was so enchanted by the idea of giant wooden ships that I could not give them up. And it occurred to me that Grandfather Hu, pushing a broom in the courtyard of the Suzhou Acrobatic Troupe, might have a secret past as a naval engineer. In fact, he might have single-handedly invented a system of iron-framing a ship.

The historian will tell you this did not happen, but a storyteller only needs to know that it *could have happened.* China at that time had extensive iron mines and foundries.

Some realities of the time had to be respected, such as the systems for measuring time and distance. As far as we know, not a single European had visited China at that time except Marco Polo (and there are doubts about him). So the Chinese knew nothing of hours and minutes, or of feet and yards. Interestingly, some Chinese measurements were similar to the Western systems we use today:

CHINESE MEASURE	WESTERN MEASURE
ch'i	27–33 cm (11–13 in.), about 30 cm (1 ft.)
li	half a km (one-third mile)
cattie	half a kg (over 1 lb.)
watch	2 hours

There is not much information about everyday life in China at the time of the Treasure Fleet. But Westerners who lived there in the nineteenth and early twentieth century believed that little had changed in China for 500 years. So I have borrowed some of their observations for my story.

Could a country really stay the same for so long? Consider this: the Panther badge that Father wore was still in use, more than 500 years later, when the last Emperor, P'u Yi, resigned in 1912.

Ray Conlogue

CHAPTER 1

IT WAS A CHILLY day in early summer when Fei Shen climbed high up to take a look at the war.

The only practical place to do this in Nanjing was the Drum Tower, which was built on an artificial hill. From the top you could see far past the city walls, into the sunlit haze over distant rice fields. In peacetime, Shen and his friend Kun liked to go just to see the slack-jawed look on the guards' faces when Shen pulled out the copper token showing that his father, Captain Fei Lee, was an Imperial Guardsman. Then they were whisked right to the top of the tower, temporary royalty.

But now the Prince of Yan's rebel army was on the march. Things had changed. The Drum Tower was occupied by soldiers who looked as if they drank vinegar for breakfast. The last time the boys had tried to get in, one of the guards whacked Shen's ear with the flat of his hand. The ringing sound hadn't gone away until sunset. "I guess your magic amulet doesn't work anymore, topknot boy," said Kun.

Because they were friends, Kun knew he could get away with making fun of the tight bun of hair in the middle of

Shen's head. And Kun never let up, because he hated his own shaved servant's head with its two stubs of hair sticking up on each side like mushrooms.

Today, Shen had come alone. Avoiding the guards at the foot of the hill, he scaled the rocks of the steep hillside, scampered across the carriageway, climbed the second nearly vertical rockface, and lay flat at the top. The tower stood in front of him.

It was hard work because, even though it was sunny, the stones were slick from the heavy rain that had been falling on and off for weeks. Sweat beaded on his forehead, and a mosquito caught in his hair complained noisily. But Shen was filled with the calm that came over him when he was spying. As his pulse returned to normal, he timed the guards pacing the forecourt. When he knew he had a clear moment, he pulled off his slippers and made for the wall of the tower.

He hadn't climbed the red-painted wall before, but the thick mortar joints between the squared stone blocks were made for the toes of a thirteen-year-old. In moments he was on the terrace of the tower's upper level, where he knew there would be nobody but an old attendant who insisted on calling himself an astronomer. The man recognized the boy, whose round face and mischievous eyes did not quite fit with his habit of standing like a soldier, feet apart, head erect, and hands clasped behind his back. But Shen was familiar to him from earlier visits, so the attendant let him in.

Shen thread his way through the giant drums that sounded the watches of the day and night until he found the roof ladder. Emerging into blinding sunlight, he blinked furiously as he checked that nobody else was there and then looked to the northwest—where Yan's army was approaching the city.

At first the view made no sense to Shen. The green fields had turned a dull red, the color of radishes. Here and there he could see a snap of yellow that came and went, which puzzled him until he realized it was the wind plucking at the Prince's banners. That meant the red was the quilted knee-length tunics of the soldiers.

Countless soldiers. How could so many defy the Emperor? Shen felt the twinge of something painful, not a thought exactly, but a picture of Nanjing in flames. He pushed it away, and a rush of anger and indignation took its place. "How dare they defy Heaven?" said a voice in his head. "We will pave the streets with their bones and teeth."

That was Father, of course. Not that he actually spoke like that, except in Shen's imagination. In reality, Father made fun of the big-talking warriors in the folktales Shen loved, the ones where Monkey was always leaping on and off clouds and striking down demons with oversized weapons. "A real soldier saves his breath for fighting," Father would mutter as he settled in to read yet another dull official document.

But that was the way Father *would* talk, now that the time had come.

Shen's eyes swept from the blurry vista of fields carpeted with enemy soldiers to rest on the city wall. It was covered with what looked like dark, segmented beetles—the black armor of the Imperial Army, made of overlapping steel plates. The soldiers stood two columns deep atop the wall, which extended nearly sixty *li* around the city—the distance a man could walk in a day.

Shen took a long breath and exhaled the sweet air of pride and righteousness through his nostrils.

———

OUTSIDE THE HOUSE, FATHER'S powerful gray mare was watched over by two sweaty and nervous foot soldiers in the green-and-white uniform of Father's brigade, the Forest of Feathers. Shen opened the gate warily, noticing flecks of blue paint dropping off its weathered stile. Father's last promotion had brought them this modest courtyard house, with its small reception pavilion for guests in the middle of the yard and the family quarters at the back.

He heard angry voices from inside the pavilion.

"How many times, Beloved Wife, have I allowed you to speak back to me? But now you must obey! This is how we will get our son safely away."

Shen's mother, Lu Ting, shot back angrily: "All this trouble because that foolish child-god, that little Emperor, has changed his mind again. Why doesn't he abdicate and take us to safety? Isn't that his duty?" The wailing, angry voice was unmistakably Mother's. There was the sound of pottery smashing. Then, Mother again, frightened: "Calm yourself, Husband. Please! I bow down to you!"

Silence.

"When he talks about getting his son safely away, I guess

that includes me?" said a soft voice behind Shen. He whirled around to see his sister Chang's round, alert eyes, as black as Father's ink stone, looking quizzically at him from her long, fine-boned face. "No need to mention me, of course."

"What are they fighting about?"

"The city can't be defended. That's what Father says. We lost too many men in the last month trying to stop Yan's advance on the city."

When Chang talked of war as if it were a girl's affair, Shen usually found something sharp to say. But this information silenced him.

"Also," she added, "we're not supposed to know that. They think I'm at the market with Uncle San. And you—" She coughed delicately and looked at the sun. Shen understood. He should still be in school.

———

BROTHER AND SISTER ENTERED the formal room where guests were received, Chang following obediently behind Shen. The effect was comical rather than dignified, since she was walking on her toes so as to see over his shoulder. But she noticed that Father was not charmed by her antics as he usually was. His face was furrowed with anxiety. She lowered her feet to the floor and bowed her head.

Father was sitting on his prized plumwood chair, with the backrest shaped like an official's hat, broad in the middle and tapered at the sides. Mother was rigid on a wooden stool.

Shen and Chang went down on their knees and welcomed Father home from the palace, where he had slept for the past three nights.

"It's good that you're here," said Father to Shen, knitting his thick black eyebrows closer together, "even if it is because you have failed to attend school."

"I climbed the tower to see the Prince of Yan's army."

"And your observations?"

"I'm sure we'll defeat them!"

Father gazed at him appraisingly, and Shen was again aware of how poorly he played the soldier. He was slender, with clear eyes and finely sketched brows like Mother's. He had full lips, and when he smiled, the smile pushed into plump, lazy cheeks. To prevent this unfortunate effect, he held his head erect and jutted out his mouth.

"Hmph." Father's eyes strayed to one side of the room. He pressed into place the emblem of a snarling jungle cat sewn to the front of his black tunic. It was a year since he had been promoted to a Panther officer, the sixth out of nine ranks. For weeks he had fussed about the threads working loose on one side. Now he glanced at it without interest. "Damned Yan has a remarkable general. One of those eunuch soldiers like they used to have in the Song Dynasty. A giant with a blotchy face. Zheng He. Not even a Chinese name. I don't know where Yan finds them." He sighed. "The rebels may break through the walls. There could be fighting inside the city. For that reason, you must all leave."

Chang shot to her feet. "Without you? No!"

Father signaled angrily for her to kneel. Chang instead sprang onto a heavy wooden chest and caught hold of a low rafter. Pausing for a moment, she weighed her disobedience and thought better of it. Remembering the new responsibilities that came with turning twelve, she descended quietly and went back down on her knees.

"I respectfully ask to be included in this conversation," she said. " I don't want to be like one of those girls in the stories—"

"—who shrivels up and dies out of politeness," completed Father. "I'm not asking you to die, or even to shrivel up. But understand this: soldiers are not permitted to send their families away. The people would think the army was afraid. Speak to nobody about this."

Shen was shocked. "You're disobeying orders?"

Father frowned. "I am ordered to stay at my post until the end, and I shall." He let that sink in. "But my family is my concern."

One of Father's soldiers appeared at the door. Father's eyes moistened with tears as he gazed at his children. Chang thought, Why does he look at us this way? But she remained silent as Father left the pavilion to return to his duty at the palace.

———

KUN, THE SERVANT BOY, had been standing outside. As Father disappeared into the night, Kun appeared in the doorway and beckoned Shen.

"There's trouble," whispered Kun as they stepped back into the courtyard. "My *ba*'s got money problems with your *ba*."

Shen hated it when Kun used *ba*, the familiar term for Father. You did not call your master *ba*. But he didn't have the heart for an argument just then, and anyway Kun's father, Old Bao, was shuffling into the reception pavilion. The children sneaked away.

Kun and his father were the family's only servants now that Kun's mother had died of fever and his older brother had left to seek his fortune. Mother felt sorry for them and tolerated the unseemly friendship between the stocky servant boy, always chewing on a bamboo splint, and her gentle son with the ever-present loose bang of black hair just above his eyes. She even let them throw dice in the inner courtyard, between the pavilion and the family quarters.

"My *ba* says we should surrender to Yan before he breaks into the city," said Kun, shaking the dice. "It's more sincere that way."

"We're going to win," snapped Shen.

Kun looked at Shen as he often did: as if studying an especially stupid mouse about to fall into a bucket of water. But both were distracted by rising voices in the house. "It's 'cause your *ba* wants his money back," spat Kun.

This was bad. Father, like many officers, had given all his savings to a merchant to invest. Bao had been the go-between, since soldiers weren't allowed to deal with merchants.

And now Father wanted the money back! Shen realized with a sinking heart that they really were going to abandon their home.

"The problem is," said Kun, "my *ba* already gave it to a man who deals in lacquerware. He can't just ask for it back, like that, because… you know… you suddenly need it."

"What do we need it for, Ah Kun?" asked Chang melodically. They had forgotten she was squatting nearby, her slender squirrel chin resting on her knees. She was idly dragging a stick through the dust, but her eyes were fixed on Kun. His squinty eyes were squintier than ever, and his mouth was bunched up defiantly. He had accidentally revealed that he knew of the family's plan to leave the city. He had been eavesdropping.

"I don't know," lied Kun, tapping his forehead lightly as a sign of respect. He flushed a bit. "Doesn't everybody need money when they're *be*-sieged?" he said, stretching out the word *besieged* for comic effect. Then he recited:

The city has fallen: only the hills and rivers remain.
The birds startled my heart in fear of departing.
The beacon fires were burning for three months.

Chang was surprised that Kun remembered the famous ancient poem. She had only recited it once. She guessed that Kun's father, who had learned to read when he was a merchant, had helped him. She felt strangely flattered by this but didn't let it distract her. "You only need money if you plan on 'departing,'" she said coolly. "And we're not going anywhere, after all."

"Oh. I thought maybe—"

"We're staying right here. If you think you heard anything different, you are mistaken."

Kun was beet red by now. He had blundered by showing off how much he knew about their plans. This wasn't the way to impress Chang, he realized, and he very much wanted to impress her. But before he could recover his lost face, a rough kick from his father landed on his backside. Old Bao had emerged from the meeting with Mother and Father, looking even more woebegone than usual.

"I have business in town," said Bao quickly. "Do my chores while I'm away. Especially make sure you oil the iron pot."

Bao scuttled out into the laneway, Kun following to see him off. Shen leaned over to his sister. "Kun is right. We have to get out of the city. Did you hear Father say the rebels might break through the walls?"

"But we're not allowed to leave the city."

"We're not asking for permission to leave. Come with me. I've got something to show you. If we hurry, we can be back for supper."

CHAPTER 2

Moving out of the military area where their home was located, Shen led Chang south past Booksellers' Square. The sun was setting over the yellow tile roofs and the discouraged flowers in the public garden, neglected because of the war.

But the street traffic thundered on. Laboring men with their hair pulled back into a bun, or with a piece of fabric knotted on their heads to ward off the sun, trod like elephants under the weight of cloth bales hanging from poles across their shoulders. It seemed as if their slipperlike shoes would fall to pieces at any moment, especially when the laborers were pushed aside by rowdy workers from the nearby bronze foundry. These men were easily spotted by the coarse hairnets that kept their long manes out of the machinery. Mother always wrinkled her nose at them. She claimed the fumes from the foundry ruined her cooking.

Chang looked right through the workers. Nor did she much notice a scholar racing by in his black-bordered white silk jacket, seeming terribly preoccupied. Her eyes did stray to a prosperous lady in a lavender knee-length tunic decorated with red-and-blue cranes. Each extended its wings to make a perfect circle.

Shen nudged Chang away from the palace compound and into Three Mountain Street. There, the Muslims of Nanjing had received permission to build the city's first mosque. Shen disliked the unfamiliar dirgelike music that its priest sang through his nose from the high tower, but Chang was thrilled by it.

Her feet slipped on the flagstones, wet from the recent rain. Shen hurried ahead. In surprisingly little time they reached the bridge over the narrow arm of the Red River that ran inside the city walls.

Chang had not been here before. On the high wall, innumerable soldiers stood shoulder to shoulder. To her right she recognized the famous Gate of Gathering Treasure, with its four entrances. She mumbled a few words to placate the powerful god that lived under the gate.

"The gate is a trap," said Shen matter-of-factly. "There are four entrances outside as well, with courtyards in between. When the enemy breaks through, archers and pots of hot oil are waiting on the courtyard walls. There's no way out. The enemy is the 'treasure' gathered at the gate."

Chang shivered.

"There's something else," said Shen. He pointed to a small iron door, just wide enough for one man, which stood a good distance to the left of the gate. "It's not worth opening Gathering Treasure for just one man. So the messengers use the iron gate over there. It's supposed to be sealed in time of war. But there's a soldier lurking nearby—see him?—he'll open it.

There's a way you have to approach him. I've watched people do it. But you need silver."

"What if we don't get our silver in time?" asked Chang. "Besides, we must do as Father instructs. He will have a plan."

"Of course he will," said Shen vaguely. "But just in case. Silver or no silver, that guard over there is only one man." He narrowed his eyes in a way that made Chang nervous.

They went home by a roundabout route. Father's horse was gone, and Uncle San was rattling around the courtyard. Bent and rheumy-eyed, with a thin beard that hung like a dirty icicle from his chin, he was actually their great-uncle—Father's only relative in the city and now a permanent addition to their household.

"Well," said San, catching sight of them, "if I've never said it before, Don't look for ivory in a dog's mouth."

Chang scowled. She was never in a mood for San's proverbs, especially obscure ones.

"It means our servant Bao is gone," said the old man helpfully. "He won't be back. He has stolen our money. It's your father's fault for being greedy."

Mother gestured urgently from the doorway, and the two of them went in. "Listen carefully," she said, pulling Chang and Shen farther into the room. "Father ordered Bao to stay here until he could talk to the merchant himself. Not a moment later Bao walked out past the gate and disappeared. This is very serious."

"Did he steal our money, like Uncle says?" asked Chang.

"We don't know that yet," said Mother. "But I have always been Husband's bookkeeper. Keeping accounts was my task.

And now I must be more vigorous about it!" The first thing she had done was to lock Kun in the storeroom. "That will make his father come back. And if it doesn't, then Kun will know where he is. I will force him to tell."

"You can't do that to Kun!" cried Shen.

"Your bad temper shames you, child," replied Mother in a fierce voice.

"Can we still get out?" whispered Chang.

"Without a silver *tael* in our pockets, it will be harder. Much harder," Mother replied.

―――――

THE REBEL ARMY STRUCK the next day at dawn, sooner than expected.

Shen and Chang heard about it from Mrs. Ling, the skinny woman next door. She'd returned from the market at a run, claiming that the enemy had wheeled wooden siege towers close enough to fire arrows into the streets. Thousands of dark shafts filled the sky, darting hither and yon like "clouds of dragonflies." But where the Emperor's arrows bounced harmlessly off the siege towers, the Prince of Yan's flew over the wall, striking the cartmen and shopkeepers and women poking at rhubarb and bok choy in the vegetable stalls.

Breathless as she was, Mrs. Ling still talked with her chest stuck out importantly. "If I were as fat as you," she observed to a corpulent neighbor passing by, "I'd be dead for sure. There were so many arrows I had to turn sideways."

Back inside their gate, Shen looked guiltily at the store-room, which sat on the east side of the little inner courtyard, its heavy wooden door designed to discourage thieves. He could accept that Old Bao had betrayed them, but not that Kun was protecting him. His playfellow's eyes gleamed through the door's tiny iron grate. Shen felt as if his heart were being twisted.

"Let me out, Chang Er," Kun pleaded, adding the syllable that turned her name into that of the moon goddess. "Let me out before the soldiers come. Or the fire. What will happen to me if the street burns?"

Shen's guilt suddenly evaporated, replaced by annoyance. He did not like the way Kun had acted foolishly around his sister recently, and the "moon goddess" remark tipped him over the edge. Kun, he decided firmly, had no business seeking a "close friendship" with his master's daughter.

Chang stalked over to the door and stood on tiptoes. "What will happen to you? The same thing that will happen to us. We can't get out without money!" Her sharp, angry tone gave Shen a grim pleasure. They were on the same side where Kun was concerned.

Mother had gone to the Military Registrar's office, hoping to meet officers' wives with connections to escape the city. Her parting words, delivered in a piercing voice she had mastered in her earlier career as an actress, were that neither child was to leave the house.

Shen, bursting to see what was happening in the streets, gave some crafty thought to Mother's order. Not fifty paces from their gate was a poster with the seal of the Grandson, as everybody familiarly called the Emperor Hui Di. It enjoined citizens to carry on with their daily routines "in order that we may impress upon the enemy our contempt for him."

Emperors come before mothers, thought Shen, and gathered up his school things. Chang wanted to come, and he didn't see a reason to refuse her.

In the market, people were ransacking the shops for food and cooking oil, as if it were New Year but with a dose of desperation and snappishness. Chang jumped aside when a merchant pushed a persistent customer down on the sidewalk.

This is what Father meant when he said the war had begun, thought Shen. The day suddenly seemed darker. Seeing the silk weavers lined up for work on the Flower Bridge, as if it were a normal day, his fear and anger overwhelmed him. He shouted, "Go home! Don't you know you're going to die?"

Chang began to laugh.

"What's so funny?" said Shen.

"You. You're acting crazy. Like the demon in that play of Mother's, the one who runs around announcing who's going to die today."

Shen's mouth worked for a moment or two, but no words came out. Then he turned on his heel and stalked down the street. Chang ran to catch up.

"Older Brother!"

Neither of them noticed they were being followed by a man wearing short, floppy green trousers. The man's lanky hair was parted down the middle and fell longer on one side of his head. He kept his hands jammed into the low-slung pockets of a dirty cotton tunic that was too long for him. His calves were wrapped in cloth tape, as if it were midwinter instead of early summer. As Shen and Chang turned a street corner, the man in green trailed them at a discreet distance, keeping himself out of sight.

No matter what was going on, Shen never completely abandoned his habit of observation. His preferred fantasy was to imagine himself a spy, behind enemy lines and plying informants with wine. The part of his mind that tended to this fantasy had registered a flash of green in the crowd behind them, half a dozen street corners back. And there it was again. Pulling up beside Chen Chao's kite shop, Shen peered intently into the four round panes of glass that made a kind of window. They weren't meant for seeing through, since they were thick and distorted. Chao had arranged them in the shape of a four-circle kite. A patch of green was reflected in one of the round panes.

Shen pushed Chang through the door of the shop and looked back out. There was nobody there.

"No kites today, children," said Chao, who was humming a song as he rolled a piece of white paper around a tube-shaped structure of bamboo sticks. "I'm making lanterns for the Hungry Ghosts."

In spite of the threat of war, the palace had ordered the city to celebrate Ghost Month. Everyone invited the ghosts of those who had not been properly mourned by their families to come back and visit the earth. In another ten days, every home would prepare a feast for them, and theater troupes would enact ghost plays in the streets. The living did not dawdle to watch.

But now, with the god of war tightening his grip on the city, there was no real appetite for festivals. Only poor, simple-minded Chen Chao really cared, thought Shen.

"You have a back door, don't you, Master Chen?" asked Shen politely. "Could we use it?"

The kitemaker looked at Shen with mild surprise. "Why not? You used it last time you were playing spies with your friends."

"We're not playing this time," said Shen, grabbing Chang and making for the door at the back of the shop.

"Why do you keep grabbing me?" she asked peevishly as Shen hastened her into the alley.

"There's a man following us. I noticed him back by the market. He's wearing green pants."

"Why do I care what color his pants are?"

"Nobody wears green pants," replied Shen, breathing heavily as he levered himself to the top of a gate at the end of the lane. Chang scampered up the gate like a monkey and hopped down the other side. She waited for him to drop down beside her, and they set off down the street toward the school.

"Damn Bao for running away," said Shen. He was annoyed at his sister for going ahead of him over the fence. He told himself that it was because she was breaking the rule of precedence, where a sister should never walk ahead of her brother. But in truth, he was embarrassed that she was quicker and fitter than he was. "Bao should be here to walk you home," he added loudly, conveniently forgetting that Chang had often walked him to school and gone home alone.

"Don't worry about me," laughed Chang. "If I see your man in green, I'll ask him to walk me home."

And now she was being flippant! "You don't understand the world at all, do you?"

Chang smiled. They had reached the imposing stone gate of the Officers' School, where only the sons of senior officers like Father were permitted to attend. "I don't assume the worst about the world, Older Brother."

Shen's eyes popped. "If Bao were here, I'd tell him to carry you home in a bag so you don't get in trouble."

Chang quickly bowed, to placate his anger. Then she affectionately touched her head to his chest before running off down the road. She glanced back from time to time, and was disappointed not to see the man in green.

The rest of the day was spent in servant's chores, husking rice, mopping floors, and sewing clothes. Remembering Father's annoyance the day before when Mother had repaired his loose Panther badge with orange thread because she had misplaced the black, Chang organized the sewing supplies so it wouldn't happen again.

Then she turned her attention to Father's writing desk.

Girls were not permitted to learn reading and writing. But Mother had been taught when she was an actress, and now she had given in to her daughter's pleadings to learn the mysteries of written characters. They would sit together at Father's table and Mother would teach Chang the five strokes that meant "sun" and the three strokes that meant "tree," and how the two could be combined to mean "east"—the direction where a tree would stand in front of the rising sun.

By now Chang could study by herself. Mother pretended not to see her using Father's brushes and ink stone when he was away. But whenever his horse whinnied at the gate, Mother whispered, "The desk!" and Chang hurried to clear her papers away.

Looking at the desk now, she knew she would never sit there again.

The shudder of iron balls falling in the streets made its way to her ears. She joined Mother at the summer cooking stove tucked into a roofed-over corner of the courtyard. Mother's shoulders were draped with the dark blue shawl she wore even on hot evenings. A strand of jet-black hair had escaped from her hairpin, and she brushed it aside as she stirred the soup. The smell of duck meat and hot peppers filled the air. Chang thought how beautiful Mother looked, even when she was doing servant's work.

"A man in green pants followed us today."

One of Mother's eyebrows shot up, but then her face became impassive. She kept stirring. "At times like this, all kinds of strange people are in the streets."

Chang watched Mother slip a manicured fingernail into the gap between her upper front teeth. She worried the little gap whenever she had something on her mind.

"You're not going to start seeing fortune-tellers, are you?" said Chang, remembering that this was Mother's weakness when things went badly.

Mother laughed briefly. "No, I know that you don't believe in them. I'll try to behave myself."

"Is Father going to die?"

The stirring ladle stopped in the middle of the soup cauldron. It looked like a boat that had struck a sandbar. Then Mother tapped the ladle on the edge of the cauldron and laid it aside.

"Come with me," she said.

They went to her room in the family quarters. There Chang saw, to her surprise, that Mother had opened the costume chest she had kept from her days as an actress before she married. Little stoneware pots of makeup were laid out on the bamboo mat, alongside a jar of walnut juice that was used to color and age the skin for "old woman" parts. Once, when Father had come to the Phoenix Canopy with his officer friends to watch her perform, he didn't recognize her in the old woman role even though he was already courting her. She still teased him about it.

But just now Mother wasn't interested in any of that. She lowered herself onto a carved stool while Chang sat cross-legged on the mat.

"I won't lie, Ah Chang," she said. "If the palace falls, Husband will die." She blinked, but there were no tears. "Of course, there is the chance this Zheng He will never reach the palace." She lifted her lute out of its case and began to strum a disjointed melody.

"That's the theater song Chen Chao the kitemaker was humming today," cried Chang. Then she gritted her teeth, because now Mother would know she had left the compound.

But Mother only nodded distractedly. "It's from a play called *Lute*. About how gods and demons pull the strings in our lives."

"Just the kind of thing a kitemaker would sing," said Chang, wondering if Mother would even notice the joke. She didn't.

Something crashed to the stone floor of the winter kitchen. "Don't be frightened, Daughter. I'll tend to Uncle San."

She rose to leave the room, pausing at the door. "I am expecting a visitor. I'll explain more when your brother is here."

Chang stayed in Mother's room, looking at the makeup pots and remembering all the times her parents had fought because Father thought that actresses were too independent. "The theater spoiled you for being a wife!" he would shout at Mother.

"And now there is a visitor," she said to a pot of makeup.

CHAPTER 3

WHEN SCHOOL ENDED THAT day, Shen walked home by his usual route. He saw a streak of fire fall from the sky into the courtyard of a nearby house. There was screaming and confusion, and men ran in from the street to help. Shen slipped inside and saw a family cowering in one corner.

It was the first fire arrow he had ever seen. As long as a man's leg, and as thick as an ax handle, it had smashed to bits when it hit the flagstones, throwing pieces of burning pitch-covered wood around the courtyard and up onto the thatched roof. A man was up there beating at the flames with his shirt. His friends below had hooked a pail of water onto a rake handle and were shouting at him to take it. He finally did and emptied it onto the flames. A puff of black smoke covered the roof. When it dispersed, the fire was out and a crowd of passersby applauded.

Shen pushed back into the street and hastened home. As he approached his house a prickling feeling ran across his neck. The courtyard gate was ajar.

Flattening himself against the short, freestanding "spirit wall" that prevented passersby from seeing the house, he peered around the corner. The storeroom was unlocked, its door hanging open.

Picking up a heavy stone, he made his way to the reception pavilion. Father's chair had been kicked over. Ignoring it, he walked on the balls of his feet into the inner courtyard.

Subdued voices came from the family rooms. One was Kun's, but there were also some men. None of the voices sounded like Father, and he didn't like their arrogant tone.

Slipping over to a window with a small tear in its oiled window-paper, he squinted to see inside. Kun was standing in a corner, blood running from a wound on his head. Chang was sitting at the table, quiet but plainly terrified. Mother was speaking in a near-whisper. And there were two scruffy men he didn't know.

"The boy Kun has already told you that our money is gone. Since you are his father's thugs, you should know he is telling the truth. You were sent here to take him. So take him. Get out of my house."

A sneering man reached forward and struck Mother across the face.

That was all Shen needed. In a rush he burst through the doorway arch and cracked the rock across the man's skull. Then something heavy landed on the back of his head, and he fell to the floor.

He didn't see the men escort Kun to the street. Nor did he see Kun's agonized last look at Chang, who stared at him with hatred. Later he learned that Chang, finding the men releasing Kun from the shed, had struck Kun with the pump handle from the well.

———

MOTHER STOPPED IN SHEN'S room, taking the wet rag from his limp hand and dabbing at the emerging duck egg of a lump on his head. "Uncle San slept through it all," she whispered.

"Ow. I'm all right. What did they hit me with?"

"The stoneware bowl," she said calmly, laying his head back on the pillow.

Chang was squatting on the porch, hugging herself and saying nothing. Mother came out of Shen's room, bent down and kissed the top of her head. As Chang looked up she saw a streak of flame pass high over the house. Mother saw it too and spat at it.

Then Mother left the porch and went indoors again. When she emerged, Chang was surprised to see she had put on white cotton trousers and a plain blue tunic of ramie, a cheap fabric she didn't usually wear. Stepping past her, Mother went to the gate and called for a boy to carry a message.

"Is it for that visitor you were expecting?" said Chang.

"Yes," said Mother. "His name is Lan Yi. He's a man you don't know. Father sent for him to help us. He wasn't to come until tomorrow, but—" She stopped because of shouting coming from down the street. "But things are happening too fast. I must decide on a course of action."

NOTICING THE COLD EMBERS in the stove across the courtyard, Mother strode over and had the fire crackling again in moments. Chang protested, but Mother waved her silent. "Those vile men would like to think we are too frightened to eat. But I for one am hungry, and I think you are too."

Mother went in to fetch Shen and Uncle San. Shen emerged with his lump and Uncle with his hangover. At any other time Chang would have laughed. But now she was struck by the pitiful spectacle the family presented.

"I told Uncle what happened," groaned Shen. "And he said something about a friend of Father's who is going to help us."

Mother nodded briskly as she ladled duck soup into his bowl. "A man who has never impressed me. A thin reed to lean on at a time like this."

The children stared at her, and Mother reminded herself that their home had just been invaded by strangers. She relented slightly. "I'm sure Father's friend will be of some use. But we must also rely on one another."

Brother and sister finished the meal in silence while Mother prepared for the journey, ticking items off on her fingers and muttering to herself. As the courtyard grew dark, she hoisted a pair of small sacks on to the table. "We must leave the city tomorrow. These are the clothes you are to wear. You won't like them, but you will be safer in them. We cannot wear anything fine."

"What will you wear, Uncle?" asked Shen.

San focused his rheumy eyes on Shen, making a little O shape with his mouth. Then he looked at Mother, as if he had done something wrong.

"Uncle can't walk without a stick," said Mother firmly. "He won't be coming."

"No point in drawing legs on a snake," chuckled Uncle San, lifting a pant leg to reveal a scrawny calf netted in bulging blue veins.

"But you'll die!" cried Chang.

"I have lived long enough," said Uncle San. "I did my fighting against the Mongols. I saw them kill our relatives. I rejoiced when Old Emperor Taizu drove them out." He glanced around, the bags beneath his eyes huge in the candlelight. Over the courtyard wall Shen noticed a faint redness in the sky to the east. Fire, he thought.

San extended a withered hand toward a small green pot of rice wine. Then he stopped, collecting himself. "But later Taizu gave the throne to his grandson instead of his son. What does he care, all comfortable in his grave, that he has cursed us with civil war." Uncle blinked at the red sky and a thin-lipped smile appeared on his face. "Fire is what we have deserved."

A sudden pounding at the gate made them jump. Mother leaped up but returned calmly a moment later. "The boy says Lan Yi can't come tonight. We'll have to try to sleep. To your beds now!"

Uncle San had begun drinking his wine straight out of the pot. "Go where you can be happy." His voice dropped. "Go to some foreign country, where there are coconuts."

Mother sighed. "To bed. Now."

IT WAS UNCLE SAN, still drunk in the predawn darkness, who lit the lamp and shook them awake. Shen drowsily pulled some clothes out of the little bag Mother had given them, then creased his brow in disbelief. "They're hemp. White hemp. Mourning clothes."

Chang was slipping into hers without hesitation. "Open your eyes! They're just poor people's clothes. And they're not all that white. Fairly dirty, in fact." She wrinkled her nose.

Shen and Chang each put a few personal things into their bags. Shen looked longingly at the fine porcelain soldiers Father had given him on his name day, then set them aside. No poor person would have such things.

"Mother told us to put in a bowl and spoon too, for eating," said Chang in a whispery voice.

As they padded to the cooking area, they found a strange woman waiting. She was old, in ragged clothes, with dry, reddened skin around her eyes and forehead.

"What are you staring at?" said Mother in a voice not quite her own.

"You're not pretty anymore!" complained Chang.

"All the better for me," said Mother, "where we're going."

Father would never have agreed to such an undignified escape, thought Shen. And it was unheard of for a wife, even one as combative as Mother, to make plans without her husband. Things were back to front, and Shen felt dizzy.

Mrs. Ling's shouting voice floated over the courtyard wall, informing them that a visitor had arrived. Seconds later a man stepped around the spirit wall and advanced with a grin toward the pavilion. He wore baggy green pants cut off just below the knee.

"Let's see now," he said, widening his eyes, "you're rehearsing a pantomime. Do I have to guess which one?"

Shen was taken aback. From the green pants he guessed this was the man who had stalked them through the city. As if in confirmation, the man bowed and the long hank of hair on one side of his head flopped down.

"This," said Mother, "is Lan Yi."

Shen and Chang bowed to the newcomer. Yi responded with a flamboyant bow, this time almost touching his head to the ground. Then he looked at Mother, nodding his appreciation.

"Still the actress, the great shining star of the Phoenix Canopy," he said.

"Hmph," replied Mother. "And you're still wearing those green pants. Do you ever wash them?"

"Alas, I have no wife, I have no scrub brush."

"I knew it was you when Chang talked about those pants. Why did you follow the children?"

"To see what they are like," replied Yi, suddenly serious. "It's a dangerous road to Suzhou. It is gratifying to learn that the boy is alert, and good at concealment. The girl has nerve." He squatted down on the floor, ignoring the wooden stools. "What were you doing two days ago by the Gate of Gathering Treasure?"

"Just looking around," said Shen, who had taken an immediate dislike to Lan Yi's flounces and theatrical mannerisms. And he had only spotted Yi on the way to school the previous day. How had he not seen the man two days earlier when he and Chang went to the Gate?

"Just looking around," repeated Yi, adopting a clownlike expression of astonishment that irritated Shen even more. "And in the many conspiracies of children, is there a way through the city wall?"

Shen said nothing. Lan Yi sighed. "An official was hanged at North Gate this morning, trying to bribe his way out. And the Brocades are watching officers' families." Shen felt a pulse of fear in his stomach: the Brocades were trained to ferret out traitors. The law didn't restrain them. Even Father was afraid of them.

Yi had one further piece of news. "I saw your father at the palace guardhouse last night. He can't do anything more for you. He told me to give you these." And he handed Shen and Chang two small dragons made of gold, which came from the grandparents they had scarcely known. "He is sorry about the silver," said Yi. "This is all that remains."

Shen cradled the fat amulet in his hand. He tried to imagine Father offering it to him, but found that it was frightening to think about Father. So he looked up at the ridiculous stranger. Who was he? For that matter, who was Mother, standing impassively to one side and paying no attention to the amulets? She seemed to be changing back into the woman she had been before he was born.

He had a sudden image of a whistling cold plain, and nobody there but himself and Chang. He put out his hand to grasp hers, and she grasped as fervently in return.

CHAPTER 4

WITHIN MINUTES THEY HAD left the house behind. Shen and Chang had embarrassed Uncle San by embracing him. They had not known their grand-parents, who perished during the war with the Mongols. Instead Uncle San had accepted the task of the grandparents, teaching them the stories of their ancestors. The rice wine made his stories a little unreliable, but they loved him nonetheless.

His bent figure was the last thing they saw as they fought their way down the crowded street. It seemed to Shen that the old man was already vanishing, taking his place with the ancestors. Shen turned away from him and was momentarily blinded by the sun. He shielded his eyes and looked down the road.

Panic was well underway in the city. The little group squeezed against walls as strangers bullied past, wielding crates of squawking chickens or boxes overflowing with household linen. A desperate few were still lugging buckets of water to the burning houses, but most had given up and were trying to escape.

Thatched houses everywhere were ablaze, and even those with clay roof tiles were not safe. Heat from nearby fires had boiled the rainwater trapped between the tiles. Now they began to explode, hurling knives of clay into the streets. Lan Yi grabbed the heavy lid from a water barrel and, holding it by its handle like a warrior's shield, tried to protect the children.

Soon they were on Zhongshan Road, the great Way that led to the south. It was lined with ancestral temples and the homes of wealthy officials, with soaring whitewashed walls and gray-tiled roofs. Beautiful in times of peace, they were now little more than a funnel for the crowds streaming northward. Among them were bloodied soldiers, their spiked helmets gone, their black armor askew. Yi leaped in front of one of them and, in spite of his torn and dirty peasant's clothes, demanded that a soldier give him a report on the battle.

He returned to the family a moment later. "Bad news, Lu Ting. The south wall is in danger."

"Where can we go then?" she said.

"South, anyway. Chaos is opportunity." Looking to Shen, he asked, "Can you lead us through the lanes, where the horsemen can't go?"

Still in shock that Yi had addressed Mother by her familiar name, Shen guided them to the private lanes behind the houses. Pointing to the first gate, made of stout wooden planks and taller than a man, he watched as Chang locked her fine fingers and toes in the decorative carving on the gate's face and hopped over it. She was closely followed by Yi.

When they released the lock on the other side, Shen and Mother slipped through, following Yi and Chang, who were already running like rabbits through the twisting lanes of fitted flagstones and past the locked back gates of great houses. Repeating this so often that Shen lost count—traveling several *li*, about halfway across the city—the four rejoined the vast Zhongshan Way that crossed the city. They were searching for the bridge across the Red River that would take them to the Gate of Gathering Treasure. And here a terrible sight greeted them.

Bodies covered the road and the gentle rise of the stone bridge. On the far side of the river, a whole section of the south wall had collapsed into a wilderness of broken stone and flat orange brick. The attackers had avoided the Gate of Gathering Treasure, with its four delicate and deceptive arches, knowing full well that steel traps and concealed archers awaited them inside. Instead they had smashed the wall beside the Gate, and Shen could see the first few red-jacketed attackers appearing at the top of the heap of broken stones. At its base, the defending soldiers who had not fled were trying to organize a last stand. Clouds of brick dust still hung in the air.

"When you were here before with Chang, I saw you point at the Messengers' Door," said Yi urgently. "What do you know? Where is the guard?"

Shen knew nothing, but at that moment he spotted a crumpled body hidden in a shadow of the wall. "He's there," he said in a hollow voice.

Yi ran to the body. Assured by the guard's glazed, unseeing eyes that he would not be troubling them, Yi considered the heavy door. Then he hurled himself against it. It didn't budge. "Why won't it open?"

Shen glanced nervously at the broken wall, only five hundred footsteps away, where scores and scores of Yan's red-coated soldiers were now screaming their battle anthem as they pushed the defenders back down the slope of fallen stones and bricks. "The guard always hid the key," said Shen in a panicky voice. Then he took a deep breath, and his spy calm came to him. It was as if the noise and chaos moved back, leaving a zone of tranquillity. His eyes moved deliberately over the course of stones behind the dead guard. During the earlier visit he had seen the man drop something and ease it into a crack with the back of his foot. It was *that* stone.

"Hurry, boy!" cried Yi.

Shen plunged his hand into the dust, wriggling it into an opening between two gray blocks. In a moment he withdrew the heavy iron key. Yi snatched it and struggled to turn the lock while Shen was distracted by a low groan, like thunder or the death throes of an ox. Looking back to the broken wall, he saw the Imperial archers turning their backs and fleeing, leaping from one heap of orange bricks to the next, throwing away their precious bows as a gardener might discard a fallen branch.

"That is the sound of defeat," said Yi quietly. He gave a push and the door swung open. On the outside, a great mass of enemy soldiers was surging toward the breach in the wall. Behind them, legions more were throwing planks across the Red River, jostling one another in their haste to reach the rich plunder inside the city.

Luckily there were no soldiers immediately on the other side of the sturdy iron door as it swung open. But a five-man detachment, only a hundred paces away, was carrying a siege ladder toward the wall. They stopped immediately, their jaws dropping at the sight of the open door. "To the river! Run!" shouted Yi, pushing Mother and Chang ahead of him.

A cloud of smoke obscured the small arm of the Red River, which gurgled out from under the walls through a nearby stone channel. They bolted toward it, but Shen lost sight of the other three. As he looked around for them he tripped and rolled. At that moment the wind rose and lifted the gray cloud that had hidden him. Towering over him were six huge cavalry horses. The lead horse carried the most terrifying man Shen had ever seen.

His face was a mass of rough dark flesh, like lava. Here and there on his skin were small red spots, as if his head were in the habit of catching fire. When wisps of smoke blew across him, he reminded Shen of a demon set loose to walk the earth.

Two enormous arms wearing gold-colored chain mail projected from what appeared to be the mouths of savage animals. They were, in fact, the artfully made shoulder pieces of the huge man's uniform. He casually balanced an immense sword across the pommel of his saddle.

"So, child," said the giant, his words sounding like rock scraping against rock, "can you tell me the way to find the Emperor?"

Shen was paralyzed with fear. Endless moments passed as the soldier's gaze remained fixed on him. At some point he realized that the man's glorious uniform, with a howling brass beast covering his belly and an ornate red sash hanging just below it, was that of a supreme commander. This was the Prince of Yan's eunuch general.

"Who has the insolence to ask such a question?" came a voice. At first it reminded Shen of the way Father spoke, and he glanced wildly over his shoulder. There was nobody there. He realized to his horror that it was his own voice.

This must be a dream, he thought. He blinked at the giant. But the broad face was still there, as ugly as ever. As real as ever. Black eyes studied Shen carefully, but he could read no expression behind them. It seemed odd that everything was so quiet. Turning his head slowly to one side, Shen saw that red-jacketed soldiers had gathered in a circle around their general. They looked on with ghastly curiosity, perhaps waiting to see a child's head rolling on the ground.

Instead, the giant on the horse nodded, very slowly, as if lost in thought. "Once before, I heard a boy speak so proudly to a general." With a crisp movement of his hand, he summoned three foot soldiers to his side. "Gather this child and his friends who are hiding where the stream comes out from under the wall. See them safely on the southern road."

Slipping the huge sword back into its scabbard, he said, "Tell me your name."

"It is Fei Shen, Honored General."

The man nodded one last time. Then, with a metallic clatter of horseshoes on stone, he and his entourage vanished into the smoke.

CHAPTER 5

THE NEXT TWO DAYS and nights were a jumble
in Shen's memory. The great southern road was
filled with barricades, some of heaped rocks and others of logs
where trees were available. A few were no more than a line of
sullen soldiers on horseback, or squatting on the road. These
military vagrants might be from Yan's triumphant army, or
tattered remnants of the Emperor's forces. The rest were common thieves, who often enjoyed strutting about in uniforms
stripped from battlefields. They saluted merrily in bloodstained
tunics. All preyed on the endless shuffling column of refugees.

Late in the second day, Lan Yi decided they would strike out
across the country to avoid soldiers and thieves "if indeed one
can be told from another." They would rejoin the road near the
port city of Zhenjiang, where Mother insisted they must stop.
It was in Zhenjiang that Old Bao had invested Father's silver
with a merchant trading lacquerware to Japan. Mother still
hoped to recover some of what had been lost.

By way of preparation, Yi instructed them to bind their
ankles with cloth to lessen the chance of sprains. Chang and
Mother set to the task, but Shen stood sullenly to one side. "I

know how to make my way across rough ground. Father taught me."

"Evidently he didn't teach you obedience," replied Yi. "If you sprain your ankle, I'll be obliged to carry you. Sit down there and do as you're told."

Shen stood.

"Why do you defy me?" Yi asked quietly.

"Why do you order me about? I never heard Father place me under your authority."

Mother paused in the wrapping of her ankle to comment that Shen had heard her say so.

Shen sneered. "You're a woman."

Shen startled himself with these words, though there was nothing unusual in a man speaking to a woman in this fashion. It seemed he had been unkind, and yet wasn't he now the man of the family? This meditation was interrupted by Yi's eyes, now less than a finger's length from his own and bulging with anger. Shen was also aware of a sharp pain in his head, caused by Yi's strong hands grasping his hair and lifting him nearly off the ground. He pleaded for mercy.

He was dropped unceremoniously into the dirt and two strips of cotton were flung in his face. "Do it quickly," said Yi, walking away.

For nourishment they had nothing but the stale bread and pork in their shoulder bags. But as evening drew on, they found a lamb bleating noisily in an empty field. Mother, whose people had not lived on a farm for generations, drew her shawl over her eyes as Yi bent the lamb's front legs to the ground and cut its throat. Chang looked on seriously, as if she were studying to be a butcher, while Yi stripped off the wool and clumsily quartered the tiny body with a knife not made for the task. They ate well that night, in front of the eager flames of a fireplace in an abandoned farmhouse.

Shen nursed his grudge against Yi while the fire crackled. But as the wood burnt down and shadows closed in, his thoughts returned to the encounter by the Gate of Gathering Treasure. His nerves still tingled. So that had been the eunuch Zheng He! Shen knew what a eunuch was—starting with the fact that a boy who was to become one was castrated at Shen's present age, thirteen. That was old enough to allow him to develop the deep voice and powerful body of a man. But a eunuch was destined never to have a family. Instead, he lavished his loyalty on his master, and eunuchs were reputed to be the deadliest soldiers in the land.

During the previous day's trek, Shen had looked back at the distant column of twisted smoke that marked his city. Where was Father? Last night he had dreamed of Father being pushed down into darkness while a pair of black eyes set in a pockmarked face leered at him from above.

This morning, though, he had made a brief prayer of thanks. He had not dreamed of birds or small animals, the usual messengers of death. Perhaps, chance against chance, Father was still alive.

The next day Yi led them down a rough road into the Ning Zhen Mountains. In Nanjing Province, which was mostly rice paddies and bog land as far as the eye could see, any hill taller than a house was called a mountain. But these ones were hundreds of *ch'i* in height and ran in a straight line to the east toward Zhenjiang. There was a broad forest trail on the lower slope that was hidden from view by groves of fir trees, of the kind called *shan mu*, together with purple holly and lacebark elm. Every so often they saw a cork oak, and Shen joked about the poisonous-tasting hot drink that Father used to make from its seeds.

The quilts they had brought with them were warm against the night chill, but not much use against the little squalls of rain that were common in summertime. Mother's teeth were chattering in the morning, and Yi reluctantly decided that they must return to the broad, sunny road. They could still see it from their vantage point on the mountainside.

Once back on the road, they heard news from those who had escaped the city after them. A man swore that the palace had burnt to the ground. No defender had escaped.

Hearing this, Mother looked so stricken that a woman put her arm around her. All Shen could think of was that he could have killed the eunuch before he reached the palace. When he looked at Chang, he saw that she had begun to weep.

Lan Yi remained silent.

A short while later, the column of refugees slowed, then stopped altogether. People were making little fires at the road's edge and setting teakettles over them. Shen shielded his eyes from the sun and peered as far ahead as he could. In the distance was yet another barricade. He glanced back to where they had come from and saw a soldier on horseback cantering into the field. There would be no avoiding this roadblock.

The four of them made for a line of cedar trees beside the road where refugees were already sheltering from the sun.

The woman who had comforted Mother came with them and offered her plum juice. Yi filled his teakettle from a murky stream and approached a circle of men sitting around a fire.

One of the strangers waved for them to sit down and place their kettle on the stones that enclosed a small but hot fire of cedar boughs. Nobody asked who they were. Shen marveled at the casual equality—and good cheer—of people who had lost everything. Soon he was absorbed in the stories the men traded with one another about the battle of Nanjing. A man with a thin mustache finally silenced the rest by declaring that a turquoise dragon had risen out of the smoke and carried the dead Emperor up to heaven. Shen was impressed. He had seen nothing but a few regular dragons in his lifetime, and those were of the white, cloud-dwelling variety.

"Come with me," said Lan Yi, shaking Shen's shoulder. The two walked off a distance into the field. "I don't know what you said to the eunuch, and I don't know why he didn't kill you. But if it had anything to do with saving our skins, I thank you."

"Very kind of you," replied Shen sarcastically.

Yi bent down so their eyes were at the same level. "My job is to keep you alive. For kind words, look elsewhere. Listen to me."

Because of Yi's agility and strength, Shen had thought at first that he was a young man. Now he noticed the fine wrinkles around his eyes. Yi was almost as old as Father. But they weren't Father's eyes. They were cold.

"There is something I have to tell you. Your father had a message, and I pass it on to you." Shen's heart raced. "The message is that he hopes to see you again."

"When? How?" cried Shen.

"He said nothing else. Face the truth, Son of Fei Lee. Your father did not foresee the destruction of the palace. He has promised what he could not grant. If it is true that the palace was destroyed, then he is surely dead. His oath would not permit him to flee." Shen's eyes widened in rage. But he forced himself to remain silent and stumbled back to the road behind Yi. Mother and Chang rose to meet them, bowing. As he returned their bow, Shen coldly decided that he would not believe what Yi had said. Instead, he engraved Father's promise in his mind.

The men had already doused the fire and were shouldering their packs. The woman who had stayed to comfort Mother returned to her family. Chang whispered that Mother seemed better, and Shen nodded distractedly.

But as the four of them joined the footsore crowd moving toward the barricade, the cold rage roiling through Shen's mind led him to another decision about Lan Yi. He would never trust a man who told him to disbelieve his own father's words.

When they reached the barricade, the soldiers demanded money. Shen caught his breath, because he knew Yi was carrying just enough silver for food and drink on the journey. And he feared for the golden dragons that were sewn into his undershirt.

But then Yi did something remarkable. He produced a bamboo cup from the folds of his dirty tunic and filled it with cold tea from the kettle dangling at his side. His face went vacant, and he spoke to the soldiers using a thick voice and very simple words. He had no money, but the tea was very good. Would they like the tea?

A soldier upended the cup in Yi's face with a casual blow. Yi burst into tears. "My tea! My tea!"

"It's my idiot son," said Mother apologetically in her old-lady voice.

"Get him out of here," said the soldier. "Before he wets his green trousers." The uniformed men guffawed loudly.

As they left the barricade behind, Mother was exhilarated by their small triumph. "There's more than one way to get paid for a performance," she laughed in a high-pitched voice.

It gradually dawned on Chang that all of this had been a way to avoid paying the bribe. It was the kind of thing that Mother called an "improvisation."

Still puzzling, though, was Mother's familiarity with the stranger in the green trousers. "Pardon my forwardness, but how long have you known Mother?" she asked Lan Yi.

"A long time," intervened Mother with a giddy voice. "I am a great actress, and he is a clown."

"I keep a circus in Suzhou," explained Yi, looking at Shen and Chang. "You will live there. And, depending on your abilities, you will be trained to perform. A new identity is the best way to protect you." The Suzhou Acrobatic Troupe occupied an old merchant hall in that sprawling city, and often toured through the countryside. As a young man, recalled Yi, he had thrown in with them. He wasn't much of an acrobat, but the company also needed musicians and clowns because it staged acrobatic plays with spoken dialogue—a new style that the public liked.

"So I became a clown," he shrugged.

"Why would Father befriend a street performer?" asked Shen suspiciously.

"I am no longer a street performer, as you put it. Because I was educated in my earlier life, I have come to be the master of the circus. I was not always a tumbler and juggler, just as your mother was not always an officer's wife. Some of us are obliged to play more than one role in life."

"Please excuse me, Master Lan, but you haven't answered my question. How did you meet Father anyway?"

"As I said, we all play more than one role in life," replied Yi grandly. "What I was doing when I met your father is none of your business."

The rebuff told Shen that the subject was closed. But with Yi, he never had to look far to find something else to be annoyed about. "More than one role in life!" he snapped, returning to Yi's earlier observation. "What an idea! Father always said that life isn't a game. You are born into the role you must fulfill. And you stay who you are."

"Honorable First Son of Captain Fei," replied Lan Yi with elaborate politeness, "with all respect to your father, I cannot agree with his sentiments. Consider your own case. Precisely because your father was an officer of the fallen regime, you must hide and take on new identities if you wish to live. So you see, we cannot always stay who we are."

———

LATER IN THE DAY, when they took a flea-ridden room in a village inn, Chang's surprise at hearing herself described as a circus performer gave way to unease. Circus people were the lowest of the low, and Mother had said that Yi was a "weak reed."

But when she questioned Mother privately, the answers were flat and tired. "What I think of him does not matter now," she said, removing the cotton wadding that gave her a matronly figure during the day. "We have nowhere else to go." Chang protested, and babbled the names of distant relatives who might take them in. Mother shook her head, not even looking at her daughter. Chang fell silent. Mother had never refused to meet her eyes before.

If Yi felt their discomfort, he didn't give any sign of it. He briskly explained that he knew people who would produce false identity papers. The Suzhou Acrobatic Troupe was so well known that officials turned a blind eye to the fugitives it harbored. "But I am worried that they may recognize you, Lu Ting. Your husband told me that the Emperor loved theater. You've performed before the court more than once. The Suzhou magistrate might have seen you there."

Mother accepted this with a tiny nod of her head. "Perhaps I could stay behind the scenes. I know how to sew costumes."

Shen cut in rudely. "I'm not very happy about joining the circus. I don't mean to be rude, but circus people are…well… *mang*," he said, using an impolite word for vagrants.

Lan Yi took no offence. "That's our advantage. We are invisible."

"But what will we do?" asked Chang.

"I have watched you, Chang, scampering like a ferret over the laneway gates. You're a natural acrobat. You won't be able to keep up with the girls who are double-jointed, but you are agile and fearless. As for Shen!" He paused.

"Well, it's not a career I was contemplating!" said Shen, offended.

"Let's see. A boy who is touchy and stiff-necked. Who fancies himself a soldier and a spy." Yi gave him a crafty look. "How are you with horses?"

"You have horses?"

"Well, then," said Yi in a smug fashion, as if he always guessed rightly. "I assume your father taught you to ride?"

"He taught both of us!" Chang chimed in.

Yi blinked. "Teaching a girl! Now that I wouldn't have guessed. But Fei Lee always was a surprising man."

CHAPTER 6

THEIR ROUTE THE NEXT day took them into Zhen-jiang, a fat and prosperous city lying at the cross-roads of the Yangtze River and the Grand Canal. Mother, as the family's bookkeeper, knew the name of the merchant who had invested Father's money. In a shop rich with the odor of newly painted lacquerware, a man with thinning hair and a friendly demeanor readily admitted that he had seen Old Bao.

"He came by to cancel the purchase, explaining that Captain Fei had died in the siege. He said the captain's widow had sent him to recover the family's silver. So of course I believed he would give it back to you." The merchant looked regretfully at Mother. "I am sorry for you, and I fear you won't find him now. Reports came to me that he and his boy took ship with a trader who goes to the southern ocean, to Majapahit. The place is forbidden to our vessels, but who truly obeys the law? And Chinese people live there. I do not think Bao means to return."

Mother's eyes grew dull, as if a lamp had been extinguished. Shen could see she had not prepared herself for this. He clumsily took her arm and led her out of the shop.

It was still early in the day, and Lan Yi decided for Mother's sake that they should leave this unfortunate city and strike out on the road again. Wagons were coming and going from a nearby yard where farmers sent loads of grain to pay their taxes. Yi flagged an empty one heading south. He had to agree on a price with the surly-looking driver, and by mid-afternoon they reached a small town called Xinfeng.

The heavy cart entered through a gate in what remained of the town's ancient walls. The driver surprised Yi by refusing payment. "You've got trouble enough. I can tell by the old lady's face."

As he rumbled away, they looked around for signs of a roadblock or soldiers. There were none. The farmers' market appeared prosperous, and the shops were flourishing.

Once they were settled at a table in front of a wine shop, and had asked for food and drink to be brought, Yi took the children aside on the pretext of examining the public announcements posted on a pillar in the village square. Mother remained at the table, chewing her lip.

"Your mother has gone quiet and inside herself. It is not her way. I would be happier if she were swearing at Old Bao and the thief child."

"I think it's the money," said Chang worriedly. "Or maybe that we shall not see Father again." Having uttered these forbidden words, she glanced at Shen. He angrily turned his back and began to study the posters, muttering their words aloud. One sun-bleached strip of paper was flapping loose, and he slapped it flat. The word *theater* caught his eye.

"You talk like an old man, Lan Yi," said Shen disrespectfully. "Look here! A theater company from Nanjing is in town. That's all she needs. Let's take her to the play."

"Brother!" cried Chang. "There will be soldiers there!"

Yi stood up and read the poster. "It's a risk worth taking, Chang. I'd like to know what has happened in Nanjing, and actors are well-informed. Let's go and see them."

Chang felt that Yi was making a mistake but said nothing.

After returning to the inn to gather up their things, they walked to the place where the play was to be presented. As Shen had hoped, Mother perked up at the mention of a performance. Even better, she became her old combative self. The players, she declared, were a troupe of scroungers who lived near the scandalous Painted Boats on the Red River. "They get up on stilts and wave their streamers about, and before they take two steps somebody's streamer is tangled in somebody else's feet. The female lead is the ugliest woman in Nanjing. The only person in the company who knows what he's doing is the man who throws out the drunks."

They found the troupe in a yard outside another inn, more impressive than their own. The actors had borrowed a farmer's wagon for a stage. A few bamboo poles had been jammed into the earth, and a ragged black cloth with the words *Demon Play* was suspended from them.

They sat on rough benches along with the rest of the audience. Mother, pushing her padded rear end between Yi and a stranger, cackled, "Sorry, neighbor" as she did so. She was enjoying her own performance as a cranky peasant.

Meanwhile, Shen's attention was drawn to the dark archway, which was the only exit from the inn yard to the street. In its shadows he saw quilted red jackets. Soldiers. In spite of what Yi had said, his heart raced.

Then a slender, energetic figure in a black silk robe emerged from the archway and strode toward the stage. The gaggle of actors that made up the company was waiting for him and bowed low. The official—for an official's square badge was sewn on to his chest—hopped up the three steps to the stage and looked out at the audience.

A small cry escaped Mother's lips. "It's Yang Rong!"

Shen had heard Mother and Father talk about this dangerous Confucian official, whose political enemies vanished or finished up in a Brocade prison. He tried to stand up for a better look. Lan Yi clamped a hand on his shoulder and sat him back down. "Don't fidget. It upsets your grandmother," he said amiably, glancing at the people around them.

Shen tried to ignore the frightened look in Mother's eyes. He listened as the official named Yang Rong droned on about Zhu Di, the rebel prince of Yan who was now the new Emperor. Did anyone doubt his mandate? the official suddenly cried in a shrill, threatening voice. Then they had better remember that the Prince of Yan was entitled to become Emperor. He was the oldest son of Taizu, the founder of the dynasty. Traitors had persuaded Taizu to put his grandson on the throne instead of his son. It was scandalous. But now Heaven had set things right.

Lan Yi sighed heavily. But Shen found that the speech was getting interesting. Even now, Official Yang continued, kings from countries friendly to China were sending tribute to Zhu

Di. And Zhu Di was going to build gigantic ships to explore all the unknown parts of the world.

"Giant ships!" whispered Shen, forgetting their danger in spite of himself. Yi shushed him.

As the official spoke, the actors wandered away from the stage, chewing nuts and letting their eyes wander idly over the audience. Shen was fascinated by an actress with tiny eyes set in a fat, wrinkled face. Could this be the ugliest woman in Nanjing? She was shoveling rice paste into her mouth as her pelletlike eyes bobbed dolefully over the audience. Shen saw her glance carelessly down their row and then shift her attention to the back of the crowd.

But her eyes quickly returned to them. She fixed her gaze on Mother.

"The actress has spotted us," Shen whispered to Yi, who stiffened.

"Walnut juice on the skin!" spat the actress, pointing at Mother's artificially aged forehead and cheeks. There was an anxious hush in the crowd. The official had stopped speaking as the actress continued, "Aren't you a colleague I've seen before? What are you doing here with a painted face?" She then swung about like a water buffalo and plodded off in the direction of the soldiers.

But she wasn't fast enough for Shen, who ran out and slipped his foot between her shuffling legs, sending the fat actress crashing to the ground. The last thing he saw, as the soldiers rushed up to grab him, was Lan Yi dragging his mother and sister toward the archway. To his relief, nobody stopped them.

Slowly descending the creaking steps from the stage, the official helped the large woman to her feet. "The one who ran, the disguised one," blubbered the actress, still shaky from her fall. "She used to play at the Phoenix Canopy. Married an officer."

At those last words, Yang Rong dropped the actress like an armload of cabbages and strode toward the archway. When he reached Shen, he grabbed him by the ear and pulled him forward. The dark arch, part of the old town wall, was more like a tunnel than a doorway. In the patch of sunlight at the far end stood Mother. She had discarded her bulky disguise.

"I've often said you were a serpent, Yang Rong," called Mother. "And the serpent always desires the larger egg. I offer you a trade: myself for the boy."

Shen felt Rong's hand knotting the shirt behind his neck until he couldn't breathe. And yet the voice that emerged from the official's mouth was as sweet as honey.

"It's a beautiful day, but the sun hurts my eyes," Rong said in a friendly fashion. "I can't see your face, good lady. Who are you?"

"Somebody who was never fooled by you."

"I need a better look," said the official, pushing Shen ahead of him as he advanced into the tunnel.

"Don't waste time," cried Mother. "Do you agree to the exchange?"

Yang Rong hesitated and then retreated, dragging Shen with him. Shen saw Mother glance over her shoulder at something out of his line of vision. He heard a faint whinnying sound and realized that Lan Yi was trying to steal the soldiers' horses. What luck that Chang knew how to ride! In a few moments they would appear and rescue Mother.

Shen licked his dry lips and glanced at the face of the Confucian who was still holding tight to his arm and neck. Shen prayed that he had not noticed the whinnying, or thought nothing of it.

But the Confucian was no fool. His eyes narrowed, and he signaled with a jerk of his head for bowmen to approach the tunnel opening. Two of them took up positions on either side of the opening, so that Mother could not see them.

When they notched their arrows, Shen saw how quickly they could kill her. They would step into the opening and she would be dead in a heartbeat. Throwing caution aside, he screamed, "In the name of Heaven, Mother, run!"

The soldiers, confused, looked to their master for instruction. But Yang Rong, seeing that Mother was not running away, motioned them to slacken their bows. Mother stood proudly, framed like a portrait in the circle of sunlight. Then she clapped her hands loudly, just once. "Release him!" she said imperiously.

To Shen's amazement, the official let him go. He bolted into the tunnel, followed by the man's mocking voice.

"I know that you'll keep your word, Wife of Captain Fei," cried Rong, who had finally identified her.

As he reached her, Shen seized his mother by the arm. "He was stupid to let me go. Let's run!"

Mother shook her head, looking deeply into Shen's eyes. "You're nearly as tall as I am. It's odd I didn't notice before. Now go! If the gods are willing, you will find me again." She tapped Shen briskly on his backside, sending him stumbling toward the huge black horse that Yi was holding for him.

As he leaped into the saddle and lashed the horse's hide with the reins, he heard his mother cry out: "Build no shrine to your father until you know he is dead!"

And as her figure dwindled in the distance, he knew that Mother was Mother once again. She had found her heart.

But would he ever find her again?

CHAPTER 7

THE SUZHOU ACROBATIC TROUPE had just celebrated the spring festival of 1405. It was nearly two years since the fall of Nanjing.

Above Shen's soft lips there was now a faint and struggling mustache. Chang teased him because there was no beard on his chin as yet—a touchy subject, since a few acrobat boys his age already had a dusting of black whiskers.

He responded with a detailed list of childish behaviors Chang must abandon now that she was nearly a young woman. It began with immodest facial expressions (quizzical, shocked, angry), laughter (too loud), and her habit of standing like a man, hands on hips and pelvis outthrust. At first she bowed to acknowledge correction, but lately she rolled her eyes. It dawned on him that the girls in the company, expert in climbing knotted ropes and jumping backward through hoops, rarely walked with the tiny, mincing steps required by custom.

She needed protection from this bad influence. This of course was what Lan Yi had promised Father he would do. But once they had their new identities and got used to the circus, Lan Yi lost interest in them. In Shen's view, the job had fallen to him.

But what did he know of the underclothes a girl should wear when her breasts began to grow? Chang had corrected his few stumbling suggestions with amusement and said that Mistress Guo, the old woman who trained the girls, supplied her with necessary things. Shen felt his face shining red like a New Year's lantern.

There had been no word from Mother or Father, and brother and sister spoke less and less about them. Occasionally they would agree that Mother was certainly alive, because there was at least a chance this was true. And sometimes they would return to the disturbing fact that Mother and the terrifying Yang Rong, her jailer, seemed to know each other personally. They made up stories of how this might have happened.

About Father, on the other hand, there was no mystery so far as Chang was concerned. He was dead, though she didn't dare say so to Shen. Her brother habitually bragged about Father's toughness and certain survival to the boys in the troupe, who laughed at him. Many were without fathers and had no patience with Shen's delusions.

The circus was located on a run-down street of old merchant warehouses. The blocky, whitewashed building had wood-latticed windows in the upper floor but none below, to discourage thieves. There were a few traces of elegance, especially two looming doors of carved cedar through which oxcarts of trade goods had once rumbled into the courtyard. Now they swung outward on screeching hinges only when the circus went on tour with its horse-drawn wagons.

In the echoing courtyard the acrobats practiced pole walking and tumbling in fair weather. Bricks and plaster that occasionally fell from the walls were swept into a corner and forgotten. When it rained, the troupe rehearsed in a poorly heated hall just off the courtyard where accountants had once weighed goods and tallied prices on abacuses. Under Mistress Guo, a retired acrobat whose face had more bumps and hairs and wrinkles than a mandrake root, they had learned the ancient tricks—balancing chairs, tightrope walking, swinging from leather straps high in the air.

Chang felt sorry for the merchants who had abandoned the building long ago, when Father was still a child. Taizu, the first Ming Emperor, had punished Suzhou with high taxes because it had fought against him. The merchants couldn't make a living. Their misery had been the good luck of the circus, which settled into the abandoned property.

Chang had been thrown into training the day after they arrived. She still remembered the rapid hammering on the door of the girls' dormitory that first dark morning. She had stumbled down from the second floor, eaten a hasty breakfast, and joined the other girls in calisthenics under Mistress Guo's tyrannical eye. The old woman kept a bamboo rod in one hand, and laid it across the back—or the stomach, or the neck—of anyone who did not keep pace. Those who refused to practice were tied by the wrists to a stone pillar and beaten. Chang felt the rod less often than others, but she winced and her back muscles twitched when she saw it descend on another girl's back.

Boy acrobats were subject to this treatment as well—and worse. They could be confined in one of the windowless sleeping rooms reserved for the boys at the back of the building, behind the practice room and eating room. Or be denied access to the shared kitchen. Most preferred a beating to days of hunger or solitude. Chang was glad that Shen had escaped the training, even if it was because he was so bad at it. He was saved, as Lan Yi had foreseen, by the horses.

To haul the circus carts there were two heavy-bodied workhorses and three nobler animals, including the two magnificent military steeds that Lan Yi had stolen from the soldiers. They were under the care of a heavily muscled Mongol named Temur, who spoke broken Chinese even though he had been born in Nanjing. His cheeks, as round and red as apples, looked as if they had been burned by the wind of the steppes, which he in fact had never seen. There were gaps in his front teeth, and his wide-set eyes were sad. His family had left when Emperor Taizu drew a line across the middle of China and declared that Mongols to the south of it could not marry or have children.

Chang felt sorry for Temur, who had stayed behind when his family moved north. He had come to the circus hungry and penniless. But she was glad he was there, because he loved horses and had made Shen into an ally, though not exactly a friend. She watched them feeding, watering, and grooming the animals together. Shen, normally impatient, listened carefully as Temur struggled to find the right words to explain. It annoyed her that later on he made fun of the Mongol to the other boys, but she said nothing.

There was a sixth horse that Shen was not allowed to touch because it was a pony from Temur's ancestral Mongolian grasslands. So short-legged that Temur could lovingly groom its shaggy black mane without rising on tiptoes, it did not seem likely to be fast. But when Temur exercised it in a field near the compound it galloped in rapid circles. It dodged and weaved while the Mongol stood in the high stirrups and whirled a curved saber in a strange, repetitive pattern. One of the acrobats whispered to Chang that Mongol soldiers slashed that way with their sabers when the enemy army was collapsing. They were "harvesting" the heads of the fleeing soldiers and their horses. Chang knew she should hate him for this—had the Mongols not ravaged her country and family?—but secretly she found Temur's ferocity thrilling.

Then one day, noticing his sister all agape about Temur's antics, Shen decided to do some showing off of his own. He knew how to ride the sleek military horses, because Father had taught him when they were younger, at the summerhouse. Now he chose the one with the shining white coat, mounted it, and galloped flamboyantly, making the horse rear and zigzag and turn in tight circles.

"You ride like horse soldier," said Temur. Shen froze and then cantered the horse back to the stable.

Temur grinned at Chang, revealing that one of his missing front teeth had recently been replaced by a silver incisor. She wondered if Temur had found the money to fix his teeth by informing to the police. Such things happened. And their false papers said they were the children of a Nanjing merchant. Not likely that a merchant's son would know military riding! But Older Brother couldn't resist showing off.

A FEW DAYS LATER they had one of the rare private meetings they were permitted as brother and sister. Sitting under the half-dead courtyard tree by the costume shed, Shen told her that Mrs. Ling, their old neighbor ("the arrow-dodging lady"), had finally replied to his demand for information.

"She got my note two months ago but couldn't find anyone to bring a reply until now." Chang waited; they had this conversation each time Shen received a reply to one of his letters. The answer was always the same. "She says the palace won't release names of prisoners. And this time they wrote down her name. Now she's scared. She says we should stay away from the city. Our house isn't there anymore. The street is being rebuilt."

"Was that all?" Chang leaned toward him. "Anything about Uncle San?"

San had broken his leg during the siege, when a wall fell into the street. He had managed for a year or so with a homemade crutch but then took to sleeping all day in a corner of Mrs. Ling's house.

"The neighbors buried him," said Shen, who had loved Uncle San in spite of the endless proverbs. But he didn't like to show his feelings. "It was three months ago."

Chang dropped her head in the warm drizzle that so often fell in Suzhou, even during the winter. A white egret at the end of the roof poked its head under its wing, as if it, too, were mourning a lost relative. It seemed to her that the rain was falling like tears from every sky, all the way to the edge of the world. Under her breath she whispered a prayer.

"They're going to let me perform in public the next time we go on tour," she said, trying to sound as though the news about Uncle San had not upset her. Shen was relieved that she had changed the subject, so that he didn't have to say anything sentimental about the old man.

He looked closer and saw that Chang had traces of makeup around her eyes and mouth. "Don't stare at me!" She pushed him away, embarrassed. "We all have to wear it. And we have to smile all the time, even if we have a top spinning on our noses."

Chang had only trained for two years, and it was unusual for a circus to put a performer onstage with so little instruction. But Mistress Guo never stopped reminding Chang that she had been "old" when she arrived—some of the children she trained with were only seven or eight—and it was time she earned her keep!

A tiny, fine-featured girl strode up. It was Chang's acrobat partner, Jade. Shen noticed that, like Chang, she had been made to cut her hair short, in a pageboy style, so it wouldn't interfere with their routine.

In spite of her size, Jade enjoyed respect because she had briefly studied at the Imperial School of Acrobats, and the proud way she carried herself constantly reminded people of it. "Lan Yi has asked to speak with you," she said, narrowing her eyes at Shen. "And he has a stranger with him. The man smells like a pigsty and looks worse. He's an outlaw, I'm sure of it. Don't ask how I know. You'll feel it the moment you go in there."

And she was off. Jade had a habit of slanting the news to make it seem as if disaster was about to strike, and Shen didn't usually give much weight to her words. But this time he had a premonition that something was really wrong.

Bowing ruefully to Chang—if it were possible to bow ruefully—he plodded toward Yi's quarters. There had been a falling-out between them months earlier about Yi's drinking. The other boys said that Yi had always been a rice-wine drunk, but it had got worse since the civil war. "Now he drinks all the time because he has to feed vagrants like you and your sister," said one of them cruelly.

To be called a vagrant by a circus boy! How could he sink any lower? wondered Shen. He had been fretting about this one day when he visited Yi's quarters and found him and several of his friends sprawled on the floor amidst a clutter of wine cups. Shen lost his temper and shouted insults at the circus master—his elder. Of course Yi had staggered to his feet and beaten Shen while scorching him with abusive remarks. Shen knew that Yi was obliged to do that. No adult could tolerate a child's insult.

But still, he had avoided Yi ever since.

Yi's quarters were in the corner of the compound farthest from the street, because he had a habit of receiving mysterious visitors. They arrived at the back gate, carrying their own key. Some seemed to keep to a schedule. Many wore rags and a few wore silk. They went directly to Yi's quarters. Shen suspected a secret society of some sort, but eavesdropping on such a place was a challenge. Not long ago Yi caught him and kicked him across the courtyard. Since each was too proud to speak first to the other, the whole thing had taken place in silence.

Now he stepped inside and bowed, thinking something important must be afoot for Yi to break the ice between them. Yi nodded him toward a stool with a small, brusque smile of welcome. The circus master's face was tense, but he was also excited, as if some great decision had been made.

There was a stranger in the room. He was an ill-looking man with long, dirty tendrils of mustache hanging down each side of his mouth. He flicked a glance at Shen and began to bite at his fingernails.

"Are you happy with your treatment here, Fei Shen?" said Lan Yi formally but also rudely, since he did not introduce the men.

"Very happy, Master Yi," replied Shen, bowing from the waist. He was determined to be polite and leave as soon as possible.

"I am going to require a service of you. You have heard of the Treasure Fleet?"

Everyone had, of course, since proclamations had been pasted on every other street corner for nearly two years. Shen had often wondered about this marvelous fleet, remembering Father's stories of the oceangoing ships that had rotted away, centuries earlier, when the Middle Kingdom sealed itself off from the world. "Since the Prince of Yan became the Emperor Zhu Di, he has got a taste for the great world outside China," continued Yi. "Astronomers have come from Persia, and diplomats from India. The borders are opening. Even this strange religion called Islam is to be tolerated. You yourself have seen a mosque built in Nanjing. Who knows where it will end?"

"Some say that beyond the Arab countries there is a rising power," muttered the man with the dirty mustache. "A land where people have yellow hair and believe their god was nailed to a wooden cross."

"How grotesque!" cried Shen, thinking mainly of the yellow hair. "May we never go to such a place!"

The others laughed loudly and coarsely. "Some of us aren't choosy about where we go!" cackled the man with the long mustaches. He popped a pistachio into his mouth, rolled it around, and neatly fired the two half-shells onto the floor.

Yi became thoughtful. "Whatever reason the Emperor may have for building this fleet, it is a great opportunity for us."

Shen found all this interesting enough, but what did it have to do with him? What kind of "service" did Lan Yi need from him? But his thoughts were interrupted by the ill-looking man with the trailing mustache.

"Why do you think the Treasure Fleet is an opportunity for us?" whined the man. "The Emperor built it for himself. He's going to use it to destroy the Confucians."

This was more interesting, thought Shen. He had good reason to hate the Confucians, who had always controlled the government. One of them had arrested Mother. Another, Qian Pu, was the magistrate of Suzhou. The circus troupe lived in fear of him. The Confucians could do what they pleased.

Lan Yi turned his attention back to Shen. "Is this a bit above your head, boy? What my friend Marmot is talking about is a war inside the government. The new Emperor seized a throne he wasn't entitled to by putting eunuchs in charge of his army. Now the eunuchs have been paid off with government ministries and high positions in provincial governments. The

Confucians are fighting back. I hear the court in Nanjing is bloodier than a cockfighting ring during a holiday." Yi paused. "This touches us directly. The Confucians run things here in Suzhou, but for how long? They're under pressure. The Horse— you know who I'm talking about?"

"Magistrate Qian," replied Shen.

"He isn't taking bribes anymore."

Shen said nothing. He and Chang had frequently been trooped out to the courtyard, along with the others, to receive one of Magistrate Qian's visits. The little man grinned at them with a long, equine jaw well equipped with oversized and protruding white teeth. His officials examined everybody's documents, and they always denounced somebody for carrying forged papers. Then, after a brief hullabaloo, they apologized. They were well bribed.

But in recent visits they had seized company members, and these people had not returned. "Even worse, I'm afraid we won't be getting any more identity papers," said Yi to Shen. "Marmot, here, forged them with a little printing press. But yesterday they destroyed his shop and all of his beautiful stamps. He was lucky to get away alive. So I'm beginning to think that we need a new patron. In particular, I'm thinking of the eunuch with the blistered face who for some reason didn't cut off your head at the Gate of Gathering Treasure."

"Zheng He? The general?"

"He is an admiral now, Shen. Admiral of the Treasure Fleet. I think you can help us obtain his protection. He asked to know your name, didn't he?"

"Yes. But I'm sure he's forgotten it."

Yi leaned forward in his chair and spoke with the chilling authority he could summon unexpectedly. "You have begun to grow a mustache, Son of Fei Lee, but you have no idea what such a chance meeting can mean." He relaxed back in the chair. "You might begin by offering respect to Marmot. You and your sister are carrying quite lovely forged papers that he made for you."

Shen studied the curiously named Marmot more closely. Jade was right, he had the shifty eyes of a cutpurse.

"Nobody has a pretty face when he's a fugitive, Shen," continued Yi, seeming to read his thoughts. "You weren't very presentable when I brought you here, and your sister looked like a bag of laundry left out in the rain. Now, let me tell you what the eunuch admiral has proposed."

Yi then related what seemed to Shen a marvelous tale. The Treasure Fleet intended not a conquest of foreign lands, but a conquest of hearts and souls. It would carry trade goods, of course: tea and silk and celadon pottery, in exchange for the treasures of unknown countries. But it would also take aboard hundreds of scholars and poets and artists. They would carry the spirit of China to the barbarian lands.

"And how will they know they have the best? Because the Admiral himself is visiting the great cities of our land. He is holding auditions."

Marmot snickered. "And of course he's going to want a clapped-out little circus from a back street in Suzhou! Not to mention its fine selection of wanted criminals, such as myself. You are a dreamer, Lan Yi."

Lan Yi ignored the jibes. "Dear Marmot, you are forgetting this wonderful boy. This Fei Shen. He is a gift from the gods. He has met Zheng He. And he is going to call upon him."

"Me?" cried Shen.

"Of course. You are the boy from the Gate of Gathering Treasure. Your presence will cause the Admiral to look kindly upon taking the circus aboard his ships."

Shen was speechless. He looked like a bird grabbed by the neck.

"Consider. Why shouldn't we be ambassadors of our country's culture?" Yi continued, getting into one of his grand moods. "I have seen in the Imperial palace, scratched on a clay tablet, a picture nearly two thousand years old of acrobats dressed as lions, balancing on trestle tables just as we do today. I have read a poem a thousand years old about aerialists on leather straps such as the ones Old Hu cuts for us in his workshop. 'Circling like a hawk, floating like a duck.' Why should we not represent our country?" He looked at Marmot and Shen as if expecting applause.

Shen's head was swimming. "I need time to think about this," he finally stammered.

"You will have a month," pronounced Yi. "At that time, one of the giant ships will make its way down the Yangtze River. Not far from here the Admiral will come ashore to hear the petitions of those who wish to join the fleet. We shall be there."

Late that night, unable to sleep, Shen cursed Lan Yi under his breath. It was bad enough that he would be forced to bow to the man who had destroyed his city and his life. A little later he realized something else and sat bolt upright in bed. If he and Younger Sister agreed with this mad plan, they would be leaving China. They would be abandoning Mother and Father.

He forced himself to calm down. Gazing at the night candle that glimmered in the corner of the room he shared with three other boys, he made a decision. He and Younger Sister must flee. Their time in this place had come to an end.

CHAPTER 8

ONE AFTERNOON NOT LONG after his visit to Lan Yi's quarters, Shen left the boys' dormitory and came across Jade in the men's section where she should not have been. In her hands was a wooden tray with tea and soup. "I'm taking it to Grandfather Hu. He's sick," she said apologetically. "Would you like to come and visit? Nobody ever visits him."

Hu was the handyman who kept the troupe's equipment in good repair. In his remaining time he swept and tidied the courtyard. Shen thought as little about him as he did about the dust that danced around Hu's broom and settled back where it had been before. "The old man?" he said, using a sharp tone of voice. "Isn't he a little gone in the head? I thought that's why we call him Grandfather."

Jade fixed him with her brown-flecked eyes. "Evidently you don't get around much or you would know that he really is my *zu fu*, my father's father. And you might be surprised by the quality of his conversation."

"*Aiow*," muttered Shen. Lately it seemed he made every possible social blunder. He bowed and apologized at length.

Jade touched his shoulder to let him know that his apology was accepted. "Grandfather is the reason I came to this place. When the war shut down the circus school in Nanjing, he arranged that I should be invited. And"—she added pointedly—"I'm grateful to him."

Silenced for once, Shen let her lead him through Hu's little workshop. It increased the impression of his unimportance. A modest set of tools was hung on the decaying wall of yellow-brown plaster, including a curious wood scraper that looked like a snake with ten little sharpened steel plates protruding from its belly. All the tools were old, their hardwood parts darkened with dirt and sweat.

"Don't say anything to get him excited," she said in a low voice. Then she lit a candle and carried it into the old man's windowless sleeping area. The room was scarcely big enough for his straw pallet. Gently awakening him, she whispered that he should take a sip of medicinal tea.

As Shen's eyes became accustomed to the murky light, a shape at the foot of the bed resolved itself into a model ship. It was exquisite, its masts and spars of a dark wood that glowed with tung oil. The lugsails were of shining white silk.

The old man's cloudy eyes were finally open. "That is the greatest ship I designed," he said with a firm voice. "It was three hundred times the length of a man's foot. Three hundred *ch'i*. The Ming sailors used to call them 'mountain ships.' How they fled from us!"

"You fought for the Mongols?"

"No, you ignorant boy!" cried the old man. "We drove the Mongols out of central China. We were the Kingdom of Han."

"Please forgive me, Grandfather Hu," said Shen quietly, noticing Jade's alarm. "I know nothing of a Kingdom of Han."

That was the wrong thing to say. Now the old man was furious. "No, you would not. Many kingdoms sprang up when the Mongols fled. Taizu ruled only one of them. But he declared himself Emperor of all China! Many bowed down to him, but the people of Han defied him. Taizu was angry." The old man was so excited that he sat up in bed, causing Jade to cry out. He ignored her. "Taizu the tyrant! He ordered that all memory of the Kingdom of Han should be erased."

The old man fell back on the bed and closed his eyes. "That is why you know nothing of us."

"Please, Grandfather, drink some soup," pleaded Jade. "Don't make him talk anymore, Fei Shen. I need to get back to rehearsal or Mistress Guo will beat me."

Shen, who was shocked by Grandfather's traitorous talk, was already backing toward the door. But Grandfather's eyes flickered open again. "Has the eunuch admiral come to Suzhou? I hear they will test one of the big new boats on the Yangtze."

"Not yet, Grandfather," replied Shen.

"When that ship comes, I want to see it sink."

This was irresistible. Shen found himself edging back toward the bed. "Why would it sink?"

"Too big. They'll need iron to hold it together." He was seized with a racking cough.

"Enough talking," said Jade. She pinched Shen on the neck and pushed him into the workshop. She was surprisingly strong for her size.

"I asked you to visit him, not kill him!"

"But what he's saying is important."

"To whom? Not to me, you can be sure. Didn't I tell you I'll be punished if I don't get back?"

They went down the corridor together. But Shen kept looking back at Grandfather Hu's door. It seemed larger than before.

IN THE FOLLOWING DAYS the encounter with Grandfather Hu haunted Shen. The old man's story, and above all the vision of great ships laced together with iron, came into his mind each morning when he awakened.

There it did battle with his earlier resolution that he and Younger Sister must not go aboard those ships. Shen was torn. And for that reason a half-month went by before he spoke to Chang.

By the time they arranged to meet one evening in the courtyard, he had banished Grandfather Hu's story from his mind. He was not free! He could not amuse himself with adventures. He was shackled—he admitted it, he did not like it—but he was shackled to his duty. And his duty was to Mother and Father.

"It's time we stood up to Lan Yi," he declared with more conviction than he really felt. "He's going to send us out there like so much baggage, as if our desires had nothing to do with it. And to foreign places! I've made up my mind to speak to him about it. We aren't going."

The springtime quarter moon was already filling the courtyard with wan light. Chang looked at him in an appraising way, the chilly moonlight pooling in her black hair. Then she said, "I like the idea of going to foreign places. I can't wait to see the big ship next week."

He didn't let himself be provoked. "Really? Well, you won't see it. And not just because I don't want you to. Grandfather Hu says it's going to sink."

They sat in a sulking silence for a little while. He saw that she had folded some papers inside a rattan bag. "You're practicing writing again?"

"Two characters a day, and working hard to remember them. Didn't Uncle San say, 'Flowing water doesn't go stale'?"

"No doubt. How many do you know?"

"About two thousand. I'm starting to be able to read books."

"That's a lot," he said suspiciously.

"Mother taught me more than you knew. And now Lan Yi is helping me," she added, answering the unspoken question. "It's only been a few weeks. He says I need to be able to take care of myself if anything happens to you."

"That drinker of loudmouth soup!" cried Shen, referring to Yi's drunkenness. "How can he give you advice? How does he dare to? We are not going on those ships! Don't disgrace me by saying you don't know your duty to Mother. We must find her here, not in some barbaric place."

Chang hung her head, her short hair falling about her ears. "I don't know. I guess you are right. Of course you are right! We must leave the troupe. But where can we go?"

THE NEXT DAY, MAGISTRATE Qian posted notices that a

special pass must be obtained by anyone who wished to meet with the Admiral the following week.

Shen saw the signposting that afternoon as he pushed a wheelbarrow from the market back to the circus compound. He was balancing baskets of cabbages on each of its side platforms while Chang rode in the middle, on the board mounted above the barrow's oversized wheel.

Both were struck by the scarlet and gold-embroidered jacket of the soldier putting up the poster. He was a Brocade Guard, and they remembered Father's stories about this terrible brigade of the Imperial Guard. Each brigade had its task. Some, like Father's Forest of Feathers, guarded the Emperor directly. Others supervised the shipping lanes, while still others were in charge of building bridges and fortifications.

But only one, the Brocades, had power over all the others. Brocades could seize any officer and his family and torture them in a prison called the Bureau of Suppression and Soothing. The "suppressed" were not seen again, while those lucky enough to be "soothed" were relieved of their tongues or their hands so they could spread no more treason. Civilians were not safe either. The soldier's jacket glinted in the sun, and the shoppers walked wide to avoid it.

Shen parked the wheelbarrow under a shop awning, where he and Chang waited for the man to pick up his bucket of milky glue and move on. Then they came close to read the poster.

It declared that Ocean Lord Zheng He would meet with those who wished to serve the Treasure Fleet at the place where the Grand Canal entered the Yangtze River.

But Chang's eye went straight to the official names at the

side of the document. Bumbling Magistrate Qian's stamp was there, of course. But beside it, and much larger, was that of Lord Yang Rong, Commander of the Brocade Guard and Minister of National Security. The slender man in black who had arrested Mother. "We must tell Lan Yi right away," she said in a muted voice.

They rushed back, only to learn that Yi already knew. "Lord Yang Rong—formerly Junior Official Yang Rong—has done very well for himself under the new regime," said the circus master. "He just managed to avoid being jailed after the civil war. Now he's the king of the secret police!"

"Will he come here?" asked Chang.

"My information is that he will. He is a true believer, Chang. He thinks that contact with foreigners will corrupt China. His Confucian cabal doesn't dare oppose the Treasure Fleet openly. Instead, they'll sabotage it any way they can."

"I don't see what this has to do with us," declared Shen. "I've already told you that we're not going! And that goes double if Yang Rong is there. He'll know me! And what use am I to Mother if I'm in jail too?"

"With respect to your mother," said Yi in a brittle voice, "right now I am tired of hearing about her. You will speak to this Zheng He as I have ordered. As for Lord Yang, we'll keep you out of sight."

It was agony waiting for the rest of the week to go by. Shen felt humiliated, as if he were a tool that Yi would use and then throw away. Looking for somebody to take it out on, he fell on Temur. For the first time he mocked the Mongol's bad Chinese to his face.

This was dangerous, because Shen was not certain whether Temur was above or below him in the circus hierarchy. But on this occasion Temur backed away. Emboldened, Shen thought he could get away with saddling up the nameless little Mongol pony he was not allowed to ride.

He was cautious enough to wait for a day when Temur had duties in the town. Then he hit the stubborn little animal with the crop to get it moving. Though the pony shook its head angrily from side to side, it finally obeyed Shen and jogged as far as the practice track down the street from the compound. With spurs and lashings of the reins Shen made it gallop around the track until the sorghum-stalk fence that enclosed it became a brown blur.

It wasn't like any horse he had ridden. Although small, its back was broad and the muscles rock-hard. Even at speed it could maneuver unpredictably. Without warning it leaped off the track and ran across the grass to the other side, then pounded down the track in the opposite direction. Only with difficulty did Shen make the pony stop.

Sitting on the cross-grained little creature, mopping his brow and wondering what to do next, he heard his sister's voice. "He doesn't like you!"

Shen dismounted and tied the pony to a post. He still hadn't looked at Chang.

"Do I have to eat your birthday lunch by myself?" she cried.

He blushed, remembering that he was fifteen today.

Chang was fumbling with a bamboo box on the ground, from which she lifted out a steaming bowl of noodles. "Sorry I couldn't come up with any good-luck birthday money."

They shared the noodles, which were flavored with chicken fat and onions, while the sun climbed over the fence and sent warm orange-yellow fingers flowing along the beaten ground. Chang would soon be fourteen, he thought.

"That man Marmot came back this morning," she said. "I think he has papers of passage to get out of the city. There will be no obstacle to the troupe going up the Yangtze to audition for the Admiral."

"I don't want —"

"I know. But I beg you to reconsider, Brother. I've been thinking about it. If we strike out on our own, with false papers, we'll be fugitives. Forever. How can we help Mother that way?"

Shen snuffled through his nose, sounding a bit like the Mongol pony. He had come to understand that his plan was terrible. The problem was, backing down meant admitting that Lan Yi was right.

And that, naturally, was the next thing Chang said. "Lan Yi is almost certain that volunteers for the Treasure Fleet will receive a pardon. We're not the only people with bad records, Older Brother! It's a chance to—to—what's the word?"

"Regularize our status."

"That means a better chance of finding Mother, doesn't it?"

Shen hated conversations where he was wrong. "Don't forget that the ships will sail off the edge of the earth," he said, repeating the general belief that the earth was flat and square. "Maybe it will fall into the Country of the Dead and we'll have a reunion with Father, if that's where you think he is! Or Uncle San, who's there for sure!"

They ate in silence for some time, avoiding each other's eyes.

"Perhaps we won't have to complete the voyage," resumed Chang, ignoring his outburst. She looked slyly to one side. "We could get off somewhere. Maybe in Majapahit."

"I knew it! You're still thinking about him!" Meaning the vanished servant-boy Kun.

Chang began smacking him with the empty lunch box, covering him with curses. But her face was beet red, and so he felt at liberty to keep laughing until he was sitting on the ground and she was trying to pull his hair out.

"Stop! That hurts," he wailed.

"Take it back."

"*Aiow!* You've totally forgotten him."

"Who?"

"*Ai!* What's-his-name. See, I forgot him too."

She sprawled behind him, bracing her back against his back. Knowing she was sulking, he studied the little green cone-headed grasshoppers. It was remarkable how long a hopper would sit before suddenly launching itself into the air. Why now, and not a moment earlier—or later? There was no reason.

He could hear Uncle San drawing some stupid moral about decisive grasshoppers. "I can't just jump like that," he said out loud, confusing Chang for a moment. "I'll plead the circus's case to the eunuch, if it will help. I owe Lan Yi that much. And great happiness to our acrobat friends if they're accepted. But they'll leave without us."

Chang kept looking in the other direction, to hide her smile.

CHAPTER 9

TWENTY MEMBERS OF THE circus troupe squeezed aboard a single-masted fishing boat Lan Yi had rented for the trip to the Yangtze River. The ancient Mistress Guo cursed as she and her acrobats were jammed up against the thwarts, while Shen's feet slid about in the greasy remnants of a cargo of fish. Pinching her nose against the odor, Chang scampered onto a framework of poles that usually supported a net in front of the boat. There she sat like a bird and watched the greenish water swirl beneath her.

Brick balconies and windows jutted out of the canal-side houses every which way, as if the dwellings had jostled one another for space by the water. Brown clay tiles were laid in crooked S-shaped lines down the roof slope, so that they looked like long, muddy snakes. Nearly every house had steps descending to the canal, where women washed clothes and children tried to trip one another into the tea-colored water.

Soon the houses gave way to irrigated rice lands. By nightfall the land grew marshy, and Shen fell asleep on the fish-smelling deck. Everybody was stiff and bad-tempered by the time the sun rose the next day, especially Grandfather Hu. His health had improved enough for him to make the journey. Chang, who had spread the fishing net over the poles and slept comfortably, wished she had offered her homemade hammock to him.

Reaching the last village on the canal, the troupe made its way to the flat spot near the Yangtze River where Zheng He had erected his pavilion.

To Shen's relief the pavilion was empty, though guards were posted around it. And the crowd was thin, even if the city of Zhenjiang was close by. There were a few sellers of grilled meat, some musicians, and a scattering of peddlers with toys hanging from bamboo rods, the better to keep them out of children's hands until they were paid for. But there was no sign of the giant ship that had been sent downriver to test its strength in the ocean. It was supposed to return that day.

Grandfather Hu went bustling off to interrogate the guards by the dock. When he returned, he grabbed a glass of barley beer from Shen's hand without asking. "I was right! There was a mild gale at sea, and the timbers sprang. The hulk has already limped back to Longjiang. There's nothing to see." Longjiang was the vast harbor that had been dug just outside Nanjing to construct the fleet.

Shen was ecstatic. "Then we'll go back right away?"

Lan Yi had quietly approached and overheard. "The Admiral's officers are here. Apparently the eunuch still intends to recruit."

"So they say," replied Grandfather Hu. "But it's anybody's guess if he's in a mood for painters and opera singers. He hasn't come ashore today." He gestured at a small warship anchored near the riverbank.

As Shen watched, tightly disciplined sailors marched out onto the deck, wearing sky-blue uniforms of a design he had not seen before. As they prepared a boat, a man with a six-pointed official's hat stepped out of the ship's cabin. He was gigantic. Shen knew right away that it was Zheng He.

And Shen bolted. He did not look where he was going and instantly slammed into a vendor carrying a tray of spiced meats. They went down in a tangle of feet and sausages. But in a moment he was on his feet and running toward the canal. He heard Yi's voice and ignored it.

He could not ignore the two pairs of powerful hands that seized him from each side. A pair of Brocade Guards were shouting at him, but he could not hear what they were saying. He was conscious of the fierce heat of the sun beating on his head.

Finally, after what seemed a very long time, Yi arrived, out of breath. "It is a misunderstanding," he gasped to the soldiers.

"Misunderstanding? This boy looks a perfect thief. See? He has a gold ornament around his neck."

Shen saw that his tunic was torn, and the gold dragon that he normally concealed inside was dangling freely. Yi ripped it from its leather thong and held it up between two fingers. "This boy is my business. Your business is to look elsewhere." He waved the shining little object back and forth in front of the soldiers. Their eyes followed it greedily.

Moments later Yi and Shen arrived back at the pavilion. Yi had given away the gold dragon as a bribe in spite of Shen's feeble protest. Then he had dragged him back by the hair, shouting at him for being such an idiot as to run away.

But the circus master abruptly shut up when he saw the Brocade Guards posted at the pavilion entrance eyeing them suspiciously. Their heavy red tunics were buttoned to the chin in spite of the great heat. Sitting comfortably under a large umbrella nearby, a servant waving a feather fan near his face, was Yang Rong. The square silk badge on his robe was embroidered with a bird, a red-capped crane. Shen saw all this as if it were a painting, frozen in front of him. He was certain that Lord Yang would see and denounce him.

But Yang never looked in their direction. Yi and Mistress Guo approached the Confucian and spread the circus's legal papers on a small folding table in front of him. The Confucian glanced briefly at the documents and languidly thumped the topmost paper with a jade seal, called a chop, which was dipped in ink. A waiting Guard escorted the group to the entrance of Zheng's pavilion.

Shen was nearly blind with the salt sweat that had run into his eyes, and at last he managed to raise a hand and wipe it away. There was blood in the sweat. He felt his forehead throbbing painfully where one of the Brocades had cuffed him.

He began to hear voices, the babble of many people speaking all around him. When their turn came, Lan Yi discreetly pushed Shen in the direction of the eunuch admiral. At the same moment, Mistress Guo stepped up to present an aerialist who called himself the Flying Pigeon. He was the best-known performer in the troupe.

At a plain soldier's field desk sat the Admiral. The formal bright-blue cloak wrapped around his massive chest was trimmed in gold, with the courtier's black cap carefully fastened to his hair. The spotless clothing made his face seem even more ravaged than before. The hideous grandeur of the man suddenly did what nothing else had. It shook Shen's belief that Father had survived.

Shen forced himself to listen as Lan Yi expressed deep regret to the Admiral about the mishap with the trial ship. Zheng He nodded in a distracted way. The short court official standing behind him impatiently waved one hand in a small circle, indicating that Yi should get on with it.

Shen listened, still with a sense that all of this was unreal, as Yi embarked on a flowery speech about ancient decorated clay tiles and old poems about acrobats. Zheng He glanced pleadingly at the little official.

"All very interesting," said the near-sighted man who blinked incessantly, "but dreadfully low class."

"Low class?" cried the Admiral, who seemed to be looking for an excuse to spar with him. "Well, I think we have engaged enough opera singers to torment the barbarians. And I happen to like the Flying Pigeon. I've seen you before," he added, grinning at the aerialist. Zheng He's gleaming teeth gave him a tiger-ish look. The Flying Pigeon stepped back a pace.

"You're next," hissed Yi into Shen's ear. "Get a grip on yourself."

Then Zheng's eyes settled on Shen, moving searchingly over his face. "And you, child? Have I seen you before?"

"When you broke the Gate of Gathering Treasure, Lord Zheng," replied Shen in a voice that he was just able to control. His lips were dry.

The eunuch's black eyes studied Shen carefully. "Ahhh... yes! Look here, Blinky," he said abruptly, tugging the near-sighted official closer. "This fellow nearly ruined the moment of my triumph in Nanjing. He proposed to cut out my heart if I went near the Emperor's palace!"

The group of officials around the Admiral laughed dutifully, and so did Lan Yi. But Shen, remembering that he had said nothing about cutting out the eunuch's heart, continued to stare levelly at Zheng He. "I wish I had said that. I wish I had done it. Then I would be with my father now."

Out of the corner of his eye he saw Lan Yi's face collapse in defeat. Chang was staring at her brother, appalled. Shen didn't care. It seemed worth it to say the truth just once.

The Admiral's entourage made alarmed noises. One pointed at the spot of blood on Shen's forehead. Zheng He waved them silent. "You speak your mind like a soldier. I'd wager my hat your father was a soldier."

"He was, Honored Lord."

"Then this one is dangerous," cried the official called Blinky. "I say turn him over to Lord Yang."

"Absolutely not," replied the Admiral. "I think I will drink tea with this boy."

The sudden and unexpected invitation brought a smile to Chang's lips. But Shen and Yi were off balance. Before they could sort themselves out to say something gracious, they were shouldered aside by the next applicant. He was a landscape artist burdened with scroll paintings. The Admiral glanced at the long line of hopefuls behind the painter and beckoned him to step forward. The guards discreetly moved the little group, and the several acrobats accompanying them, toward the pavilion's exit.

As they joined the rest of the troupe in the bright meadow, however, the short official named Blinky came running after them. "You're to return at sunset," he said to Shen with a smirk. "Lucky boy. But keep your tongue in your head." And he was gone.

Lan Yi turned to Shen. "The gods watch over you and your big mouth. Or maybe the eunuch just wanted to annoy that blinking dwarf." He took Shen's arm and pulled him away from the others. "The eunuch has invited you on a whim. Be agreeable. Nod like a wooden puppet. And don't remind him of your insolence here. We may have made a good impression in spite of you." He seized Shen's neck in a tight grip. "I'll be here when you come back."

———

IT WAS LANTERN-LIGHTING TIME when Shen returned from the Admiral's warship. Lan Yi and Chang had waited for him on the dock. Against the evening chill his sister had nothing but a rotted straw rain cape a farmer had discarded.

Yi had decided to send the rest of the troupe back in the fishing boat and rent a smaller craft for the three of them to return in. As its tiny sail tugged them down the canal, and the boatman shifted the wooden sweep to keep them away from shore, Yi prodded Shen to narrate the happenings of the evening exactly as they had occurred. As Shen did so, he put his arm around Chang, who was shivering. The comforting embrace and the familiar softness of his voice in the night silence soon lulled her to sleep.

Looking at the net of bright stars overhead, Shen recalled first that the cabin on the Admiral's small warship had been crowded. All his principal officers were there, and Shen noticed right away that they did not speak of the Treasure Fleet as the merchants did. They called it the Star Fleet, because it would sail beneath unknown stars.

Then Shen recalled his strange conversation with Zheng He. The Admiral was nervous and overexcited. He told a story from his childhood about when the Prince of Yan—the man who was now Emperor—came to Yunnan Province looking for fleeing Mongol soldiers. The young Prince had seen the child Zheng He playing by the roadside and asked for information.

Shen tried to imitate the Admiral's gravelly voice, causing Chang to stir in her sleep. "'Who are you to ask me?' this little boy roars at the Prince. And then he refuses to tell the Prince anything, not even his name. Then the Admiral says, 'The Prince was so impressed a little country boy like me would talk back that he took me into his service and had me cut for a warrior eunuch!' Then Zheng He got all thoughtful, and he said to me, 'You, boy, back in Nanjing. You reminded me of myself. The idiot bravery of the young. I wish I had it now.'"

Shen loved repeating that last remark because it was about himself. Then he recalled that the Admiral had spoken of the ship that had almost been lost. He challenged his officers: "'We've made ourselves ridiculous to the common people. Soon the whole country will know. The Emperor will be angry when the news reaches him, and it will strengthen our enemies. What can we do?'

"None of the officers said anything," Shen continued. "So the Admiral mocked them"—Shen made a very unconvincing attempt to reproduce the Admiral's facial expression—"and he pointed to me. And he said, 'Be like this boy! Say what you're thinking.' Then an old captain with muttonchop whiskers stepped forward and said, 'We can tell the people that the goddess Tianfei laid her hand on the ship to warn us. Her spirit generals broke the planks so that we'd know we're not ready.' Then Captain Zhou dared to add, 'And we aren't.'"

Shen's voice trailed off. He looked at Chang, snoring in the crook of his arm. Lan Yi nodded. "You did well, Son of Captain Fei. So you remind the eunuch of his younger self! That will be worth a hundred golden dragons to us."

As the boat skimmed down the canal under the gentle moon, Shen finally nodded off. He dreamed that he was in a little boat being blown in every direction on an empty sea. Every so often a figure would call out from the depths, a flickering white image of a relative or priest. There was even Chen Chao, the bumbling kitemaker from back home, trying to fly a kite underwater. Shen felt his arms moving heavily, as if the ocean currents were unfriendly spirits.

He startled awake and saw that Yan Li and Chang were asleep. The dream had left him in a cold sweat.

———

NAVAL OFFICIALS HAD TOLD Lan Yi that the fleet would not sail until the ninth month—still more than five months away. The circus would not learn for many weeks if it had been selected, because the Admiral's first business was to get the merchant ships assembled on time at Longjiang.

Grandfather Hu had also learned a good deal. Using his knowledge of shipbuilding, he had loosened the tongues of some officers who had serious doubts about the giant ships. He had learned there were four more under construction, but work would be halted until the engineers understood why the first had failed.

"They nearly lost the *China Harmony*. Just one little gale that wouldn't hurt a Fuchow trader! How do they think they're going to sail to the edge of the world?" said Grandfather Hu with obvious pleasure.

What had been dreadful news for the Admiral left the old man in unaccountable high spirits. He spent as much time as possible in his dark little room, calling for extra candles and lamp oil all day long.

Jade was embarrassed. "It's that boat. He's becoming obsessed again."

Shen found himself probing Jade to see if she was one of those who would go with the troupe onto the ships. "It's not possible," she replied. "How could I go off for years on a sea journey with no chaperone? What would happen to the marriage planning?"

This silenced Shen. Chang was also of marriageable age, he realized. What would become of her?

With these thoughts still preying on him the next morning, he decided to clear his head by going for a ride. He secretly saddled Temur's little chestnut pony and walked it out of the stable. As he did, he noticed Temur's heavy Mongol bow, crafted from animal horn and strips of steel, hanging on a peg by the door. Without thinking he slipped it over the horse's pommel and cantered through the courtyard toward the street gate.

It had been a warm spring, and in the intervals between acrobatic classes and training, Chang was trying to make honeysuckle grow up the courtyard wall in a place that got good sun. She was digging more black earth into the stony, beaten-down soil when Shen stopped to look on. She squinted up at him, wiping a smudge from her forehead. "Brother, you shouldn't ride that horse. I meant to warn you the other time, when you rode it on your birthday."

Shen shrugged to avoid talking about the pony. "I dreamed on the boat that I was paralyzed. I'm going to undo that dream."

She caught sight of the bow. "Did Temur say you could take that too?"

"He's not around."

"But it's his father's bow."

"Eahh! Mongols aren't sentimental. And I won't be long."

The little horse became more comfortable with him as they cantered down the alleyway that led to the rice tribute field. This was where farmers brought the grain they used to pay taxes once a year. The rest of the time it was empty, and the circus used it to exercise the horses.

As Shen and the chestnut pony cantered around the track, he wondered why he had taken Temur's bow. He loved the feel of it, but it came into his mind that he had committed a violation by laying hands on it. Temur's father's bow.

Wagering that he wouldn't get caught, he gazed at the magnificent weapon. Only a grown man could pull a Mongol bow, because of its laminations of horn, wood, and steel. But Shen found that he could bend it a little way. So he whooped along on the horse's back, using the bow to weakly fire sorghum stalks at some children who had collected at the edge of the field. The activity lasted only a few minutes before he saw a shadowed figure standing underneath a tree at the field's edge. Its arms were folded and the shoulders leaned forward, hunched and tense. He knew it was Temur.

A cold wash of shame came over Shen. He lowered the bow and tugged the reins, bringing the animal to a halt. He dismounted without being asked.

Temur's face was as dark as a cloud shadow on a hill. He roughly snatched the bow from the saddle. "Not for fun, this bow! It is for killing."

The Mongol was so upset he forgot to mention the horse. But he jerked it cruelly by the reins and led it back toward the compound. "You shame your father," he said loudly over his shoulder, with great effort producing a correct sentence.

Shen waited till Temur was gone and then followed him at a distance. Temur knew by now that Shen's father was a cavalry soldier. It had been common gossip in the company since he had blurted it out during the interview with Zheng He. Now Shen burned with shame, because Father would never touch another man's horse without permission. Even Mongols didn't do that. He shuddered to think what a low opinion of him Temur must have.

But by the time he reached the street gate of the circus building, the jangling and booming of ceremonial music distracted him.

The music announced the arrival of Magistrate Qian, who was approaching on his gold-painted palanquin. It was supported by two strong horizontal wooden poles, each one carried on the shoulders of three hefty attendants. They wore the loose robes of minor officials, including long, floppy sleeves that covered their hands and hung down to their knees. Two higher officials with impressive angled hats carried Magistrate Qian's scepter of office and led the procession. Behind them were four musicians, one with a small goatskin drum he was steadily beating, two with flutes, and one with a curious wind instrument held upright against his chest that emitted a long drone from its chanter. A short column of police constables brought up the rear.

The procession stopped outside the circus compound. Shen raced inside, just in time to see Lan Yi and Mistress Guo hastily emerging from the building.

"It's the police," he said.

CHAPTER 10

T HE CONSTABLES ROOTED THROUGH the men's and women's dormitories, noisily overturning beds and emptying the wicker baskets where the troupe kept their personal effects. Then they returned to the compound where the performers waited in straight lines, holding their documents—many false—in front of them.

Chang watched the magistrate warily. Then she noticed that Marmot, who had been hiding out in the compound, was nowhere to be seen. Since the warrant for his arrest was still active, he would have fled as soon as he heard the music.

What worried her the most, though, was that Shen was not there. She was about to ask the people beside her if they'd seen him when the magistrate suddenly stepped in front of her.

He glanced at her papers, suspicious as a dog outside a closet full of kittens. "Tell me about your family," he said in an unfriendly voice.

Chang recited the story she had memorized. She and her brother were the children of a wealthy Nanjing merchant, she said, repeating his name with what she hoped was daughterly piety. "Both of our parents died in the war, Honorable Qian."

"A touching tale, and a sweet face. A man would almost believe you."

Lan Yi had moved in closer. "Is there a problem, Revered Magistrate?"

"I have good reason to believe this girl and her brother are holding forged papers. And where is he?"

Where was he indeed, thought Chang. Her heart began to pound.

"You have approved the girl's papers before, Honored Qian," said Yi. "Please understand that her father was a particular friend of mine. She is under my protection. Since I respect your diligence, I will happily make a further contribution of silver *taels* to your office." He opened his hand to reveal two little lumps of silver so heavily stamped by the Imperial mint that they had a squashed-up fringe around their edges.

Magistrate Qian smiled evilly. "Those two little boats are not large enough to carry this child to safety."

"How much silver do you require?"

"It's not a question of silver," replied Magistrate Qian, who was now wriggling uncomfortably. "Remember, I must satisfy other people." He leaned in to whisper confidentially, "I have been asked to bring these children for questioning."

"Were you asked by the Brocade Guards?" said Yi.

"I can't say that. But as you know there have been quite a lot of Brocades in this city the last while. They'll be back soon. I'm just as afraid of them as you are."

"I sympathize. And you know I have always done as you required. But this is awkward, you see, because I have sworn on my honor to this girl's father. Can you give me a little time?"

"My masters will arrive in a week. During that time I expect you to find her brother and keep them both here until I require them."

Yi bowed. "I solemnly promise that I will find the brother, and that both of them will stay by my side."

Chang had a funny feeling that Yi had not agreed to quite the same thing the magistrate had asked. But the bony little man did not seem to notice. He backed away, bowing politely. Soon the clanging of processional music grew faint in the street.

Chang darted her eyes around the courtyard, expecting Shen to emerge from a hiding place. But he wasn't there.

AS SOON AS MAGISTRATE Qian asked Chang about her family, Shen knew that the game was up. He had been watching through the latticework window of a small door in the compound wall, where he had hidden as soon as he saw the magistrate. This door led inside the building to a concealed passageway. It in turn was connected to the merchant's compound next door. The merchant was paid to provide an emergency exit if the company had to flee, and everyone knew where it was. Several others had already slipped away.

Watching from the doorway, Shen tried to think of a way to free Chang if the constables seized her. But then Yi stepped in. He couldn't hear what the two men were saying, but the magistrate soon lost interest in Chang.

Relieved, but still nervous, Shen slipped out through the merchant's compound and wandered the streets for the rest of the day. Every so often he stopped to flick idle pebbles into the turf-colored canal water.

A constable was now standing guard outside the circus compound, so Shen crept back in through the merchant's building instead.

By this twisty route Shen found himself in Lan Yi's quarters. Yi was there with Grandfather Hu and Chang. He could see that she had been crying.

"Good evening," said Yi, squinting at him by candlelight. "How did you know to run away?"

"I can't say exactly. Something in the magistrate's voice when he asked for Chang's papers. I knew right away we'd been denounced."

Yi nodded. "Grandfather Hu and I believe that Yang Rong is behind this. He must have spotted you that day by the Yang-tze River. But why is he going to so much trouble over you? You're nobody, after all. There must be a thousand Forest of Feathers orphans running around the country." Yi looked thoughtfully at Shen. "Whatever the reason, we're not safe here any longer. And the Admiral seems to like you. Maybe it's time we paid a visit to Longjiang."

"You can't!" protested Shen. He stood up and straightened his back in order to tell them what he had decided that day. "I'm grateful for your protection, Friend of My Father. But I have decided that we will not go on this journey. And as you admit yourself, you can't protect us here any longer. My sister and I are leaving. Tonight."

Chang shrieked and looked at him in horror. "To go where?"

"That is for me to decide!" declared Shen, who kept his gaze on Yi even as he spoke to his sister. "You are under my authority, and I am of age. It's time we found Mother and learned what has happened to Father. We'll return to Nanjing and start the search there. After that we'll go wherever we have to. We're old enough now to look for them. And you know I'm right, Honorable Lan. Their flesh is our flesh."

This speech, which he had delivered in spite of himself in a spluttering voice, had exhausted him. But he remained standing, breathing heavily and with his eyes glittering.

Yi scowled at him, but bit his lip and looked away. When he finally spoke, it was to commend Shen for taking charge as his father would have done. "But much as I admire you, I must overrule you. You owe me a debt for protecting you and your sister, and you will acquit it by accompanying our troupe to Longjiang. We need your influence with the eunuch."

"I won't do it!"

"You will. And soon. I have decided that the company will flee Suzhou before Magistrate Qian's seven days have elapsed. We'll throw ourselves on the Admiral's mercy, and you will help us do that. After that, you're free to leave."

Shen gaped at him.

"Furthermore, Temur will keep you under guard until then. Although I hope you will come to your senses and see that honor binds you to do this much for us." Grandfather Hu looked at him with pitying eyes. So did Chang, but in her case the pity was false. She had been terrified of going out onto the roads of China. Truly, Older Brother understood nothing of what might happen to a girl.

CHAPTER 11

SINCE BEING NAMED AS Shen's guard, Temur had accompanied him everywhere, sitting comfortably on the little horse's back while Shen trudged alongside. Chang was confined to the compound.

"This day, I give the horse a name," Temur had said on the first morning of Shen's captivity. "He is Merk. You call him this name."

The name meant nothing to Shen. The only thing he cared about was the utter impossibility of outrunning the pony.

But today, on the third day of his captivity, an unexpected opportunity arose. Shen had the wheelbarrow, which he was to fill with vegetables and grain from the market and take directly to the large boat Lan Yi had procured for the company's trip to Longjiang. Since time was short, Temur had been ordered to help Shen load.

At the seller of sweet potatoes, Shen watched as the Mongol dismounted, something he rarely did. Temur was prudent enough to keep the reins looped around his wrist so Shen could not gallop away with Merk. But Shen had expected that.

It was promising that the Mongol was off the horse at all. This would give Shen several moments of running time before Temur could get back in the saddle. And Shen had chosen this shop because there was a narrow footpath beside it that the pony could not enter.

A short while before, Shen had noticed a few Brocade Guards patrolling the perimeter of the market. They were not supposed to arrive in Suzhou for two days yet. He knew this would disturb Yi's plans, but that was not his problem.

He breathed deeply, and just as Temur grunted to lift a sack of potatoes into the wheelbarrow, Shen sprinted for the little lane. As he reached the entrance, a Brocade Guard stepped out of a doorway and grabbed him.

Temur was not far behind. He tried to take charge of Shen but could not make himself understood to the guard, who apparently didn't have much use for Mongols. Temur struck the man heavily on his windpipe, driving him into the wall, and seized Shen.

But it was too late. Other Brocades had appeared, and within moments Temur and Shen were dragged up before an officer. Shen noticed the man was wearing a Panther badge. The officer shucked off his helmet and ruffled his sparse hair, which sweat had plastered to his balding skull.

"My name is Chu," he said amiably, bowing. "I believe I saw you two at Lord Zheng's pavilion some weeks back. You belong to the circus, don't you?"

"Yes," grinned Shen. "We're buying kitchen supplies."

Panther Officer Chu pursed his mouth and nodded thoughtfully. "Your Mongol struck my man. Since I must deal with this questionable circus company sooner or later, I shall take you there now. Your head man will pay reparations."

It could have been worse, Shen knew. But all afternoon Lan Yi was furious. He had to hand over a good deal of money to the Brocade officer. Even worse, the officer was suspicious. He had posted guards at the compound's front and rear gates.

"You are a colossal fool, Fei Shen!" raged Yi. "Magistrate Qian's constables are easy to evade, but how am I to get fifty people past the Brocades?" Calming himself, but still breathing heavily, he added, "We will leave tonight. And to make sure you behave, you will be lashed to your horse. When we dismount, you'll walk with your feet tied. We'll see how you like a long journey, mincing like a servant girl!"

Yi's plan was for most of the company to slip through the courtyard door into the adjacent merchant's compound. A very few, including himself and Shen and Chang, would ride away on the circus's horses. All would meet up at the shipyard in Longjiang. Two Brocade Guards had been set at the back of the company's compound to prevent escape, but those on foot would depart unseen through the merchant's building.

To distract the guards, Marmot had gone out to offer some warm wine against the evening chill. Although they looked warily at his long mustache tendrils and greenish teeth, they accepted the wine. Being well disciplined though, they refused a second bowl when Chang came out later to offer it. One stood up when he heard a thump behind the merchant's compound but sat down again.

After the last of the company had slipped away through the neighboring merchant's building, Chang stood in the courtyard and gazed at the moon rising. She knew that Lan Yi was waiting patiently for one more of the night's six watches to go by, to give the circus people who had left on foot time to get to the river. Lan Yi had calculated they would arrive there when the moon reached a certain point above the top of the compound wall. Meanwhile, Temur kept up appearances by putting out the lanterns and locking the gates at the customary time.

Chang was relieved that Lan Yi had agreed to let her stay with the little group that was to leave on horseback. She had threatened to raise a fuss if they didn't, because she would not be separated from her brother. And she had reminded Yi that she could ride a horse.

She saw that everybody was there—Yi, Temur, Marmot, and Older Brother—looking sullen with his feet lashed to his stirrups. Only Grandfather Hu was missing. But just then he came huffing into the stable with a bag full of rolled-up papers and his model ship.

"Grandfather!" barked Yi. "You cannot bring the ship."

"But it's my ship!" he whimpered, and tears spilled out of his eyes.

"It doesn't have a god living in it, so far as I'm aware," said Yi carelessly. "It's the drawings we need. Take good care of them."

Still complaining, Grandfather Hu rested the wooden ship in a haystack. He had carried the model with him for forty-six years. By the time he mounted his horse, he had fallen silent.

Moments later Temur unbolted the rear gate and swung it open. Five horses, followed by a small Mongol pony, thundered into the lane as the two Brocades fell over each other to get out of the way. Fortunately, they lacked horses to give pursuit.

The group trotted down the dark lane, picking up speed as they turned onto the short road that led toward the tribute field. They urged the horses onward with tight, breathless voices, glancing back for signs of pursuit. Only the old man was silent, riding stiffly and gazing ahead. After a while Shen heard him mutter, "My ship. My *Leaping Tiger.*"

So the little boat had been a real ship. Shen decided to winkle the story out of Grandfather Hu before they reached Longjiang.

ALL OF THE YANGTZE delta country was flat and marshy. By the first light of morning, they had ridden many *li* in a northerly direction on the road that ran along the Grand Canal. They looked for the boat that should be carrying the rest of the troupe in the same direction, especially since Grandfather Hu was worried about Jade. But Yi finally decided that they must have passed it in the darkness. And there was no going back to look. Each group was on its own.

Drainage canals extended in all directions through a bright green empire of rice paddies. After a while the Grand Canal slanted in a northwesterly direction toward the Yangtze River and the country became marshy once again.

By midday, Grandfather Hu was dozing in the saddle. Chang rode alongside to gently slap his hands. "I am very well,

Granddaughter," said the old man, rubbing his tired eyes. "Don't fuss about me. This is a journey I have looked forward to."

At the gate of the small city of Wuxi, Marmot spoke with the duty officer, who seemed to know him. The man warned that their escape was known, and Brocade cavalry were searching the countryside. After that they rode as quickly as they dared through the town, thankful that they encountered no Brocade sentries. Yi didn't relax until they cleared the gate on the other side, and he didn't stop to feed them and the horses until the city was out of sight. Then he told them they would have to ride right through the night, putting the Brocades well behind them.

Temur had chosen to ride a big military horse so he could deal with any soldiers who might interfere with them. As a gesture of goodwill, he allowed Shen to ride Merk. The little grassland pony had trouble keeping up with the long-legged animals on a straight road. But as darkness fell the big horses had to slow down and pick their way. Merk, to Shen's delight, cantered onward as if the landscape were flooded with daylight, leaving the other five horses behind.

At daybreak they pitched camp behind a ruined wall of brown bricks that had once been the entrance to a farmyard, now vanished and replaced by a field of ripening millet. The wall hid them from any Brocade patrol they might happen by. Yi declared that Shen need not be tied to his horse any longer, since there was nowhere for him to run to. Shen sat on the ground, rubbing the rope burns where his ankles had been bound to the stirrups. He was too angry to go to sleep. Instead he asked Grandfather Hu to talk about his lost model ship.

The old man was exhausted, but the mention of the ship roused him immediately.

"You must think me foolish to keep a toy of a ship that brought me nothing but sorrow," muttered Grandfather Hu as he wrapped himself in a dirty quilt and lay on the ground. Then he told a long story, with many details about how the ship was built. But the most vivid part was about the disaster that befell it on its maiden voyage.

"The King of Han asked me to build the biggest ship ever seen, nearly three hundred *ch'i*, so that we could pursue our enemies to their home ports. I called it *Leaping Tiger* because I imagined it was long enough to leap from one giant wave to the next.

"And so it did. But when it did—and this was its first voyage—the ship broke in half. I watched our soldiers spill out of her belly like seeds from a pomegranate.

"From that day to this I have never stopped thinking about it. And finally it came to me how such a ship might correctly be built."

"How is that, Grandfather?" asked Shen. But the old man's eyes had closed and he was far down the path of sleep. Looking around, Shen saw that Chang and the others were already snoring.

It was a pattern that would be repeated each day: an exhausting ride through the night, over uncertain roads, followed by fitful sleep in whatever daytime place they could find that shielded them from the view of passersby.

The only city on their route was Zhenjiang, and Lan Yi kept them well inland on the south shore of the Yangtze in order to avoid it. Only when the city was behind them did they approach the great river at last. They took a ferry to the north shore.

As they moved through the last stretch of open country before Longjiang, Yi pushed them harder. They rode not only through the night, but also far into the morning. Military patrols appeared. These were infrequent and easy to evade at first but became more numerous as the group drew closer to the heavily guarded port where the Treasure Fleet was under construction. So did lumbering wagons stacked high with heavy hardwood planks, and others carrying boxes and bales of unidentifiable goods.

On their last day of travel, they were hailed by a distant group of red-jacketed cavalry. "If they're guardsmen, I've had enough of running from them," Yi said, spitting out a grass stalk he'd been chewing. He signaled Temur.

The soldiers were already notching arrows on their bowstrings. Temur quietly pulled three arrows from the quiver attached to his saddle, spacing them between his fingers. Then he fired them in three rapid swoops, like a girl strumming a harp. They arced high in the air, making a loud whistling sound, before falling to the ground on the far side of the guardsmen.

That was all the Brocades needed. The whistling told them the arrows were Mongol, and they knew they couldn't match the range of the Mongol bow. They wheeled about and departed.

Now the group had to make speed for the rest of the day in case guardsman units were sent in pursuit.

That evening, as they wearily made camp in a small wood at the base of a vast grass-covered hill, Shen thanked Temur.

The Mongol stared ahead without saying anything, his dark face as blank as a door. Then he turned away.

"Well," said Lan Yi, walking up to the frozen sculpture formed by Shen and Temur, "more proof that the Chinese army needs to adopt the Mongol bow."

Shen wasn't sure why Temur had turned away from him. But he realized he had to say something to defuse the Mongol's anger. "It's a … a superb weapon, Temur. My Uncle San used to say—well—I won't repeat exactly what he said. But your bow cost us a lot of battles."

"Chinese people do not… learn from savages," said Temur slowly. "Unfortunate for them." Then, pulling a pipe out of his leather jerkin, he walked into the little copse of trees and sat alone by the fire.

"He's still mad because I got away from him in Suzhou," said Shen proudly.

"He's mad because you look down on him," said Yi with a flinty voice. "It's time that stopped."

As the others rolled into their sleeping blankets, Shen sat awake. He felt a tiny pang of guilt about Temur but a much bigger resentment about being made to feel guilty. So, putting the Mongol out of his thoughts, he looked curiously at Grandfather Hu. The old man had stoutly kept pace for six days. But exhaustion was written on his face, and his chest rose and fell shallowly in sleep. His hand, as always, clutched the roll of papers as he slept. But a couple of pages had worked loose, and without hesitation Shen scooped them up and moved a few steps away to unroll them.

The moonlight was so faint that he had to hold the first page near the embers of the dying fire to make out the images. The spidery lines slowly became the high stern of a sailing ship. Horizontal lines drawn through it at intervals indicated the width of the aftercastle deck, the broadness of the ship's waist, and the greater width of its vast hold: one hundred and ten *ch'i*. Shen knew that a *ch'i* was about the length of a grown man's foot. The big river junks that carried cargo up the Yangtze past Nanjing were rarely more than a hundred *ch'i* in length. This ship was wider than that!

The other paper was a series of strange-looking shapes. Beside most of them was written: *This must be of iron, with no impurity.* As he puzzled over the words, Shen noticed that the fire had gone out. And yet the pages were still illuminated with reddish light. A shiver went up his neck, and he whirled around, expecting to see strangers with lanterns.

Nobody was there. But the entire hill was bathed in light, reflected off a low cloud. It seemed to be coming from a fire on the other side, accompanied by a deep groaning sound.

"Lan Yi! Lan Yi!"

The circus master lurched to his feet, a short sword in his hand. His eyes darted to the red light at the top of the hill. With a frown, he delivered an emphatic kick to each of the four remaining sleepers, not sparing Chang. Blankets were flung aside. Marmot and Temur were quickly on their feet, and Grandfather Hu was not far behind. He snatched the papers out of Shen's hand.

"Thief!" he cried, still half asleep. "What are you doing with those?"

"Quiet!" hissed Yi, gesturing with his palm down. "Take up weapons and follow me."

They padded silently up the hillside, whose top did not seem to come any closer. But the sound grew louder. Shen could hear now that it was intermittent: a few seconds of silence punctuated with a grunting tone that seemed to vibrate in the ground.

And then they froze. Rising above the top of the hill was a line of solid red. It kept climbing, looking at first like a long, slender banner and now like the side of a building. It was vast, it was unthinkable, and yet it continued to get bigger.

Yi shook his head in disbelief, and Marmot swore. But Grandfather Hu grinned like a cat, showing the stumps of his teeth. "How beautiful!" he breathed. "Just as it should be!"

"What thing is this the King of Hell has sent?" demanded Yi.

"A sail! A sail that will carry us around the world!"

CHAPTER 12

THEY MADE THEIR WAY to the top of the hill, crawling on their bellies to avoid being seen. By now the scarlet sail had reached its full height and stood swaying in the light of unseen fires below.

"But we're nowhere near the river," said Lan Yi. "So far as I know, there's no water here at all."

"No ship either," said Grandfather Hu, who seemed delighted. "This is a sailworks. And this sail has just received its lucky red color. It's sopping wet."

The rhythmic chanting of a horde of workers hidden behind the hill began again, and the sail shuddered and seemed to move toward them. Marmot backed away on all fours, like his namesake animal. So did Shen, though he noticed that Temur stood like a block of wood, with Chang in his shadow.

Only Yi stood up boldly and walked across the crest of the hill.

"It's hanging on a wooden truss," he said, "mounted on wheels below."

As the others came forward, they saw that the far side of the hill had been cut away to make an almost vertical drop. Workers on ladders were hauling on ropes, easing the great sail as close as they could to the dug-out hillside, and then lashing the ropes around pulleys fixed into the hillside. Next they pulled the ropes as tight as possible, stretching the sail so that it would dry in its proper shape. Shen squinted, trying to see what it was made of. "It's silk," whispered Chang, who had crept up beside him. "Imagine how many villages to make one sail!"

As they edged across the brow of the hill, the scene below came into view. Workers swarmed like caterpillars around a long gray slash in the ground that was filled with red fluid. Farther away a smaller sail, also on large wooden wheels, was slowly moving toward the bath of red dye, pushed by a line of nearly naked, sweating laborers. Fire pits dug at regular intervals threw off light and waves of heat that illuminated the whole scene.

"It's time to introduce ourselves," said Yi. "Marmot, get out the papers."

They made their way to the shoulder of the hill, where a steep slope presented them with a route to the bottom. Grandfather Hu grumbled about a strange "slaughterhouse smell" in the air as he picked up a fallen branch to help himself down the hill. He promptly fell, scraping his shoulder.

The others helped him to his feet and then descended, slowly at first. But soon they were all clambering and half-sliding. At the bottom, several rough-looking guards were waiting for them. "You're noisy, for thieves," said one.

"You mistake us," replied Lan Yi. He unfolded a document bearing the seal of the Suzhou magistrate. "We'd like a word with the headman."

None of the guards could read the document, but one of them fondled the golden seal. Then they hastened off to find the headman.

Grandfather Hu and Shen moved toward the great slit in the ground filled with dye. Chang tried to follow, but Lan Yi—who for once seemed to remember his promise to keep Fei Lee's children safe—held her back.

"Wake up, old man!" cried a boy about Shen's age who balanced two pails of red fluid on a yoke across his scrawny shoulders. His hair was pulled back from his narrow face into a bun on the back of his head and held in place by a net so it would not catch on the yoke. Grandfather Hu hopped out of his way, and the boy deposited the square pails on the ground with relief. Then he lifted each in turn onto the edge of the clay wall that lined the trench and emptied it into the rippling scarlet pond.

"What is that stuff?" asked Shen, overcome by a repulsive odor.

"Treasure, my friend," said the boy. "Pigs' blood. They can't get enough of it. They're paying so much, I don't think there'll be a squealer left alive in my village this winter."

The boy, who introduced himself as Ru, explained that the dye was a mixture of blood and pulverized mahogany bark. Shen followed him back to a crowd of peasants guarding the buckets and barrels of blood they had carried from their villages. Ru's starved-looking father stood over his last two wooden pails. As the boy leaned to hook them onto his yoke, Shen noticed a red welt dug deep into Ru's shoulders.

"Let me take them for you."

Ru flashed a suspicious look at him. "Why? I don't know you."

"'If you are generous, you will win all,'" quoted Shen.

"Ooo, fancy. Where I come from, wise sayings get you a kick in the head," said Ru, putting the yoke across Shen's shoulders.

As Shen tottered back toward the steaming trench, he realized that he never would have spoken to a low-born village boy like Ru in his old life. What an idiot he must look, quoting from books.

"My friends and I want to meet the Admiral of the Treasure Fleet," he said, trying to sound like a man of experience. "Maybe you can help us."

"*Ai!* You're not as posh as I thought," crowed Ru. "And your big Mongol looks like an assassin. Who are you, anyway? And who's the girl in the shadows?"

"You go first."

Ru sized him up and said, "All right. The best thing I can give you is a warning. If you go near the gates, the guards will knock you over the head and you'll wake up in chains."

"Why?"

"Why? Because the master is a lunatic! He wants to sail to the edge of the world! No seaman in his right mind will sign on. It's come to where they're emptying the prisons to man the ships." He jerked his head in the direction of Lan Yi and Temur. "Your friends look strong, but they haven't a chance." He hoisted one of the pails and emptied it as easily as a teacup. "Now it's your turn to tell me something."

Shen took a moment to absorb the bad news. He decided to be direct. "We're in trouble. We need to leave China, for a while, at least." Ru was still looking at Chang. "That's my sister."

Ru squinted. "She'll be worth a lot." Seeing a dark frown flash across Shen's face, he added quickly, "I'm talking about the bride price. She's marriageable, isn't she?"

"We have no parents."

Ru looked stricken. "That's bad luck for you."

Chang came forward and bowed. "This is Younger Sister Chang," said Shen.

"Good health to you, Brother," said Chang to Ru, politely addressing him as if he were a member of her family. Her voice was steady and melodious in the way that Mother had taught her. Ru stared. This was not the place he expected to meet an upper-class girl.

The second sail was approaching the dye trench, and Hu put his arms around the three to push them away. "Make way for the mizzen!" he cried.

Yi and the others approached. "What does that mean, Grandfather Hu?"

"It's the sail that attaches to the *wei-wei*, the aftermast. Normally it would only have one halyard, but this one is so big it'll need two, together with quite a strong topping lift."

Yi nodded sagely. "Well, given what I know about sails, you could tell me it needs marinating sauce and I'd believe that too. Come along, we're going to the shipyard. The headman says he'll bring us to the gatemaster."

Ru laughed crudely. "Each of you is worth half a silver *tael* to him!"

Yi looked inquiringly at Shen. "His name is Ru," explained Shen. "He says they seize strangers at the gate."

Yi studied the undernourished peasant. "Then what shall we do, boy? You seem practical."

"There's a transport wagon ready to take a sail to the yard. If I'm with you, I can get you onto it."

"And why would you do that?"

Ru grinned at Lan Yi. "'If you are generous, you will win all.'"

———

LEAVING MARMOT TO TAKE care of the horses, which had been left on the other side of the hill, the others climbed aboard a long, sail-bearing wagon with wheels made of solid wooden slabs. It was still pitch-black when it lurched toward the Longjiang Gate, lanterns swaying. Blue-uniformed sentries glanced at the driver and waved him on. The two oxen, one with a splayfoot, dug in and heaved.

Ru was sitting up like a ferret, looking intently about as the wagon trundled down a smooth road lit with torches on poles.

"What should we do now?" asked Shen.

Ru hesitated. "Stay aboard until we reach the sail storage." Every few moments they passed a torch, and a dancing pool of light washed across Ru's face. Shen saw that the boy was appraising him with hard eyes.

"Do you know the Admiral?" said Ru finally.

"We met him. We're circus people. He said he might take us on the journey."

Now, in the shadowy lantern light, Ru's face had an expression Shen couldn't read. It was avid, almost hungry. But hungry for what, there was no telling.

"Listen to me!" said Ru suddenly. "You can't just go to the Admiral. And with no papers for here, you could still get grabbed. But there's somebody I could show you to. Somebody high up."

"Can we trust you, Ru?" said Chang suddenly out of the darkness between the road torches. Shen groaned at her simplicity. But then, to Shen's surprise, Ru replied:

"Usually not. But just now, yes."

"Who is this somebody high up?"

"He's a general with one eye and his chest bent out of shape. An old killer named Ho Fu. Comes down to the sailyard sometimes. People avoid him, but I like him. He talks to me. So maybe...see over there? That's the warehouse the wagon is going to. But up that road"—he pointed to a stately building blazing with light—"is the headquarters of the Ocean-Spanning Guard. The general lives there, and it'll soon be morning."

"I can't keep my eyes open till morning," grumbled Grandfather Hu. His shoulder, injured from the fall on the hill, was bothering him. Picking up his stick, he whacked the wooden deck of the wagon until the driver halted. Then he hopped down with surprising agility, though Shen saw him wince with pain.

Yi grabbed a handful of Ru's rough cotton shirt and pulled him out of the wagon. "You'll come to that headquarters building with us, peasant. If it's a trap, you won't live long enough to collect your pay."

"No trap," cried Ru. "This is good for both of us. You'll see."

Sitting on the veranda of the headquarters sipping tea were several guards and a man with a helmet of short gray hair. He had one eye and a loathsome puckered spot where the other one should be. He wore a Tiger badge.

"Welcome to Longjiang," smiled General Ho Fu, revealing teeth that were, like his eyes, incomplete. He nodded to Ru and tossed a silver *tael* to him. Then he said to Shen, "You are the circus boy that came to our warship on the Yangtze. So it is true what they say. A sleepless night brings many surprises."

———

THE OLD SOLDIER FELL into conversation with Lan Yi and Grandfather Hu. Shen took Ru aside. "You did all that for a silver *tael*?"

"A silver *tael* is a lot of money in my village. General Ho Fu tells me to bring him anybody that might have something interesting to say. I'm pretty good at spotting people like you."

"Why don't you come on the fleet yourself?"

Ru rolled his eyes. "Because you'll go to the middle of the ocean and never come back. But I'll remember you to my grandchildren."

Laughing, he trod off into the night. And Shen, after listening awhile to Lan Yi droning on with the old general, fell asleep against a post that supported the veranda roof. Chang, who could sleep anywhere, was already curled up like a cat and gently snoring.

SHEN AWOKE THE NEXT morning on a couch in a large room with walls painted the blue of the sea. Sunlight poured in through a window with a metal lattice. Above it were two smaller windows with dark wood latticework carved to resemble knotted ropes.

The floors were of green Dalian marble with whirls that looked like clouds and mountains. The couch where he had been deposited at some point last night was upholstered. It had a cylindrical, red silk-covered pillow. With tassels.

Looking around, he saw Chang still asleep on a bed that had draperies on all sides. Strewn about the floor was the rest of the company. Lan Yi slept on a thin but fine quilted mattress. Grandfather Hu lay snoring beneath one of the latticed windows. Shen noticed that the injury on his shoulder was black-yellow and bulging with infection.

Facing the door, on a carved chair not unlike Father's, sat Temur. Shen could tell from the Mongol's erect posture, and the way his hands rested on the arms of the chair, that he was awake. His swordbelt was empty, the weapon apparently confiscated.

"*Hé!* Temur! Is the door locked from outside?"

"Yes."

Shen lay back on his couch. Were they prisoners after all? What an idiot Lan Yi was to think they could visit the Admiral of the Treasure Fleet and then leave when they pleased! The lucky one was Marmot, lounging on a hillside with the horses. But how long would he wait for them to come back?

He dragged himself to his feet, still feeling queasy from the stench of pigs' blood and the swaying of the sail cart. Outside the window was an endless line of warehouses with upswept roofs and windows covered with elaborate iron fretwork to ward off thieves and ill fortune. Wooden doors were carved with the writhing shapes of sea creatures.

A thumping of spear shafts on the ground outside the door alerted them that visitors had arrived. Yi's eyes opened and he sprang to his feet.

Two soldiers bearing slender *pudao* spears were first to enter. Then Blinky swept in. Shen thought the Admiral's tiny official in his rumpled robe looked like a stray cat between the well-turned-out Brocades.

"Have you been comfortable?" said Blinky.

"Superbly," replied Yi, still a little dazed with sleep. "How good to see you again, Official Fourth Class."

"Yes. Delightful."

A howl emerged from behind Yi's back. Grandfather Hu was crouched amidst the bedding, flinging it away. "My drawings!"

"Calm yourself, old man," said Blinky. "Your papers are safely in our hands. You are summoned by the Ocean Lord. Regrettably"—he paused, his eyes taking in Temur's leathery arms and worn jerkin and Hu's grass-stained robe—"regrettably there is no time for matters of personal hygiene."

Chang rose with the others, but she already guessed what the outcome would be.

"Don't imagine that you are included, girl!" said Blinky,

who was suddenly, furiously blinking. "You and the Mongol wait here."

The soldiers escorted the three of them to a wide five-bay house with gleaming golden roof tiles. It had upswept roof corners supported by a carved octopus rather than the customary dragon. Shen was craning his neck to get a better look and so failed to notice the heavy wooden doors silently sliding open.

And there, glaring at him from underneath black eyebrows that made a broken line like seagulls' wings, was Zheng He. The Ocean Lord himself.

CHAPTER 13

THE UGLY EUNUCH SEEMED to take up all the space in the room, but Shen quickly noted a half-dozen men in cedar armchairs forming a semicircle around him. He spotted the one-eyed general, Ho Fu. He was a beauty, Shen thought, compared to the dark-skinned giant. He coldly observed that the man who had destroyed his city was now displaying the badge of a supreme commander, embroidered with the image of the Qi'lin, a sacred animal that resembled a lion with horns.

Much friendlier in appearance was a strongly built, neck-less man with large, rabbitlike front teeth and an odd, whispery voice. He wore old-fashioned gentleman's clothes. A red silk gown with a broad blue band at the bottom hung comfortably from his shoulders, and a decorative silver-stitched red girdle slumped beneath his ample belly. He was chatting amiably with Zheng He.

Shen's eyes were drawn to the walls of the room, where Grandfather Hu's drawings were pinned to tapestry cloth. Grandfather himself was in bad shape. He gingerly held a dirty rag to the wound on his shoulder.

"Speak first, Ho Fu," said Zheng He.

The one-eyed man rose. "The Brocades are out of control, my Lord. They blockaded the Suzhou Acrobatic Troupe in their own quarters to stop them from coming here. The troupe fled six nights ago. This group arrived on horseback, and the others are coming by water."

"What else?" said Zheng He.

"Lord Yang is directly involved. His local agent, Magistrate Qian, was ordered to arrest this boy and his sister."

Zheng looked levelly at Shen. "We meet for the third time, boy. Do you know any reason for Lord Yang's interest in you?"

Shen rose, feeling as if he were caught in the jaws of the Qi'lin on the Admiral's badge.

"No, sir. Except that Lord Yang arrested my mother two years ago. I believe he was acquainted with my father during the time of the Grandson, Hui Di."

"And what was your father to Hui Di?" asked the Admiral.

"A Panther officer of his guard, sir."

"And so dead, as you indicated at our previous meeting?"

"That's what everybody says, sir."

One-eyed Ho Fu was impatient. "It doesn't explain anything that Lord Yang knew the boy's father! And it's normal he arrested the mother. But why is he chasing these children two years later? Has he nothing better to do? Something is afoot here."

The man with the rabbitlike teeth intervened. "My dear Ho, not everyone has the strength of a soldier," he whispered. "Have a thought for the old man sitting here. He has been injured." He stood up and went over to Grandfather Hu. "If you please, elderly sir, my name is Ma Huan. I am a scholar of barbarian languages. Are you unwell?"

"My name is Ang Hu," said Grandfather Hu, "former naval architect to the King of Han. And I feel like a dog spat me out."

Hearing the old man's high title, Interpreter Ma turned pink with embarrassment. "We have failed in hospitality. Lord Zheng, please let me take him to a private chamber and have a doctor attend him."

"But the matter of the ships is urgent!" said a good-looking officer wearing a third-rank Leopard badge.

"Let the boy explain all that," croaked Grandfather Hu, his skeletal fingers squeezing Shen's shoulders. "Come to me for the details, after I have rested." Supported by Interpreter Ma, Grandfather Hu tottered out of the room.

Shen's mind was as white and featureless as a sandy beach. Zheng He leaned his head to one side and said, "How many years have you?"

"Fifteen," replied Shen.

"Old enough to collect your thoughts. Did the old man explain his ideas to you?"

Shen tried to remember the conversation several mornings ago beside the crumbling brick wall, when they couldn't sleep for the sun shining in their faces. "Grandfather said he once built a great ship with nine masts, and many bulkheads, like your ship that was on the Yangtze. But it sank on its maiden voyage. He said your ship will also fail."

Shen was conscious of silence in the room. "What broke his ship?" said the Leopard officer eagerly.

"Wood," said Shen. "It was all made of wood." He searched his memory. "Grandfather said...that the ship was lifted on two great waves. It...broke in half. Even with bronze bolts as thick as fence posts." Shen remembered the livid light in Hu's eyes. "Grandfather saw this with his own eyes. He thinks the gods were warning him that such a ship must be made in a new way."

"And then the Kingdom of Han was destroyed," said Zheng He in a soft, rasping voice. "The new ship was never built."

Shen cast his eyes down and looked at the floor.

"I have just one more question. My friend Hong"—Zheng He gestured at the handsome Leopard officer—"is our chief naval engineer. He finds it difficult to believe that the ribs and beams in these drawings are to be made of iron. Where would a man find so much iron?"

Shen chose his words carefully, realizing that everything depended on him explaining Grandfather Hu's ideas correctly. "Grandfather believes that inside the ship's belly there must be a cage of iron. And from this cage must hang the wooden parts of the ship."

Leopard Officer Hong snapped his head back and huffed indignantly. "There is not enough iron in the Empire to do as the old man wishes," he said, gesturing at the drawings. "And in some places, he wants sword steel! In a ship! Sword steel is like white jade, obtained after long labor and in very small amounts!"

The giant eunuch grinned balefully. "Hong does not wish to trouble the Emperor with more demands. He fears the Emperor. But I fear something more."

Shen realized that he was expected to ask the question. "What do you fear, Ocean Lord?"

"Drowning!" said the eunuch. And his eyes grew huge.

———

IN THE FOLLOWING DAYS, Shen decided that what he feared was the return of Officer Chu and the Brocade Guards. The shipyard was defended by the marine brigade of the Imperial Guard, who went by the wonderful name of Ocean-Spanning Guards. But Father had often said that regular soldiers feared the Brocades.

Fortunately the rest of the troupe soon began to arrive at the great Longjiang Gate. They came in twos and threes, each little group accompanied by an Ocean-Spanning Guard wearing civilian clothes.

"They came out of nowhere, all these young men," Jade told Chang in an excited voice. Shen sat nearby, his arms crossed. They were sitting in the public room of one of the shipyard dormitories set aside for women. "They said we had to leave our boat because the Brocades had a blockade across the Grand Canal. So we split into small groups and went overland. Our guide had sleepy eyes. As if he had seen terrible things that he wouldn't talk about."

And they laughed, in a shrill kind of way. Did girls lose their minds, wondered Shen, about any boy with sleepy eyes who happened to be a few years older than he was? Annoyed, he left without saying anything and heard them, still laughing, as he went.

Grandfather Hu was approaching, accompanied by the rabbit-toothed interpreter Ma Huan. Without waiting for a greeting, Grandfather clapped an arm across Shen's shoulder.

"Walk with us, boy. I see my granddaughter has arrived safely. And they've sent for Marmot, whom I expect to see soon unless he got bored and gambled the horses away. Interpreter Ma has been telling me wonderful stories of the places the Star Fleet is going to go. Did you know he can speak five languages?"

"In most quarters I am considered a great bore," added the stout man modestly.

"He tells me that the Muslims have a sacred city in the middle of the desert, all the way across the Southern Ocean."

"That seems far away, Grandfather," said Shen. As he walked, a picture of the Southern Ocean appeared before him in its roiling immensity. "What do their chopsticks look like?"

"They don't have any," said Interpreter Ma. "An Arab who survived a shipwreck told me they eat with their right hand. Sometimes they use a spoon."

Worse still, Shen learned, there were no gods in the Muslim country. Just empty desert and a few trees with no spirits. Their city walls had no ghosts to protect them, and their ancestors were far away in the sky. Their one god had sent a book through a prophet, according to Interpreter Ma, then had gone away, never to be heard from again.

"What a lonely place! How can anybody live there?" Shen moaned.

Interpreter Ma laughed at this, but Grandfather Hu was thoughtful. "When I was young, we built our big ships for war.

We never thought of going out to explore the ocean." As he spoke, he thrust his chin deep into the cowl of his cloak, causing deep wrinkles to spread up his cheeks.

But then he looked up with a smile of wicked delight. "You remember our first meeting with the eunuch Admiral? When we arrived here last week? He went to Nanjing the same day to plead for ten thousand more *catties* of iron. The ships shall have the iron skeletons I asked for! The Emperor has commanded it."

———

SHEN LEFT THEM AND WALKED alone at the edge of the water. Grandfather Hu's triumph was immense. Shen half-expected that some god would change the old man into a young man again, now that he was to build the ships he had spent his life longing to build.

He looked around the shipyard with fresh eyes. It was astonishing that such a decision was made so quickly! But then he remembered that the Emperor's prestige was wedded to this expedition. The endless lines of workers hastening past him were proof of that.

And, of course, there were the ships themselves. Longjiang had been specially created for the Star Fleet. The five giant ships were to be built in huge holes, called dry docks, which had been dug in such a way they could be filled with water when the ship was complete. He was walking beside the canal that had been built for that purpose. When the time came, the giant ships would be floated down the canal to the Yangtze River.

The vessels' great bodies were still hidden within the dry docks, which had been built at the western side of the Longjiang lands, near the city wall of Nanjing. But Shen could see their masts and spars rising in the distance like leafless trees. He wanted to go and look at them, but then he remembered that he was here as Lan Yi's prisoner. He would lose face if he showed any interest in the ships.

Thanks to Grandfather Hu's drawings, it seemed that the troupe had won favor with the Admiral. Shen was certain that his services, such as they were, were not necessary any more. He thought of Mother and Father every day, and his feet yearned for the dusty roads.

But Chang would not go. The older she was, the more insufferable she became, he thought. She had actually called him a fool for not listening to the soldiers who had been part of the attack on the Imperial Palace. "They're stationed outside your barracks," she would cry. "Two steps away. Just ask them. Not a single guardsman got out alive! Not one!"

Shen had taken to ignoring her when she went on like that. In his head, he had made up a story to explain Father's silence. Now, as he walked along the canal, he told it to himself one more time. Father had been terribly burned in the palace fire. His men rescued him, but then they had been ambushed. Now Father was a beggar with burnt hands and lipless mouth, unable to communicate, sitting by the road near a farmhouse. The kind people there let him sleep in the granary. Usually a girl who looked like Jade helped him in when the sun set.

The daydream was distressing but also reassuring, because it ended with Father alive and cared for. Letting it run in his thoughts soothed him. Today, though, it was so engrossing that he did not notice where he was going. He nearly fell into a dry dock. Pulling himself up short, he saw a soaring wall of sweet-smelling timbers rising in front of him. A ship. It plunged into shadowy depths where workers milled about on the earthen floor far below. Others were suspended on rope seats at various points on the ship's flank, sinking spikes into the timbers with blows of heavy hammers.

Shen's attention was caught by a section of hull that had not yet been timbered over. He ran to it and gazed into the blackness of the interior, teased here and there with shafts of dusty sunlight filtering through the ribs and braces.

It looked empty and lonely. But as he gazed, a new day-dream took shape in his mind. The vast cavern within the raw ship filled up with lanterns and gangways and bent-backed laborers filling the holds with sacks of food. Scholarly men were placing instruments on little desks.

This pleasant vision was inspired by the shipyard talk Shen had heard, by the alchemists and instrument-makers who were already arriving there, and by Grandfather Hu's excited descriptions of what he called "the ship's guts."

In Shen's reverie, the walls and floors of the skeletal vessel in front of him were quickly completed. Its four decks emerged with a strange clarity. There were quarters for astronomers and doctors and the students of new kinds of plants and animals. They were making beautiful sketches on their scrolls.

On the third deck above the hold would be the sharp tang of grapes and peaches stored in jugs of sand, and the odor of fermented vegetables and salted meats. The vast third-deck galley was filled with sprouting soybeans that would save the sailors from scurvy. And on the topmost deck, where the workers were now throwing the remnants of their lunch overboard, he saw a luxuriant garden of fruit trees and rich vegetation.

Then he remembered his fantasy of a crippled Father sitting by a roadside. He recognized it for a fantasy. The ship in front of him was real. It would carry him into the future, a real life. Foreign lands, a chance to show his mettle, to gain face and return home to become—whatever he wished!

And what did he propose to set against it? A long, dusty, and desperately sad trek through distant provinces searching for a man whose very bones (the Truth whispered to him) were lost.

———

SHEN'S REVERIE WAS INTERRUPTED by a group of guards on horseback towing three bronze cannons on wheeled carriages past the dry dock. As he ran back to the distant barracks, he saw marching columns dispersing toward every corner of the vast Longjiang territory. He guessed there were more than a thousand men.

Lan Yi was just outside the door. "Where have you been? We've been summoned to the Admiral's quarters."

"But what are the soldiers doing?"

"Defending the shipyard, Captain Fei's Son. Our worst nightmare has come true. The Brocades are on the march. A patrol that came in a while ago said they couldn't see the end of the column. It may well be that we are at war again."

CHAPTER 14

THERE WAS AN OCTOPUS carved in the gleaming oiled wooden door of the Ocean Lord's headquarters. For Shen it had become a bad omen. As the guards pushed the door open, the tentacles seemed to move. They made Shen think of columns of Brocade soldiers encircling and strangling the Longjiang shipyard.

The Admiral's private quarters were surprisingly plain compared with the grandeur of the building's exterior. While Lan Yi kowtowed, Shen examined it carefully. The walls were whitewashed rather than painted, and there were no pretty landscape paintings displayed on them. Instead, there were a couple of dented and carelessly hung weapons that Shen guessed were mementos of the Admiral's early fighting days. The tables and chairs were simple and sturdy.

But one object arrested Shen's attention: a hollow brass sphere that glowed with a dull luster. Large, round, and carefully polished, it was suspended from a curved iron hook and could be spun like a child's toy. Looking closer, Shen could see fine lacquer-filled curving lines scratched over part of its surface, with characters inscribed here and there.

"That is *shi jie*, the world," said Zheng He, who was seated at a table inking his chop to stamp a letter. "Look closer. You will see the names of countries."

Shen's first thought was to protest that the world was not a ball. Instead he said, "Why are there so many places without names?"

"Because nobody has gone to see them. And if the cannons gathering outside our walls have their way, nobody will."

The Admiral handed the letter to a guard, who took it outside and returned a moment later. The guard was the only other person in the room besides Shen and Lan Yi, who stood in front of the Admiral's table. It seemed odd to Shen that there was no scribe to record the meeting.

Zheng He addressed Lan Yi. "You greatly amuse me, Lan the Circus Man." He idly spun the brass ball. "It was impressive that you found a boat and organized your people for flight. Well beyond the abilities of a clown, I would say. Where did you learn your art?"

"In the streets of Hangchow, Great Lord. My family was poor, and my antics brought some money. Later the city circus trained me for a time."

"And then?"

"I pursued a different career. A dark time about which I prefer not to speak."

"I see. Do you think the Brocades will attack us, Lan Yi?" asked the Admiral, still idly spinning the globe.

"I am honored that a general would ask such a question of my humble person," replied Yi. "My thought is that they have only come to make a show of force. To gain face. So many of us have escaped from them!"

"That is what I think as well," said the Admiral. "Although I fear they will not leave unless I give them something. We shall see. In the meantime, I have a service to demand of you, Lan Yi. In the days to come you shall organize the care of others who will arrive here. Yang Rong may command the Brocades, but he has failed to stop me in spite of his many efforts. Nowadays there are eunuch magistrates in many cities, and eunuch officers in many garrisons. They have made the way safe for those who wish to come to me. My staff will instruct you on what to do."

Seeing that he was to leave, Yi kowtowed once more and backed out the door. He did not so much as look at Shen.

"Am I to remain, Lord Zheng?" said Shen.

The Admiral looked amused. "Yes. Lord Yang has arrived at the main gate. He is wearing an old-fashioned Hanfu robe with wide silk sleeves and vulgar chunks of jade sewn into the sash. I loathe such things, but I guess I am supposed to be impressed. He is waiting rather conspicuously for an invitation to see me. The letter I sent a few moments ago was that very invitation, and I want you here when he arrives. I want to know what you are to him." He gestured at the scribe's cushion on the floor, where brushes and ink stone were set out. "Please seat yourself. So long as Lord Yang is in this room, you are my scribe."

CHANG HAD DISCREETLY FOLLOWED Shen and Yi as they made their way to the Admiral's quarters. Her brother had fallen into one of his silent moods, and she was tired of being ignored. She watched the two of them enter the building without difficulty. They were invited, she thought.

When Lan Yi emerged, she stayed out of sight. It was Older Brother she needed to confront. A short time later a squadron of mounted Brocade Guards, escorted by a much larger number of Ocean-Spanning Guards marching on both sides of them, appeared on the road from the southern gate and stopped outside the building.

Servants put portable steps beside a horse bearing an official wrapped in a blinding white-and-gold Hanfu robe with a black cape over his shoulders. Yang Rong stepped delicately down. He and his entourage entered, and the immense carved doors closed behind them. Chang wished they had been the doors of a prison from which the Confucian would not return.

Inside the building a steward with fleshy and unhappy-looking lips opened the door and made a signal. The Admiral nodded, and Yang Rong entered the room.

Lord Yang looked at Fei Shen with puzzlement. Zheng He's game would not work, Shen realized, if Yang failed to recognize him. And with his new mustache and two years of growth, that was very possible. But there's nothing I can do about that, Shen thought, as he pinned the open scroll in place and poised his brush over it.

"Minister of Imperial Security, welcome," said Lord Zheng.

"I am your servant, Lord of the Oceans," replied Lord Yang, who continued his searching appraisal of Shen.

Etiquette prevented the Confucian from speaking to Shen. But his eyes felt like a heavy stone against the boy's head.

The two men exchanged ceremonial greetings. Then Lord Yang observed, as if it were a matter of no importance, that a good deal of iron was now being directed to Longjiang. The army generals were unhappy about this. "Of course, my Brocades are always well armed. But the new brigades being raised against the northern barbarians will not have first-quality swords and pikes, as they should."

Lord Zheng nodded sagely and said nothing. He had won the fight to have much of the year's iron production directed to the Treasure Fleet, but there was no point in rubbing it in just now. The silence stretched out until Shen's hand, hovering above the paper, began to ache and he had to rest it on his knee. He didn't dare lift his eyes, so he stared at the page until the characters he had written seemed to move around by themselves.

Finally, there was a splashing of tea as Lord Zheng's guard delicately filled two cups.

"And I, for my part," said the Admiral, "have heard that you wish to sail with the fleet."

Shen's brush left a dripping of ink on the page. He was certain he had heard wrong.

"It is more than a wish," replied Lord Yang. "I came here today to tell you the good news. The Emperor has accepted my petition to come aboard. He has declared that the fleet is so great that it is like a part of the Middle Kingdom. My colleagues in the Ministry of Rites have ordered that each ship have its Confucian priest. For the respect of religion!"

Shen risked a glance at the Confucian. He seemed as happy as a newly engaged girl on her way to the fortune-teller. Were these men friends after all? Had he misunderstood? Or, he thought darkly, was that the smile of the cat that has swallowed the mouse?

"After religion, of course, comes the law," continued Lord Yang. "Which brings me to a delicate matter. As Brocade commander, I shall be responsible for the loyalty of the fleet. I speak here of the common sailors—common criminals, more like. The Emperor requests Brocade officers on each vessel."

"How thoughtful of the Son of Heaven," replied Lord Zheng. Shen heard a loud clink from his teacup as he set it on the low table. "You are welcome to join our family. But we are expecting many guests. I must impose on you to make camp outside the perimeter until we sail. Please excuse my rudeness."

A calculating look flickered across the Confucian's face. "I do not take offense. My guards will remain outside."

Shen saw that this was not good. If Yang's men stayed there, they could seize captains, navigators, and notable people who had not yet arrived in the shipyard. There was a chess-game kind of intensity for some moments.

"Please excuse my silence. But the sudden appearance of so many Brocades exceeds the modest hospitality I can offer," said the Admiral slowly. "There is room inside our gates for perhaps two hundred of your men. At the same time, I shall set two hundred of my men outside the gate. They will create a passage so that your soldiers may not be inconvenienced by our guests."

The insolence of this gambit took Shen by surprise. With a single move the Admiral would prevent the Brocades from interfering with new arrivals. If Lord Yang refused, the Admiral could fairly complain that the Confucian had refused his hospitality.

"You are gracious," replied Lord Yang, setting his cup back on the small lacquered table. "And a more able diplomat than most of your Purified Brethren. Before I return to the Imperial Court, may I beg leave to speak to your scribe?"

"Certainly," replied Zheng.

"My dear Fei Shen, what happiness to see you! Do you know, your mother asked me to send word through Magistrate Qian that she is well? But due to some misunderstanding, you and your sister left the city before the message could reach you."

At first this made no sense to Shen. How could Mother have known where he was? Did Yang tell her? Was Yang telling the truth? But all of this was like a puff of wind. It was swept away by Shen's great longing to believe that Mother had sent word to him. "Is Mother still in jail?" he cried.

"Sadly, yes. I cannot change the law, even for such a dear friend as Captain Fei's wife. But she is under my protection, and she has not been harmed. I will bring further word from her when I return."

The Confucian rose to his feet like a dancing cobra, all in one sinuous movement. The impression was accented by his short black cape, which flared out like a snake's hood. Bowing deeply to Lord Zheng, shallowly to Shen, he backed out the door.

Shen stared at the door with large eyes.

"Well, he identified you easily enough," said Zheng He. "Do you believe that he will protect your mother?"

"I need to believe it," said Shen weakly.

The Admiral looked at him with what seemed to be pity. "You are not a match for that man, Fei Shen. Take care." Then the ugly man seemed to remember his own predicament. "Nor am I, perhaps."

"Will he bring the Brocades aboard your ships?"

"I will tell you what I think about that, but first you must swear loyalty to me. In fact"—he picked up the paper on which Shen had been writing—"I may retain you as one of my scribes, so long as you learn to write down alarming things without blotting them." Then he rested his black eyes on Shen. "And so long as you do not repeat anything you hear in this chamber."

Shen lowered his eyes. "May I ask why the Ocean Lord would bestow this honor?"

"To restore harmony between us," said the giant. "I am to blame in the disappearance of your father. And Lan Yi has said that you still wish to go seek him. I pity you, child. If you do that, you will lose your life among the ghosts. To gain virtue for myself, I offer you a place here instead. A life among the living."

"I am sorry Master Yi spoke to you about my father," said Shen stiffly. "Of course nobody believes I will find him. But there is still Mother. I have to look for her."

"And where will you look? Yang Rong holds the key to her freedom. And he will be here, as you have heard him say. Stay. Seek his good will. But be very careful."

CHANG WAS WAITING FOR Shen when he left the octopus building. "What was Lord Yang's business with the Admiral?" she asked. "And did Lord Yang recognize you? Tell me everything."

"I spoke to him." Shen wrestled briefly with his new vow of secrecy but decided that Lord Yang's intention to join the fleet must be known to everybody in the government. It wasn't really a secret, he convinced himself without much effort. "Lord Yang wants to go on the ships," he announced briskly. "That means that we're going too."

Then he set off at a brisk walk toward Lan Yi's compound, forcing Younger Sister to run after him.

"What are you talking about?" she said breathlessly.

"Another thing. Mother sent for us in Suzhou."

"Mother? Will you stop walking like that! Stop and make sense!"

But Shen was angry, and the object of his anger was Lan Yi. He strode into the men's dormitory. Chang could not follow him there.

Yi's room was down a long corridor and around a corner. Shen's head was still whirling as he pushed the door-curtain aside and found Yi sitting at a small table.

"You told Zheng He that I want to look for Father! All my private thoughts, everything!" Shen sneezed from the smoke in the room. Today Yi was smoking hemp rather than drinking. The odor was worse than spilled wine.

"Another reason to hate me," Yi said affably. "I dragged you here against your will, and now I've got you locked into a job that the richest scribes in China would give anything to have. What infamy will I commit next?"

"That's not funny."

"Well, funny or not, it's done. Now tell me if it's true, these rumors about Confucians joining the fleet."

Shen gave up on getting an apology from Lan Yi. "Yes, the rumors are true," he said, letting the circus master change the subject. "The Emperor had to give the Confucians a role in the Treasure Fleet in order to buy some peace in the Imperial Court. That's what Zheng He says."

"And how does Zheng He feel about this? Isn't the Emperor his old friend?"

"He's not angry about it. He says politics always outweighs friendship."

"Zheng He is a smart man. What else did you find out?"

Shen had saved this for last. "Yang said that Mother is alive. He will bring me word from her."

Yi nearly dropped his pipe. "Let us thank the protecting gods on Ting's behalf! I am happy for you and your sister, Fei Shen!"

———

HIS SISTER! REALIZING HE had brushed her off in his hurry to confront Lan Yi, he raced back to the dormitory entrance, hoping to patch things up. But she was no longer there.

His head was splitting. Wasn't it bad enough to be caught between two powerful men who hated each other? Did he also have to keep track of Younger Sister's complicated moods? And why was she always trying to watch over him?

Shen walked toward the canal, turning these thoughts over in his head. He was distracted by the chanting of a barge crew as they poled their way up the canal. It was a groan more than a chant, although the barge seemed to be carrying only a few timbers. As it pulled closer, however, Shen saw that the timbers were iron beams, black and oily-looking, wider in the middle than at the ends. The roughness of their casting had left sharp fins of rusty metal sticking out here and there.

As the splash of the barge poles faded away, Shen thought that Grandfather Hu at least should be happy. But what could he do about Chang?

Then his thoughts brightened. Chang would be thrilled to learn that he was to serve in the Admiral's office. And doubly thrilled to know that Mother was well. When he had a chance to tell her. And she could also stop worrying about him running away.

He breathed deeply. Things were fine! He had to admit that the honor of working in the building with the octopus roof ornaments was going to his head. He was touched that the Admiral had admitted, in a roundabout way, feeling responsible for Father's disappearance. Even the powerful were human! That was good to know.

CHAPTER 15

THREE DAYS PASSED. The Admiral was a day late returning from Nanjing, where he had gone to thank the Emperor for the first shipment of iron beams. But his real mission, said Interpreter Ma, was to get rid of the Brocades. Or reduce them to a manageable number.

"Don't fret, Fei Shen," said the interpreter. They were sitting in the Admiral's whitewashed office. Ma, who was a boyhood friend of the Admiral, was allowed to occupy it when he was away. "Perhaps he is staying to admire the Emperor's new palace. It was built on the ruins of the old one, you know." Shen flinched at this reminder of Father's last battle, but Ma didn't notice.

"In the meantime, since there's nothing else to do, would you like to hear the sounds of the Arabic language?" asked the interpreter.

Shen couldn't think of anything he wanted to hear less. Interpreter Ma loved to show off strange languages to people who didn't understand them. Fortunately, the agony had not gone on too long when Shen heard the urgent tramping of the Admiral's boots in the hall. But when the door flew open, and he saw the dark look on the giant's face, he lowered his eyes. The interpreter knelt beside him.

"Stand up, Huan, for pity's sake. And Shen, make a record. The cursed Confucian has succeeded. He can bring a thousand Brocades on board. A thousand!"

Shen was hard put to keep up as the Admiral spat out a series of instructions. The one-eyed general, Ho Fu, was to meet with the Confucian's aide-de-camp, a Panther officer named Chu, and agree on the billeting. Shen realized that this was the same Officer Chu he had met the day he tried to flee from Temur.

"Not one of them, not one, is to set foot on the munitions ship!" bellowed Lord Zheng. But there would have to be a full company of one hundred Brocades on the flagship, which was to be called the *China Harmony*. The Emperor had decreed that the Confucian would share the flagship with the Admiral. "He'll rue the day," swore the Admiral as Shen's brush pattered down the scroll. "I'll keep two hundred of my best soldiers on board. Yang will never be out of my sight, and I like it that way." He smiled wickedly.

"Not to upset you, Friend He," said Interpreter Ma hesitantly, "but who shall we remove to make room for all these soldiers?"

The Admiral breathed noisily through his nostrils. "That is an unpleasant business I haven't thought about. I will make a list. In the afternoon, send the circus man to me."

After three days of peace, Shen felt that his world had been shattered once again. He and his sister were vulnerable to expulsion because they were "paperless."

He was sent away early in the afternoon, and waited anxiously until Lan Yi returned from his meeting with the

Admiral. Yi's news was not good. The professional acrobats could stay. But all the "paperless people" among the several thousand civilians invited to join the fleet would be left behind. In principle, that included Shen and Chang.

"You, of course, are saved by your special status as the Admiral's scribe. But Chang must leave." He held up his hands ineffectually to ward off Shen's howl of protest. "Please believe me, Shen. It was Interpreter Ma who told me this. I pleaded like a condemned man. You know I promised your parents I would protect both of you. I told Ma that. But now you must plead for her yourself. Do it quickly."

———

THE NEXT DAY SHEN TOOK UP his place beside the Admiral's ornate elmwood chair with its arms shaped like a horseshoe. It had been specially made to accommodate Zheng He's sprawling physique, but it still creaked when he was restless, as he was at that moment. With every creak the attendants around him flinched.

In his hands the Admiral clenched a document he had been studying for some time. Finally he handed it to his official, Blinky, with a sigh that reminded Shen of a fireplace bellows. "You had asked to speak with me, boy?"

"I plead for my sister to remain aboard the fleet."

Zheng cocked his massive head at Shen, and one dramatic eyebrow shot up.

"You have a sister? What use is a sister? 'Feeding girls is like feeding cowbirds,' isn't that the saying?"

"She is a 'small happiness,' sir. She and I are what is left of our family."

"And I am a Purified Body," said the eunuch lazily. "I care nothing about families."

"Chang cannot manage if she is put out on her own. There are no relatives to care for her."

The Admiral was silent for a moment. "So may it be for many who must be sent away. They weren't my responsibility before they came. How can they be my responsibility now?" Zheng glanced at Blinky, but Blinky bowed his head and said nothing.

The interpreter, Ma Huan, however, spoke up. "There is another solution. Do you wish to leave with her, Fei Shen?" This caught Shen off guard. "Because it is obvious that you may not leave your sister alone," pursued Interpreter Ma. His firm tone was a reproach to Shen. "It is terrible to think what would become of her."

The truth of this pressed down on Shen. "Of course you are right, Honored Ma. I am contemptible. I did not think about it as I should have. Of course I shall go with her."

The Admiral cleared his throat and picked up the document again. "And yet you may not. You are in my service, and I do not release you. You shall have to find others to care for your sister. At this moment, I require you to take up your brush and write down an answer to the harbormaster at Nanjing, who ridiculously pretends that he cannot prevent all manner of wretched boats from coming into my shipyard."

Shen picked up his brush, but he could not feel it between his fingers. Interpreter Ma looked shocked. Shen wondered why Blinky hadn't spoken up. Weren't Confucians supposed to be guardians of the family? He had never felt more alone.

THAT AFTERNOON SHEN MET Chang in the receiving room of the women's quarters. She stood in the light of a window, calm and dignified. Her eyes resembled black polished stones.

He knelt on the floor, gesturing for her to do likewise. Facing each other on their knees was the customary posture for a solemn conversation. But Chang looked out the window instead. "I will stand," she said.

A bolt of anger flashed across his eyes. "Why are you so rude?"

"Why are you so touchy, Older Brother? Is something troubling your heart? Let me tell you that I do not wish to anger you. It seems to me that I am alone in the world, cut off from all things. Since there is no one to offer counsel, I must take counsel with myself."

Shen knelt without moving. He held his head up so he wouldn't look ashamed. "So you want me to disobey the Admiral? You want me to escape from here like a criminal, with the constables on my tail? So that I can stay with you?"

Her face brightened. "Would you do that? You will, won't you, Brother? You're so clever, how can they stop you? I know you will do it."

Shen hadn't expected her to take him seriously. "Are you mad? How can I escape a thousand Ocean-Spanning Guards?"

She looked at him silently. Then she did what she had refused to do earlier: she slid to her knees in front of him and lowered her eyes. "You promised we would never be separated."

SHEN LEFT CHANG'S ROOM in a state of total confusion. He would need to be a magician to escape. And it wasn't even what he wanted to do anymore.

As he walked along the brick pathway by the dry docks, he saw Grandfather Hu giving orders to the men who were lowering iron beams into the *China Harmony*. In spite of the dressing on his shoulder, the old man was hopping about like a flea, directing the sweating man who operated the wooden crane.

The crane groaned as it hoisted an iron rib high into the air and swung it over the ship's side. It was lowered out of Shen's view, but from the banging and clanging that followed, he knew that it was being moved along to its proper place inside the hull.

Silence fell. Shen remembered Grandfather Hu talking about how the ship's carpenters would fit the steel bits of their heavy hand drills into holes that had been made in the iron rib when it was forged. That way they could drill directly into the hull planks at just the right place to bolt them to the iron rib. Even as he watched, several auger bits came slowly twirling through the sheathing planks, like ship-eating sea worms. Once the bits were pulled back inside the ship, carpenters on the outside pounded iron bolts through the holes. The bolts had been wrapped in a waterproofing mixture of lime, hemp, and tung oil.

Shen was sheltering from the sun in the shadow of a pile of tung oil barrels. Grandfather Hu came over and sat beside him. "A wonder that nobody used iron bolts before," he said happily, uncorking a flowered ceramic flask that Shen knew contained wretched medicinal tea. "Want some?"

Shen shook his head. The smell made him nauseous.

"You look like you need something," said Grandfather Hu.

Shen struggled to control himself, but tears began to roll across his round cheeks. The story about Chang came spilling out.

Grandfather Hu was enraged. "The eunuch is a damned tyrant! I'm going to have a word with him." He grabbed an oil barrel to pull himself to his feet. Shen pulled him back down.

"You can't do anything," said Shen. "He doesn't respect anything. Not even that you're old."

"Don't I know that?" said Grandfather Hu. "But he needs me to float his ships. You stay here."

And Grandfather Hu walked off with the stride of an athlete, as if he had dropped his years like a sack of coal.

When Grandfather Hu was out of sight, Shen walked the perimeter of the dockyards. He had no faith in the old man's mission. Gazing at the rude little kitchen boats and music boats that had invaded Longjiang's artificial harbor to make money from the workmen and soldiers, he envied their freedom to come and go. But, of course, dozens of guards watched them constantly.

The harbor was festooned with a flotilla of these vessels. They carried nearly as large a population as the legions of workers whipping ox-drawn cartloads of materials down the stone way and the further legions rumbling by with wheelbarrows of lime, tung oil, and braided rope for caulking.

Shen dangled his legs over the edge of the wharf and studied the boats. Clustered around the hulks of the five giant ships was a buzzing hive of kitchen boats, with their brick ovens amidships and little houses at the stern. Each house came complete with a curved roof and ornamental tiles, to shelter the cook and his helpers. The flat, broad prow sloped down until it met the waterline, so that customers could row their sampans in close and order fast food without having to climb a ladder.

Floating by was a haircutting sampan, the barber ringing a bell with one hand while stropping a razor on a mounted leather band. A doctor on his sampan was beating a small drum with great and solemn dignity to signal that medical assistance was available to anyone who could pay for it. A theater boat, with a stage built on the high stern, was angling for a good spot to anchor for the evening performance. On its foredeck, singing girls waved their tambourines at the soldiers on the wharf.

Nervously approaching several boatmen, Shen learned that it would be costly to bribe passage. On a kitchen boat he offered the remaining gold amulet, which Chang had agreed should be used, and the little money he possessed. The man wiped his greasy hands and glanced meaningfully at the military guards lining the wharves. Then, holding up two fingers to indicate he would want twice as much, he turned his back and his knife flew across the chopping board again.

Shen thought it a bad omen that he caught sight, just at this moment, of a white-painted funeral boat far out in the harbor. This was where workers unfortunate enough to fall from their perches were sprinkled with lime and neatly stacked until their families could claim them. Even worse, the next thing that crossed his field of vision was a boat full of highly infectious lepers with shreds of skin dropping from their arms. Their long begging poles, with a little tin pot at the end, waggled at the nearest sampan. Though the harbor was jammed with boats, Shen noticed that this one had no trouble finding open water.

Tired and discouraged, he fell into daydreams about disguising himself as a leper, or even a dead body that could be stacked on the funeral boat.

Just at that moment, with a crewmember energetically beating a gong and shouting, "Make way!" a big freight junk labored down the harbor with a heavy load of pine logs. The crew's wives were cooking on a stove atop the logs, while their children swung from the rigging and got underfoot. A woman on the foredeck emptied a bucket of slops into the heaving swell of orange peels, chicken guts, and wildly diving seagulls.

The rolling panjandrum of logs, chaos, seabirds, and laughter would normally have lightened Shen's heart. But now it seemed a dream of a life that was farther away than ever.

ARRIVING THE NEXT MORNING at the Admiral's quarters, Shen was surprised to see Interpreter Ma's broad profile awaiting him in the shadow of the entry door.

After an exchange of greetings, the interpreter smiled.

"Your sister will stay. The old man came by yesterday and threw a terrible fit. He said that Zheng He was destroying an innocent girl. He said he would do no more work on the ships."

"And the Admiral relented?" said Shen, incredulous.

"For a time he just sat there, as if in a spell," recalled Interpreter Ma. "Then the Admiral's Confucian spoke up, which surprised me. He's a timid fellow. But he managed to repeat one or two proverbs about the sacredness of the family."

"Blinky did that? He didn't say a word when I pleaded for her myself!"

The interpreter shrugged. "Perhaps he felt badly for letting you down."

Then Interpreter Ma shooed him into the building so he wouldn't be late for his duties. Shen worked silently all morning, not daring to mention the matter to the Admiral.

CHAPTER 16

CHANG HAD ALREADY HAD the news from Lan Yi. But she assumed that Shen was the one who had come to her rescue.

"I thank the goddess Kwan Yin that you changed the Admiral's mind. A boy can't imagine what it's like for a girl to be thrown out on the road." She shuddered, thinking of it.

"I wouldn't let that happen," Shen said flatly. He was calculating the chances that he could take the credit for what Grandfather Hu had accomplished with his mighty temper tantrum. He guessed that the old man would never say a word. It was always tempting to be the hero.

Chang was making tea. The oolong leaves were tiny and costly, and he didn't know how she had laid hands on them. But it was clear that she had got them specially to thank him.

"Grandfather Hu did it," he said.

She paused in mid-gesture, holding the bamboo jar of leaves over the teapot. She blinked, meaning she didn't understand.

"Me begging the Admiral didn't work. It was Grandfather Hu who convinced him. Shouted at him, apparently."

A little sigh, almost like a gentle breeze, passed through her lips. She shook the leaves into the pot. "Then we will drink our tea in honor of Grandfather Hu, and I will seek him out and thank him." She came close to him and placed her cheek against his cheek. "But even more, I honor my brother, who did all that he could."

"ALL THAT HE COULD" was not enough for Shen. It seemed to him that he had accomplished nothing since the city had fallen and Mother had been lost. He had not chosen the Suzhou Acrobatic Troupe. Certainly—as his ankles reminded him of being tied to his horse—he had not chosen this ship-yard. He had never thought of being a scribe. As a wagon groaned past, he watched a wheel spoke slowly turning. "Hello, brother wheel spoke. They didn't ask where you wanted to go either, did they?"

What did he want? Some words of Confucius came into his head. "When the father is dead, watch the son. If three years later he has not veered from the father's way, he may be called a dutiful son indeed."

It would soon be two and a half years. Even if Father were alive, the injunction applied. He should not veer. But what did that mean? What did it mean he should do?

He had left Chang about a half-watch earlier. Now the sun was directly overhead. He found himself sitting, as he had the day before, not far from the *China Harmony*. The iron ribs had all been installed, and the carpenters were closing in the deck just above his line of sight. Hammers rang as spikes were driven into long, thick cedar planks.

Without asking permission, he climbed a rickety bamboo ladder. On a completed portion of the deck, the sailmen had arrived to attach another giant sheet of silk to a yardarm. They winched it up the mast a little more than a man's height and set to work at each edge of the cloth, attaching a wilderness of ropes in different thicknesses.

Remembering his fantasy of the other day, when the decks of the ship had magically populated themselves, he realized how close it was to becoming true. One day soon, old Captain Zhou with the muttonchop whiskers would climb onto the command deck of the huge wooden "castle" that was taking shape at the stern of the ship. At his word, the red sail now lying obediently on the deck would climb to its full height.

What would it feel like to give that order? All at once an ache and a longing went through his body. His mouth shaped the order, and he could see the great sails rising.

A voice cut into his reverie.

"Scribe Shen! What are you doing up there?"

It was, of all people, Blinky. Shen had never seen the official outside the Admiral's quarters, imagining that he slept in a kennel in a back room like a faithful dog. Yet here he was, gazing up and sheltering his eyes from the sun. "Come down. Walk with me."

Shen, puzzled, climbed down the ladder. The two ambled in silence along the close-fitted brick pathway beside the dry docks. Blinky glanced at him every so often in a calculating way that made a shiver go up Shen's back.

"I was present when Architect Hu pleaded for your sister," said Blinky at last. "He was most dramatic. I added a few words of my own in support. It was shockingly callous of the Admiral to think of putting her out."

"I am pleased she is safe," said Shen carefully. "But I wonder you would speak so harshly of your master."

Blinky laughed, the first time Shen had heard him do this. He laughed unpleasantly, with his mouth open, so that Shen could see his delicate little teeth. "Well, I am a Confucian first and foremost," said Blinky, gesturing at the badge on his robe. "It is a great sin to separate brother and sister, particularly when the parents are already lost. Eunuchs do not understand these things."

Shen nodded and said nothing. They walked in silence a while.

"Of course I am delighted that Lord Yang will accompany the ships," continued Blinky, "because there is much in the doings of a great fleet that offends Heaven. Some of the sailors are convicted murders, living like kings below decks. And the 'flower girls' to entertain barbarian diplomats! I am ill thinking of it." When Blinky got excited his face puckered and turned red. "But what can a junior official do? At most I have helped persuade Lord Zheng that we need a great Confucian like Lord Yang aboard. He is fierce and righteous. He will put things in order."

Shen had no use for Lord Yang, even less for Blinky, but he couldn't help feeling that this odd, red-faced man made sense.

Blinky was still observing Shen carefully. Now his voice

grew softer. "You know, it was Lord Yang who told me to speak up for your sister. He was angry I didn't do so earlier, when you made your plea. Do you wonder why he takes a particular interest in your case?" Shen's ears pricked up. "It is because he and your mother once formed an attachment."

A look came over Shen's face that made Blinky laugh out loud again. "Young men think their mother never noticed any man in the world until their father came along! But your mother was famous. Lord Yang went to all her performances, and invited her to the palace. He courted her—but very politely, with no impropriety!

"Unfortunately for him, your father was among those invited to her concerts in the music room. Seeing your mother sing and perform by lamp-light in front of the great men and their wives, all of them rustling in silk, struck dumb by the beauty of your mother's voice—I can tell you, your father was charmed! He arranged to go riding with her, and a cavalry officer on a golden horse can turn a woman's head. Your mother forgot Lord Yang rather quickly."

"That's why he hates her so much," spat Shen. "He's just small and jealous, like any man."

Blinky blanched. "Lord Yang is not like other men. He has done everything he can to release your mother."

Shen looked fiercely at Blinky. Was Blinky toying with him?

"If he's so worried about Mother and me," said Shen angrily, "then why haven't I had a letter from her in thirty months!"

"But we didn't know where you were, Fei Shen! Please be fair. Now that we have found you, you shall have a letter. I will see to it. It is even possible you may visit her."

"Where? In the middle of the ocean?"

Blinky smiled with his sharp teeth. "I can't say more. But there are surprises ahead. And I see we have reached the Admiral's quarters."

He bowed and was gone.

Shen was shaken by this news. A "surprise ahead," if it meant seeing Mother, should have overjoyed him. But Blinky's story didn't quite hang together. If Lord Yang wanted to know where to send Mother's letters, why didn't he just ask her? She knew where her son and daughter were.

But then again, maybe Mother didn't trust Lord Yang. He was a jilted lover, after all. That made sense too, though it also made his skin crawl. He thought he should recount the whole conversation to the Admiral as quickly as possible. But first he would go to Lan Yi.

Yi had treated him roughly, but some part of him still believed the circus master was on his side. And Yi had known Mother. Shen wanted to hear Yi say that Blinky was lying through his teeth.

Since being appointed overseer of the newcomers, Yi had been given his own room, which he had chosen to share with Marmot.

And here was Marmot, sitting on the front stoop of the barracks with his scrawny chest absorbing the last feeble rays of the sun. He was combing his snakelike mustache. Nodding to him, Shen lit a candle and moved slowly down the corridor toward Yi's room.

Calling softly at the door, he heard no movement or answer inside. He looked back toward the porch, intending to ask where Yi was. But Marmot was no longer there.

Shen reached out his hand to try the door. It was unlocked. He stepped inside, not really knowing what he hoped to learn.

A sour smell emanated from the corner of the room where Marmot's sleeping pallet lay. The quilt was neatly folded but in need of washing. A mah-jongg board was tucked against the wall beside a small heap of clothing and a few mementos, including a broken knife and a woman's silver hairpin.

He turned toward Yi's sleeping-place. It was pleasantly lit by the evening sun, which came in through a window above the mattress. There was a small, finely made wooden chest with a drawer at the top.

On top of the chest was a book of Taoist wisdom, which surprised Shen. He had never heard Yi talk about such things.

Tugging on the drawer, he found it was secured with a little brass latch. He hesitated. It was one thing to open an unfastened drawer, entirely another to turn a latch that was meant to keep it shut.

These qualms barely slowed his hand. He slipped the latch and looked inside. What was there was in plain view; no need to touch it. Shen's head bobbed slightly, as if he were nodding in agreement with an unseen companion.

Sliding the drawer shut, he turned and looked down the corridor toward the entrance of the building.

Marmot had returned! Had he seen Shen come out of the room?

Shen walked casually back out on the front stoop. Marmot had come back with a flask of rice wine and sat himself down on the small stone step to drink it. He waved amiably at Shen and resumed drinking. He gave no sign of noticing anything.

"Enjoy the sunset," said Shen. He felt distaste for Marmot, drunk, as he often was, his most cherished possessions a broken knife and a woman's hairpin. Shen shivered and, holding the candle aloft, made his way down the other corridor to the room he shared with several of the acrobats.

Squatting on his sleeping pallet, he thought what remarkable luck it was that Mother had repaired Father's badge with orange thread. If it weren't for that, he could not have been certain that it was his.

Because Father's Panther badge was sitting in Lan Yi's drawer. It couldn't be any other. It was stained with soot, which showed that he had stayed in the palace after the fire began. But not actually burned. The fire had never reached the badge.

The fire had not reached Father.

CHAPTER 17

IN THE SILENCE OF his heart, the day after finding Father's badge, Shen renounced Lan Yi. "By the ropes that bound my ankles," he swore, rubbing his left leg and remembering the humiliation of being tied to his horse, "I cast that man out of my life. Never will I rely on him. Never will I confide in him."

He made it official by swearing on his grandparents and the ancient founders of his family.

Then he renounced the Admiral. It was a day for renunciation, and he had a bitter taste in his throat, as if he had eaten some foul weed from the roadside. But now that Father was alive—and the badge proved it!—would not he and Shen stand shoulder to shoulder one day and take revenge on the blotch-faced giant?

Even the fact of working in the Admiral's office was a gift from Heaven. Shen knew his every move and every thought. The Admiral would be his subject, and one day he would tell Father all of the eunuch's secrets.

Then Zheng He would pay for destroying the city of his childhood.

Shen felt light-headed, as he imagined Lan Yi did when he was drunk. Was this a kind of drunkenness? he wondered. It certainly felt good. Felt powerful. Felt definite, as if the fog were lifting and a road was emerging in front of him.

———

FROM THAT DAY SHEN withdrew into himself. He kept up the forms of politeness, even joked with Lan Yi. But Chang saw that something had changed. She decided to keep a close watch on him.

The problem was how to do it. It was difficult to get away from Mistress Guo and her wicked bamboo rod. Shen, on the other hand, was at liberty when not working for the Admiral. He was harder to keep track of than a lizard in a leaf pile.

But luck presented a solution. One day a junior official called together the circus troupe and nearly a hundred other civilians on the *China Harmony's* unfinished deck. The "guests," he announced in an earnest voice, were to take basic training in the handling of the ships. Great dangers lay ahead. Professional sailors might die in storm or battle. The civilians must be able to bring the vessel safely to land.

Chang saw Older Brother sitting not too far away as these words were spoken. She smiled as she realized that he would be within view during the mornings at least. And for once he seemed interested. His eyes strayed up the masts and yardarms of the ship, and she knew he was imagining himself up there.

The girl acrobats were angry to learn that they would not be allowed to climb the rigging. The junior officer complacently explained that sailors would not tolerate women aloft. "Especially not acrobats," shouted Jade. "We would make them look bad!" For this, Mistress Guo had rapped Jade's knuckles with her bamboo rod until the young girl wept.

The girls in the company instead became expert at repairing torn sails with needle and thread, and coiling endless ropes around windlasses. They looked enviously at the boys, who were climbing the masts and learning how to slide down the ropes that held the sails in place. In the afternoons, the whole company resumed training as usual. But here Chang lost sight of Older Brother because he went off to his scribe duties in the Admiral's quarters.

Chang and Shen boarded the *China Harmony* in its dry dock at the same time each morning. The women, who were mostly singers and actresses, were herded into an enclosure made of temporary posts with panels of cotton fabric fastened between them. It was erected after noisy demands from the actresses, who did not like the idea of the male crew seeing them without makeup and wearing dirty sailors' tunics. Hidden behind the fabric panels, they wielded the sailhooks fiercely and cursed the Admiral for making them do so.

That day there was trouble farther down the deck, where Captain Zhou spoke to the sailors and sailor-trainees like Shen. He announced that the mountain-sized sails were too large to be reefed in the customary fashion. Reefing meant to reduce the size of the sail when the wind was strong, and it was usually a simple matter of releasing the deck windlass that held the sail ropes tight. As the ropes spun out, the great sail would collapse, starting at the top. Because it was divided into sections by the bamboo battens, it would hit the deck with a clattering sound and fold up like a noisy pack of playing cards.

But Captain Zhou wanted men to climb to the sturdy wooden yardarm at the top of the mast and learn to drop the sail bit by bit without losing control. The experienced sailors shouted that this was madness. Who would want to be up there when a storm struck? A fall meant instant death.

When Captain Zhou repeated the order, they sat on the deck and refused to move. A detachment of Ocean-Spanning Guards dragged a dozen men to a place near the women's enclosure and flogged them with bamboo rods until their backs reddened. The actresses pulled one of the cotton panels aside and shrieked at the guards to have mercy. But the rest of the sailors, far down the deck, stood up and hooted at the guards and still refused to move. Chang looked on silently, especially at the blood running down the beaten men's backs. She had seen men beaten before—a girl could not live in Nanjing's military precinct and not see such things—but it had not occurred to her that the fleet would be like that. How foolish of me, she thought.

"Let the cowards turn their backs!" came an abrupt shout from Captain Zhou. "Let the brave men volunteer!"

"I volunteer," cried Shen in a stout voice. "I am no coward."

And without another word, carried forward by sheer impulse and showing-off, he scampered up the climbing ladder attached to the mast. Captain Zhou, who had no intention of sending untried civilians on such a dangerous errand, tried to persuade him to come down, but Shen kept climbing until he was nearly out of sight.

Cursing Shen violently, some sailors went up the mast after him. Chang realized that the men, many of them hardened criminals, would rather defy the captain than be humbled by a boy. A pang in her stomach told her that they would fling Older Brother off the rigging. Captain Zhou screamed orders until his voice was raw, but only one of the sailors obeyed. The others were still clambering upward. She saw that one of them had Shen by the leg while another struck out at him with a knife.

At that moment the resonant thunder of the gong rolled across the deck. Everybody stopped, including the sailors climbing the mast. A diminutive figure in a black robe stepped down from the gong platform and walked to the mast. Chang saw that it was Blinky. He had observed the morning training before.

"Every sailor descend," cried Blinky in a screeching voice that carried far. "Beating and the brig for those who do not."

Chang watched the sailors climb meekly down. Shen was last, and she shivered when she saw a trickle of blood on the side of his neck. He stood beside Blinky as the little official spoke to Captain Zhou. She held her breath, afraid Older Brother would be beaten for insubordination.

Instead, something mystifying happened. Blinky and Shen left the ship together. The sailors who had pursued her brother were manacled to punishment blocks.

Chang couldn't get it out of her mind that Shen had gone with Blinky. For the rest of the morning she could hardly see the needle and thread. She and Jade exchanged worried looks but couldn't talk. When the gong signaled the middle of the day, Chang hurried toward the dormitory to prepare for rehearsal.

"Slow down!" cried Jade, coming up behind her. "What possessed your brother to do that? Has he lost his mind?"

"It's barely attached to his head at the best of times," muttered Chang as she caught sight of two familiar silhouettes up ahead.

Lan Yi and Temur were watching a very large ship moving slowly down the canal with its sails furled. A double bank of long oars projected from its sides and dug fiercely into the water. The ship's movement set off a shrieking and howling inside, as if it were peopled by demons.

"It's horses!" cried Jade. "How cruel to put them in a ship. I don't want to listen!" And she strode away, hands over her ears.

Chang remained, mystified by Jade's recent tendency to squealing and fluttering. After all, the horses weren't really being harmed; they were just in a panic from being on the ship. Their cries did not perturb her, and she saw no reason to pretend they did—even if girls were expected to be upset by that kind of thing. Instead she was taken with the magnificence of the horse ship, which she had been told carried three hundred animals.

And when she saw Temur go to the very edge of the canal, leaning out as if listening for something in particular, she smiled. Merk had been accepted into the Horse Guard, which meant that he would travel as a fighting animal with the Treasure Fleet. He might even be on this ship.

Moreover, this wasn't Temur's only victory of late. The Admiral had decreed that the Treasure Fleet would not practice discrimination against Mongols. Temur had dug out the wrinkled paper proving his father had been a guardsman during the enlightened reign of Taizu and nervously asked if that meant he could enlist as well. To his amazement, the answer was yes. Now Temur had the two things he wanted most: his horse and his soldier's tunic.

Lan Yi, less interested in horses than Temur, decided to walk Chang to the barracks. They glanced back to see Temur still absorbed in the task of trying to hear Merk's whinny in the general din.

Chang told him what had happened with the mast and the gong, and waited anxiously for his thoughts. Yi walked silently for a time, taking it in. "There is something amiss with your brother. For two weeks he's refused to speak to me, except the smallest greeting to avoid giving offense. I'm afraid he's going to do something stupid and jeopardize all of us."

"He won't talk to me either," said Chang.

"Please try harder. As far as I can tell, you're the only person he's not mad at," replied Yi.

"Excuse my directness," said Chang, speaking politely because the subject was delicate, "but you are wrong. There's Blinky. They're friends."

Yi had not known about this. He surprised Chang by laughing. "That's what happens when you mix up the eunuchs with the Confucians. We'll have a miniature Imperial Court aboard the ships. People like Blinky, they live for intrigue. And I'm very sorry to say, so does your brother."

SHEN HAD GONE FIRST to the hospital, where they put a poultice on the ragged wound that ran down his neck and onto his shoulder. It wasn't deep, the surgeon said, expressing no particular interest in how it had happened. Every sailor had a knife.

Shen's neck was stiff by the time he arrived at the Admiral's quarters. Blinky had gone ahead to explain why the scribe was late. As Shen entered, raucous laughter greeted him.

"Haaaaaaa!" mocked a Brocade officer sitting opposite the Admiral and General Ho Fu. "Even your scribes are warriors! I am very frightened for my poor Brocades."

It was Officer Chu. Shen wasn't happy to see him again, but he bowed politely as the morning scribe departed. Then he took up his brush as one-eyed Ho Fu began to list the distribution of Chu's Brocades aboard the ships. "Twenty-five on the *Falcon*, forty on the hospital ship, ten on each of the oared warships—"

"You have not allowed any aboard the munitions ships," said Chu, interrupting Ho Fu.

"Nor will I," grunted the Admiral, intervening in the conversation. "My weapons are none of Lord Yang's business."

"Of course not," said Chu, bowing from his sitting position with what struck Shen as too-eager agreement. "We have no wish to challenge your authority."

Then Chu and Ho Fu read through the rest of the list and declared that they were both satisfied. The two soldiers left, and the Admiral called for Interpreter Ma. While waiting, he asked about Shen's wound. "The sailors are rough company," the Admiral concluded. "I wonder how a soft-handed boy like you will fare with them."

Shen bristled. "The gracious Admiral remembers that my father was a soldier."

"Sons are not always like their fathers," replied the Admiral, toying with a letter he held in his hand. Shen saw that the seal had been broken. Interpreter Ma scuttled into the room. "Have the final orders arrived from the palace?" he asked

"Yes," replied the Admiral. "Emperor Zhu Di grants no delay. The fleet must depart on the first day of the eleventh lunar month. That is less than a month from now. We shall have to complete the ships' fitting at sea." He tapped the unsealed letter on the arm of his chair. "The scribe will note that a final communication was received from the Emperor this morning."

Shen dipped his brush again. Interpreter Ma's eyes darted curiously at the letter.

"The Son of Heaven informs us of an additional mission. We are to stop at the great island of Sumatra, two months' journey by sea from China. There, in the city of Palembang, we are to engage and destroy a fleet of pirates under the command of a man named Chen Zuyi. He controls the city."

"What have we got to do with pirates?" asked Interpreter Ma indignantly.

"As you can tell from his name, this pirate is Chinese. He has attacked the Kingdom of Majapahit."

"Ah, Majapahit!" said Ma with satisfaction. "They speak

a curious variety of the Malayalam language in that place. I shall be very interested to study it."

The Admiral's laughter had an alarming boom to it, like a small cannon going off. When he stopped, he wiped a tear from his eye and grinned with his huge white teeth. "The pirate has a hundred ships, my dear old Ma Huan! But still you find it more interesting to know whether the local people chitter like a monkey or a baboon." The Admiral respected barbarians but could not master their languages. It was a sore point with him. "Well, you will have your chance. We shall stop in Majapahit to meet with its king. Because we have shunned trade with them, the only Chinese people they know are renegades like this Chen Zuyi. By destroying him, we restore our good name."

Then the Admiral signaled Shen to stop writing.

"There is a further matter, which is secret. Some record must be kept, but perhaps that is better done by an experienced scribe."

Shen held his breath.

"The older ones know that the penalty for a loose tongue is death," said Interpreter Ma, worried. "It does not seem right to trouble a boy with this."

"I am an officer's son," said Shen with dignity. "I do not veer from his path."

"Hm," grunted the Admiral. "We'll see. Make a note, Fei Shen. The deposed Emperor commonly called the Grandson has been located. He is alive. He is under the protection of the pirate whom we will destroy."

CHAPTER **18**

THE MOON WAXED and waned. The month passed. The Star Fleet was ready to depart.

Several days earlier the dry docks had filled with water, gradually lifting the five giant ships into full view. It was like a slowly unfolding magical spell. The first part of the vessel to become visible was a shrine to the many gods of the sea, thunder, and wind. Next to appear was the "castle" on which the shrine was built. This was a three-story structure erected on the ship's stern for the use of the Admiral, the officers, and the navigators. Each floor stepped back from the one beneath, so it looked like an immense staircase. Each "step" was a wide wooden deck with thick teak railings. Behind it were the officers' rooms and meeting places.

Finally, the vast main deck rose into view, like a sea dragon surfacing. First the prow, like a monster's snout, climbed above the edge of the dry dock; next the "eyes," one painted on each side of the ship to let it see its way across the ocean; and finally the midship deck, where the heaviest of the nine masts was fixed. The releasing of the giant ships into the canal took a full day.

Over a hundred small warships were also built in Long-jiang to accompany and defend the fleet. But these were standard ships, easy and familiar to build; and they had all been launched and sailed down to the Yangtze River in previous weeks. There they joined the 150 merchant ships that had journeyed from the great trading ports to the north and the south. Their treasure-laden holds would carry Chinese commerce to the world.

The balance of the fleet, just over thirty ships, was between 200 and 250 *ch'i* in length. They were huge, though not nearly the size of the five giant ships. There were three ships for horses; three that were loaded with rice, barley, and millet; another where pigs and goats were kept for food, together with chickens that were sacrificed to foretell the future but never eaten!; two were hospitals; while three carried swords, spears, cannons, and rockets.

Others were military transports, carrying altogether about four thousand soldiers.

A week earlier the Admiral had moved his staff onto the *China Harmony*, where the carpenters had labored extra hard to make sure his quarters were ready. Shen had dreamed so often of stepping onto the polished cedar deck that he actually whooped and laughed like a child when it finally happened. Then he looked abashed, because he was part of the Admiral's official retinue, and the officers scowled at him.

Blinky was not part of the Admiral's quarters in the tall castle at the stern. Shortly before the move to the ship, the Admiral had cursed the Confucians one morning, and he cursed

Blinky with them. "There's a place on the ship for people who wear your black robe, little man," Zheng He had snarled at him. And Blinky had been banished to the rooms set aside for the Confucians at the faraway prow of the ship.

So now every day Blinky would slide up beside Shen when he walked on deck, asking insinuating questions about what the Admiral was planning for Lord Yang. "You know I can't talk about what he says in his office!" protested Shen.

But the little man persisted, always smiling with his delicate white teeth. As the days went by he winkled away at Shen, learning bit by bit of Shen's hatred for the Admiral. And Blinky sucked on his teeth sympathetically, looking at Shen with soft, tragic eyes. "We are both much abused by Zheng He! Much abused!"

Shen avoided Lan Yi, who had moved in to the artists' quarters two decks below the main deck. Staying away from him was made easier by the fact that Yi, like all the civilians on the ship, was not permitted to climb the magnificent teak staircase up to the castle except when invited. He sometimes tried to start a friendly conversation with Shen on the main deck, but all Shen could think of was that this man had Father's badge in his possession and hadn't said a word about it. These conversations were short and awkward.

And so the days passed.

And then one day it was time for the Treasure Fleet to go out into the great unknown world.

THE EARLY-MORNING BUSTLE of nearly eight hundred crew and passengers vibrated through the raw timbers of the great ship.

The morning gong had sounded a while back, and Shen hurried to splash his face with water and climb into dark blue dress sailor's clothes. It was a special day, for the fleet was to be blessed by the Emperor himself. The Admiral and Lord Yang would leave the *China Harmony* to visit the Emperor on his royal barge.

Glancing at a brass mirror, Shen decided that he would pass inspection even if he weren't going to meet the Emperor.

He mounted the back staircase from the second-level quarters of junior staff like himself. Entering the Admiral's vast quarters on the third and topmost level, he nodded at the Ocean-Spanning Guards in their blue-and-yellow uniforms. Like the rest of the ship, the room smelled of new wood: the clean odor of pine, the pungent, cheesy smell of freshly sawed teakwood.

The Admiral's quarters occupied the middle third of the third deck with a wood-paneled meeting room that was much more lavish than his former quarters in the octopus building. Nobody but a guard was there at this early hour, and Shen walked quietly past him to the wide double door that led to the observation deck.

Now he was looking down to the main deck below, where he saw Interpreter Ma and Captain Zhou approaching. It was a glorious early autumn day, and Shen closed his eyes, feeling the brisk, still-warm wind that hummed through the rigging. Banners and pennants atop the tall masts snapped in the breeze.

Then he hurried over to the gleaming wooden staircase that Ma and Zhou were climbing. He bowed to greet them. At the same moment the Admiral emerged from his quarters and, ignoring them, strode directly to the teak railing. He dug his fists into his broad hips and let his huge white silk cape flap in the breeze.

Spanning the Yangtze River were the other four giant ships, each under the authority of one of the Admiral's senior eunuchs. They were making their way slowly downstream under the least possible sail. On the distant northern shore of the Yangtze, Shen saw an endless crowd of commoners come to bid the ships farewell.

And then one-eyed Ho Fu approached him with an intent look. "General of the Tiger Badge," said Shen politely, bowing.

Ho Fu bowed in a perfunctory way. "Fei Shen, you will have the honor of assisting me in a small task today."

He led Shen down to the main deck, to a gated place on the ship's railing. The gates were decorated with ribbons and pennants and posted with guards in rich ceremonial costume. "At this place the Admiral and Lord Yang will descend a gangplank to the royal barge, where they will greet the Emperor. You see here a yellow pennant, wrapped tightly around its pole. Mark it carefully: the Confucian will stand beside it, in front of the gangplank. On the other side of the pennant will be a small group of Ocean-Spanning Guards. At a certain moment I shall order you to hide yourself among them. They will expect you. You will see a small cord dangling from the pennant. When the thunder drums begin to beat, pull the cord. It will come free in your hand, and you must quickly conceal it on your person. Slip away. That is all."

And he left, leaving Shen dazed.

The stiff onshore breeze ruffled Shen's hair. He noticed that it blew against his back as he stood beside the yellow pennant. Returning up the staircase, his stomach churning, he tried to guess what trickery he was now a part of. Somewhere in his mind a memory half-awakened. A wind, a pennant, an ill omen.

Shen returned to his place with the Admiral's personal staff on the castle's high observation deck. Staff officers, senior scientists in scholars' robes, and several important Daoist priests from the Ministry of Rites who had been commanded to join the expedition were arrayed in their finest gowns. Even the servants looked resplendent.

Standing before them was the Ocean Lord himself. He was a vision of power, if you could overlook the tiny shrine to the sea goddess Tianfei that he had ordered built just a bit farther along the observation deck. Unlike the public temple on the castle roof, the shrine was reserved for his personal use. Tianfei was a specialist in saving sailors who fell into the ocean, and it was by now well-known that this was the reason for the Admiral's devotion to her. The sailors laughed and called it Death-by-Drowning Temple.

Shen's eyes strayed to the main deck's garden. Thousands of copper pots, set in a shallow depression so that hatches could be rolled over them in the event of a gale, had exploded with leaf mustard, red bean, spinach, and eggplant. There was sweet melon set beside wax gourd and celery, and edible live mosses in flat trays. All were nourished by water tanks concealed beneath the deck.

A forward hatch opened, and a group of monks in green robes dashed to their place on a raised dais running alongside the gardens. They were followed by a column of Daoist priests in white satin, together with science officers and astronomers wearing four-sided, black-lacquered official's hats and formal Hanfu robes. They lined the deck railing on the side where the ship would be pulled up to the Emperor's reviewing barge.

Finally the artists emerged, each in dramatic costume. The great acting company from Beijing wore the flowing robes of the ancient plays for which they were famous. The Suzhou Acrobatic Troupe was turned out in bright-colored cotton costumes, the men with tight red caps on their heads and the women's faces powdered in pink. Lan Yi had put on the robes of a *chou*, or clown, a floppy black gown well-suited for making fun of officials and pompous people. On his face was the clown's trademark makeup, a triangular patch of white that enclosed his eyes and nose.

Coming into view was a vast floating platform. Anchored in place, it was covered with rich carpets and seated ranks of noblemen who gazed at the approaching Star Fleet. At the back was a wall covered in rippling yellow silk. It would prevent the crowds gathered on shore from seeing the Emperor, the Son of Heaven, which they were forbidden to do.

Viewed from the ships, the Emperor's throne on the barge was still no more than a speck in the distance. Shen intended to steal a look at him when they got closer, because Father had looked upon Emperors while in the palace guard.

"Older Brother?" came a nearby voice. He looked around to see Chang standing nervously at the side of Lord Yang. The Confucian would have come to the ship the previous night.

"I thought you would like to share this great moment with your sister," said Yang in a honeyed voice. "The Admiral has permitted it, and it pleases me to see you safely together." He bowed deeply, politely withdrawing with his guards.

Chang slipped in beside Shen and twined the fingers of her right hand through his, squeezing them intently. The gesture took him by surprise. It made him realize that he had been alone and angry for more than two weeks, since finding Father's Panther badge. Suddenly there were pesky tears on his round cheeks, and he remembered how he used to feel... before. He glanced down and saw Chang's open smile—as well as her alert, searching brown eyes.

"Why did Lord Yang bring you to me?" he demanded, trying to sound distant and commanding.

"I wanted to see you," whispered Chang in reply. "The guards wouldn't let me up here, and he intervened. What of it, Brother? Why does he make you nervous?"

Before Shen could say anything about the yellow pennant, a guard cried, "Avert your eyes!"

Shen obeyed the guard for many long moments, counting the beats of his heart. Then he furtively half-opened his eyes, seeing nothing at first but the glistening black hair of the back of his sister's head. Straining his eyes as far to the right as he could without moving his head, he saw a high raised throne set against a gigantic lotus painted in black on the silk. It set off the tiny figure of Zhu Di himself, wearing a seven-paneled ceremonial silk robe the same yellow as the wall. It suggested the Emperor was one with it, an immense and superhuman presence.

Though Shen wouldn't have thought anything could distract him at this moment, his attention was caught by two bizarre animals standing to each side of the royal throne. They were as tall as trees, with spotted bodies. He did not believe they were alive until one turned its head at the end of its long, stalklike neck.

There was a gentle bump as the flagship attached itself to an anchored buoy.

"Boy," said one-eyed General Ho Fu, who seemed to appear out of nowhere, "do not seek to see what you should not." He drew Shen away from Chang. "When the Son of Heaven is concealed within the jade screens, go to the place where you have been ordered!"

A guard barked the order that all might now open their eyes. Shen immediately left the observation deck, leaving a puzzled Chang behind.

The flutes, two-stringed erhu, and the shrill, many-reeded instrument called the *sheng* began to play ceremonial music. The Emperor behind his jade screens had moved to a spot just outside the shadow of the *China Harmony*. Lord Yang took his place on the deck, a few paces from Shen. Looking down the gangplank Shen saw, inside the wall of screens, the Emperor's flat-topped black silk hat with twelve strings of tiny white jade beads hanging down to hide his face.

At that moment the thunder drums began to beat. Shen, his heart pounding, tugged the little cord. The pennant fell loose, the wind picked it up—and blew it around Lord Yang's body.

A collective gasp emerged from the dignitaries below. The flat-topped Imperial hat looked upward, and Shen saw the Emperor's astonished eyes behind the strings of beads.

It wasn't until later that Shen understood why everybody was shocked. At the moment the only effect of his sabotage that he could see was that it allowed the Admiral to start down the steps ahead of Lord Yang.

But it was clear that Lord Yang's Brocades took the matter seriously. They were hurling themselves against the little knot of Ho Fu's Ocean-Spanning Guards, who protected Shen and kept a small opening against the deck railing for him to slip away. He dropped the cord into his pocket like an errant noodle into a hungry man's mouth and escaped. He saw one of Lord Yang's Brocades break through and yank the pennant out of its socket. Others roughly stretched it on the deck and searched every corner of it. But they found nothing.

As he climbed back to the observation deck, Shen's heart was still pounding. The Admiral's kitchen staff was screaming, "The Qi'lin! The Qi'lin!" which confused him until he realized they meant the two strange creatures below. Everybody could see them now.

Were these in fact the Qi'lin, the sacred animal nobody had ever seen? Shen stopped on the staircase and studied them. Two soft horns jutted from their heads, just like the pictures of Qi'lin in old books, where they were seen only in the company of wise and just rulers. These two creatures also had liquid brown eyes and improbable eyelashes. Perhaps, he thought, the gods had reached down and touched the world. But why so much magic to bless a man who had stolen the Throne of Heaven from his own nephew?

He felt a strong, bony hand grasp his elbow. "Well, aren't we in the middle of things?" hissed Marmot. "You better decide who you're working with, boy."

"Don't call me 'boy.'"

"Very well, Captain Fei's Son! Lan Yi says you're to wait for him in his quarters this evening."

Shen climbed the rest of the way to the observation deck. Disoriented by the encounter with Marmot, he had missed part of the Emperor's speech. It was amplified by courtiers with loud hailers who were just then proclaiming "the great mission of the black-haired people to the nations across the ocean."

Far below, on the royal barge, he saw the Admiral and Lord Yang laying on their stomachs on the carpeted deck in a gesture of submission. Shore cannons fired and ragged smoke blew down the river like a banished ghost.

The ceremony was complete. The Emperor vanished behind his jade screens, and both the Admiral and the Confucian climbed the long set of steps to the *China Harmony*. With no further ado, the great ship turned heavily toward the sea.

Shen made his way to the castle. So this was the way of things, though Shen. Especially if there was dirty work, and a fifteen-year-old boy who could be ordered to do it.

Interpreter Ma was sitting in the Admiral's chambers, waiting for the dignitaries to come back. After a few words with Shen about the ceremony—ceremonies meant no more to Ma than sugar to a cat—he blurted out an interesting observation. "Lord Yang has had a great misfortune."

Shen said nothing, knowing that with Ma the best thing was to let him talk.

"A bad omen for him, I think," Interpreter Ma continued. "The day the founder of our dynasty entered Nanjing, thirty-five years ago, a flag blew around his general. It turned out the general had meant to assassinate him. The flag prevented him from giving the order. What happened to Lord Yang was so very similar that I fear it will cost him dearly."

Shen saw how he had been used. The coarseness of it was brought home to him when the Admiral and his officers entered the cabin. The Admiral guffawed and beat his hand noisily on the teak desk.

"What should be my first order to Yang Rong, Captain Zhou? Should I have him polish my jade belt while I'm wearing it?" His voice was rich with pleasure at his triumph.

The old captain clasped his hands behind his back. Licking his lips thoughtfully and setting his white muttonchops into motion, he looked even more sheeplike than usual. "Do nothing provocative, Admiral. Summon him for a quiet talk in the morning. Do not fail in respect. He is dangerous."

"Zhou, you are a woman! Boy, what are you doing here?" He paused a moment and rubbed one of the small craters on the skin of his cheek. "There is no need of a scribe today."

An attendant steered Shen out of the room.

Shen stood awhile on the foredeck, watching morosely as the sailors raised the massive sails. A seaman, far away at the prow of the ship, lifted a piece of wood attached to a rope and hurled it overboard. Holding tight the other end of the rope, he walked the floating wood from the front to the back of the ship as a drummer tapped monotonously. The sailor counted the drumbeats and, as he reached the ship's stern, cried out, "One hundred and forty-one." Depending on how fast the ship was moving, the piece of wood would float from prow to stern in a lesser or greater number of drumbeats.

Shen made the calculation automatically. The vessel was moving at a prudent fifteen *li* per watch. When a sailor in the rigging shouted, "Lang Mountain!" he realized with surprise that they were already approaching the town of Nantong. His bitter reverie had taken up a good part of the afternoon.

The town's five mountains fell behind them and the country became pancake flat. The Yangtze broadened into a treacherous network of sediment-filled shallows and ever-changing river bottom. A ship could not trust this river, thought Shen, just as a man could not trust the men around him.

Looking upriver, he saw that the other four Treasure ships had formed a single line behind the flagship because the navigable channel was very narrow from that point on. The giant vessels were followed by a lengthy single column of other ships, like pearls on a string, over three hundred strong. The last ones, far out of view in the river mist, were crammed with fat merchants who wondered if they were out of their minds to have agreed to this adventure.

For different reasons, Shen was asking himself the same question. Today was a great moment in the history of his people. At least, everybody said so. And yet, even in the presence of the Son of Heaven, powerful men still thought of nothing but humiliating their enemies.

Where, he thought, was the "nobility" in this noble quest?

CHAPTER 19

THE MOON WAS LOW on the horizon when Shen left the castle, showing his deck pass to the guards, and descended to the main deck. He was obeying Marmot's summons to come to Lan Yi.

The faint light of a fishing village named Shanghai was the last sign of human presence as the *China Harmony* eased toward the open ocean. A half-*li* ahead, a small military junk churned through phosphorescent algae, leaving a sparkling blue wake in the darkness. A lantern swaying off its prow threw a sphere of brightness in which Shen could see two sailors dropping and lifting weights on ropes. He knew they would be quietly calling the depth to the sternman of their boat. Beside the sternman was a small cannon he would fire if the shallow bottom threatened the *China Harmony*.

Shen stopped to watch the navigator take a sighting on the just-risen Pole Star. The rising moon whitened the cedar planks of the deck and seemed to create a soundless hush.

"Are we truly in the ocean, Sir Navigator?" said Shen, startled by his own voice. Ahead was a vast expanse of water, as still as a painting. The ship moved through it without so much as a tremor.

"By the next watch," said the man. "After that we sail directly south, sighting on the Pole Star as long as we can. After sunrise we use the compass."

He fiddled with the compass, a magnetized iron needle on a bit of wood, which floated in a stone basin filled with water. With a caliper and an ink brush the navigator silently drew on a paper the angle of difference between the true north of the star and the magnetic north of the needle. That would keep them sailing straight during the day. The flame of his tiny lantern guttered.

"Isn't it remarkable how we go into the great world guided by a little iron needle?" said a voice behind him. Whirling about, Shen was greeted by Lord Yang's weary smile. "Greetings, Fei Shen. Did you find your sister well?"

"Quite well," said Shen nervously. "What were your feelings about the ceremony today?"

Lord Yang leaned on a railing, one forearm flopped casually across the other. "You know, the Pole Star is a symbol of the Emperor. The other stars circle around it. Well," he laughed, "if I am one of those stars, I am much dimmer tonight than I was last night!"

Shen looked at him warily. "I understand that the... difficulty... with the pennant may bring you bad fortune. But you don't seem upset."

"I was upset when I thought it was a trick of the eunuch. But my men found no evidence. I am a victim of Luck, and a man must laugh at his luck."

Relieved that Lord Yang didn't suspect him, Shen relaxed. He found himself leaning on the railing, his forearms crossed like the Confucian's, as if they were old friends. Then he thought how very strange that was.

"Why are you so generous to Younger Sister and myself?"

"I am ashamed of arresting your mother," said Lord Yang in a familiar and even friendly tone. "I was once attached to her, as I think Blinky told you. But the new Emperor ordered me to imprison people from the old regime. It was a test of my loyalty, and by the strict rules of my order I was bound to do it. Helping you and Chang is a way of making up for that, I suppose."

"But Mother disliked you."

The Confucian looked sadly at Shen. "I should say, by the time the final days of the Grandson's reign arrived, she detested me. Not only because she had fallen in love with your father, but also because she had come to dislike politics. She disapproved of me. But I would like to be her friend again. And yours."

"Blinky said I might get a letter from her." He wanted to ask if Mother could be released, but he sensed that would be too big a thing to ask. For now.

"Indeed, the letter arrived just before we set sail. There will be a delay to make certain no message is encrypted in it. How may I deliver it to you? My people are not permitted to visit the castle."

"I don't know," said Shen.

"May I make a suggestion? A section of the foredeck has been allocated to my people. There is a small deckhouse just behind the foremast, with a flat roof. My guards will place one of their red jackets on the roof when the letter is ready."

"But how can I come to your quarters? I'm not allowed on the Brocade part of the deck."

"Nothing easier. There is a lively traffic below decks, with a checkpoint at the boundary of my quarters. The guards there will know you. You may enter whenever you wish."

Shen bowed and thanked the Confucian profusely. Then, pleading his rendezvous with Lan Yi, he took his leave. He was glad to have the excuse, he thought as he walked away, because he was so excited about Mother's letter that he was afraid he might babble something stupid.

In general, Lord Rong made him nervous. But at that very moment he realized why. It was because the man was so likable.

Yi, Marmot, and Temur were waiting for him while drinking red tea in the common room off the artists' quarters. There was no wine in sight, which meant that Yi had decided to be alert this evening. Bad news for me, thought Shen.

But he was happily surprised to find Chang with them.

Yi, still wearing the white triangle of clown makeup from the ceremony, was nestling his teacup in both hands and bringing his head close to enjoy the fragrance. He offered Shen a cup with a loopy smile and well-bitten fingernails. "Please accept my tea, sirs. It is good tea," he said, recalling the simpleton he had pretended to be back on the road nearly three years earlier.

Shen accepted it with a blank expression. When he saw Yi, he thought of nothing but the Panther badge. Maybe it was time to confront him.

But Yi spoke first. "I called you here, Shen, because I am perturbed. Marmot saw you on deck among the Ocean-Spanning Guards. He saw you pull a cord that released a pennant. Who told you to do that?"

"I can't say."

"Great gods." Yi shook his head. "They have put your head in a noose for some scheme of the Admiral's."

"Well, what else was I to do?" shouted Shen, seeing that he had been observed in the act. "I didn't know what the string was attached to. And it was an order."

"The boy is right," said Marmot indifferently "He is their cat's paw. They'll use him to get at Lord Yang."

Shen considered the situation. He thought he would play for sympathy. "And you should have seen the Admiral and his people gloating afterward. It was like a den of thieves. Even Lord Yang has more nobility than that."

"Real-ly?" said Yi, using his simpleton voice again. It set Shen's teeth on edge.

"Yes, really. I just spoke to Lord Yang. He apologized for what he did to Mother."

"Hm," said Yi, looking at his neatly chewed fingernails. "I haven't always been a good guardian, but here's some good advice: Get away from Lord Yang and stay as far away as you can."

Marmot spat a pistachio shell on the floor. "They're well spoiled, these two officer's children. They prefer the company of a-ris-to-crats."

"At least aristocrats don't lie to me and conceal things that concern me," cried Shen, glaring at Yi. Then he bit his lip and squeezed his eyes shut.

"I don't know what you mean."

It was too late to stop. "I mean that you have my father's badge in your room!"

Silence around the table. Chang put her hand to her mouth.

"I have a Panther badge in my room," replied Yi calmly. "Whose it is, I do not know."

"You know that Mother sewed the orange thread on it! I told you that."

Yi's face was bathed in astonishment. "I swear, Fei Shen, if you told me such a thing I have long forgotten. As for the badge, I did mean to speak to you about it. It was one of several that Marmot bought from a battlefield scavenger." He hesitated. "I have a confession to make. I have been trying to find Fei Lee. Not because I believe he is alive, but because it seemed the only way to end your obsession with him. I thought I owed that much to your parents."

"And does the badge prove he is alive? Or dead? Does it prove anything?" said Chang from the shadows in the corner. Her voice shook.

Shen's eyes were stony. "That he's alive, obviously."

Yi stood up angrily and walked to a corner of the room.

"You remember, Yi, I told you this badge hunting was a waste of time," muttered Marmot, rolling another pistachio inside his mouth, delicately separating the meat from the shell, and firing the two half-shells on the floor like small missiles. This was a sign that he was thinking. "The girl has more sense than you do, and ten times more than her brother. The badge proves nothing. If he's dead, it was scavenged. If he's alive, he sold it." Shen yelped. "There's no such thing as a storybook soldier, boy. A man is running, he does anything to survive."

A tangled kind of silence settled over the group.

"Has the Admiral told you anything else?" demanded Yi after some moments. "If you're doing his dirty work, at least he ought to throw you a morsel or two."

They looked at him expectantly. Shen rummaged in his mind for something to say. "Nothing I can share. I'm under oath."

"Heard two navigators say the name Palembang," said Marmot. "Some old friends of mine live there. They make a good living stripping the ships of the King of Majapahit. Heard anything about them?"

"Pirates?" said Shen innocently. "Nothing about pirates."

"Does the eunuch talk about the Grandson?" asked Yi. Shen sensed that pieces were falling into place in the man's mind like the tumblers of a lock.

"No," said Shen. He was uncomfortable with lying, and agitated that everybody seemed to have forgotten about Father. "Please excuse my abruptness, but I must soon leave. May I have my Father's badge?"

Yi slumped against the wall, apparently discouraged. "Forgive me, Fei Shen. I should have spoken to you long ago about the badge, even if I didn't know it belonged to your father. And how could I remember about the damned orange thread?" Yi was scrubbing at the white makeup on his face with a rag, which made it worse. Shen laughed.

Yi stopped in mid-scrub, eyes blazing. "You are certain the eunuch said nothing about the Grandson?"

"No. Nothing," whined Shen, feeling caught off guard.

"Are you sure?" The makeup had smeared around Yi's eyes.

Shen looked calmly into Yi's eyes. "I told you. The Admiral didn't say anything else."

CHAPTER 20

FIVE DAYS WENT BY. One morning, standing on a footrope about a third of the way up the scarlet mainsail, Shen watched the Daoist priests below make offerings to the undersea dragons that cause storms. Lifting his eyes, he thought he could see the slithering blue-green beasts making their way patiently beneath the waves.

Blinky had removed Shen from the sailors' roster after the attack. But the days on the empty ocean were long, and sometimes he skylarked in the rigging if nobody stopped him. He liked the danger. Somewhere in the sails above was the man who had cut his neck. And if he glanced down, grinning back at him was the mouth of the ocean, its foaming whitecaps like broken teeth.

And finally, far to the front of the ship, was the little deck cabin that led to Lord Yang's quarters. There had been a red Brocade jacket on it more than once, and more than one meeting with Yang Rong.

It had been frustrating. Lord Yang always postponed the handing over of Mother's letter to the next meeting. Then he went on about the many trials and sufferings of his Confucian brothers. This made Shen angry at the beginning, but now he was flattered that a powerful man found so much time for him.

A steady southern wind was blowing the fleet down the passage between the mainland and the great lozenge-shaped island of Taipei. The ships stood well off the Chinese coast, which was peppered with shoals and islands and treacherous currents. Sometimes they were so far to sea that Shen could see the dim mountain peaks of Taipei to the east.

On calm days the acrobats set out the chairs and equipment on the deck. While some jumped on the high end of the teeter-totter, propelling a colleague into the air, others began to build a chair pyramid. A strong man would place a chair on each shoulder. Smaller men would climb onto them and do handstands, supporting yet more chairs on their feet high in the air. Then a slender girl would climb to the top of the pyramid and balance splendidly. The sailors in the rigging shouted their approval, except one or two who shouted for a wave to hit the ship.

In the evenings Chang tried to practice written characters in the stale air of the girls' dormitory on the fourth deck down. One hot night she decided to go on deck. Rolling up her work paper, she set her brush in its box, bundled everything together, and picked up a small lamp. Moments later she found herself in the comforting warmth of the tropical night air, watching the last fierce glimmers of a scarlet sun debating its fate with the unmoving horizon.

Lan Yi, who was also enjoying the night air, came by and asked whether she had seen Shen. Ocean-Spanning Guards had told him that her brother crossed the main deck earlier.

She shrugged to indicate she knew nothing, and Yi went back below. As she looked about for a place on the crowded deck to set down her writing tools, she realized she was annoyed. He was here somewhere, but out of sight. Typical! For days Older Brother had been disappearing during his free daytime hours, and she suspected he was visiting Lord Yang. But when she tried to follow, Shen easily shook her off.

Pushing her way through the thickness of sailors and passengers admiring the stars, she quickly assured herself that Shen was nowhere on the public deck. She squinted at the distant Brocade perimeter. If she could get past it, she might catch him where he shouldn't be. Then it would be time for some answers.

Tucking her materials under her arm, she moved toward Lord Yang's domain. It occupied roughly a quarter of the deck, all he had been able to negotiate after losing face over the yellow pennant incident.

She smiled and showed the Brocade Guards her writing book. Just as she was explaining that it was too busy on the public deck, two noisy drunks came dancing by. Would the guards mind if she found a quiet place in their zone? She would feel safer, she said, making her eyes large and panda-bearish as she did so.

As she had expected, the guards were sympathetic. They got into a good-natured argument about whether girls should write. Why should these delicate souls be troubled by the things you find in books? said one, putting his arm around her. She wriggled away, darting her eyes pleadingly at the others.

In due course a young Brocade with deep-set, intense eyes declared that he didn't see any reason why women shouldn't read. Wouldn't it make them better company? This occasioned lewd observations from the others, which the young guard silenced by clapping his hands sharply. "These monkeys have never seen a genteel girl before," he observed, leading her to a quiet spot on the starboard side. He cautioned her to stay away from the portside deck.

She worked until the guards lost interest and then blew out her little lamp and looked curiously toward the portside deck. There seemed to be Confucians in robes over there. Was Shen among them? She moved furtively to the forbidden area, settling down amidst some coils of rope in the bluish shadows made by the rising moon.

After a time she was certain Shen was not there. But just as she was about to leave, she caught sight of a group of men in dark clothes swinging a small wooden boat out over the ship's side. Their feet seemed to be wrapped or padded, and they made no noise at all. She crept closer and watched them heave a heavy cylindrical object into the boat. One let his end slip, and there was a hefty metallic thunk. In the moonlight Chang caught a glimpse of a cannon. Then, with the tiniest squeal from the winches, the boat was lowered out of sight.

Before Chang could move, one of the men who stayed behind abruptly stepped in front of her. It was the one who had told her to stay away from there. "I see you hiding there, girl. I'm not blind."

"I'm not hiding," replied Chang coolly. "I'm enjoying the evening. I have a pass." She unfolded it, and the young Brocade examined it. Then he tore it up and threw the bits into the wind.

"Why are you so unfriendly? Why don't you sit down and talk with me?" He made her nervous, but she was determined to find out more about the boat.

The guard flashed an uncertain look, trying to make out how old she was. "You're not a child. Don't be familiar with me."

Chang remembered that she now had to obey all the rules applying to young women. "I am sorry," she said. "I forget sometimes." Then she added, as innocently as possible, "Isn't it dangerous to put a little boat into the ocean at nighttime?"

"Not as dangerous as asking about it. Go below. Stay off the deck after dark." And his eyes followed her until she left his zone.

———————

SHE LAY AWAKE THAT night, anxious because she had provoked the Brocades. But even more, she was troubled by the cannon and the small boat. The next morning before everyone went upside for daily exercises, Chang visited Lan Yi. At the news his sleepy eyes reddened with surprise. "A cannon! It can't be. The Admiral has dispersed the Brocades over many ships. They can't concentrate themselves for a mutiny. You must have seen something else."

He sent her away, much to her annoyance, without believing her.

Chang worked mechanically through the acrobat exercises of the morning. She noticed Shen in the rigging and kept an eye on him. He was often up there, doing nothing, it seemed. Then, for no particular reason, he would rapidly slide down the ropes and vanish into the crowd on deck.

Today she sneaked away from her exercises to follow him.

This was harder than it might have seemed. Such was the Admiral's hatred of Yang Rong and the Brocades that he had divided the ship into two zones. The smaller belonged to Yang Rong, and Chang had broken the rules by sweet-talking her way past the Brocades guarding its perimeter last night.

She didn't want to do that again. But there were other ways. The *China Harmony* hadn't been built to be divided in this fashion, and below decks many narrow corridors ran from one zone into the other. These were closed at night, but during the day there were checkpoints. She had tried to follow Shen below decks once before, but he got away—into the Brocade zone, she suspected. Which meant he was expected there.

Today, she promised herself, she would get some answers

She tracked Older Brother through the crowd of sailors— moon-faced coastal people, high-cheeked mountain tribesmen, convicts with gimp legs—who were always busy about the ship. Then he slipped through a door quickly enough to throw off a less determined follower. But Chang came through almost directly behind him, and followed his hank of black hair as it bobbed among the scholars and scientists who worked on that deck.

This particular corridor zigged and zagged a good deal. Chang could hardly resist glancing in doorways where a collection of bats was pinned to a wall, or a doctor was mixing alchemical potions, or a library had a shelf of rare and ancient books written on banana leaves.

But she kept moving, pushing harder as the crowd thickened at the checkpoint. She lost sight of his hair for a few moments but wiggled around a pair of riggers bringing a coil of rope up from the hold. Then she saw him again

He had reached the table where a Brocade was examining papers. The man waved Shen through with barely a glance.

Without her papers, which would take several days to replace, Chang knew she wouldn't get through. So she sat on the floor and waited. It seemed half the ship had tripped over her feet before Shen came whistling back through the checkpoint. She jumped up, but he didn't flinch. "Good day, Younger Sister."

"Good day, Older Brother." She blocked him. He was coming from the wrong side of the checkpoint. There was no need for her to say anything more.

Crossing his arms on his chest and looking sulky, he said, "Remember when we were small? 'Secret silence?'"

"We're not small anymore. But all right. I won't tell."

"I visit Lord Yang sometimes. I find out lots of things."

"Share a few," she said softly.

"Well, I know who Lan Yi really is. That's not his name, by the way. He's a wanted criminal."

"The man who has sheltered us?"

"Used us. And used Grandfather Hu as well."

She shook her head fiercely. "How can you be so foolish? You're in the Admiral's service. Even if you don't tell anything to Lord Yang, this—this skulking—makes you look guilty. Surely you know what would happen if you were caught?"

"Nobody pays attention to me," he said airily, pushing past her, "except my interfering sister."

"Our safety is with the Admiral," she said urgently as she ran to catch up.

"I agree with you. And if the Confucian lets slip anything interesting, I'll see that the Admiral hears about it."

"But this is a dream! You are too proud! You cannot outwit"— she realized she was shouting and ran up beside him, ramming her elbow into his spleen—"outwit Lord Yang, Brother," she finished in a whisper. "Our safety is with the Admiral."

"So long as he's in charge here, I'll agree with that," said Shen ominously. "But things can change."

———

AND THAT NIGHT SOMETHING did change. The fire gong awakened everybody below decks, and guards hurried them up the narrow wooden staircases. On the foredeck, a bucket brigade of sailors was trying to put out a blaze in one of the ship's landing boats. It was located within the Brocade zone, and the Brocades were pushing the sailors away, shouting that it was their fire and their business.

A patrol of Ocean-Spanning Guards jogged down the deck with their spears leveled, forcing everybody to jump out of the way. "Stand aside to cut down the boat! The ship is in danger!" they cried.

But the Brocades slashed with their swords at the lowered spears. The surprised patrol fell back and called for swordsmen. These appeared soon enough, and the outnumbered Brocades were slowly pushed back toward the heavy wooden railing near the burning boat.

But they fought fiercely, and finally an Ocean-Spanning Guard let out a shriek. Chang's hand covered her mouth as she watched him slump to the ground. He was quickly kicked aside by his fellows as they pressed the fight.

Then a great flash of redness, like a giant firecracker, enveloped the burning boat. Chang thought it strange that it made no sound, but then she realized she couldn't hear people screaming either. The blast had temporarily deafened her.

As she slapped her ears to restore the hearing, a gravelly voice called out, "Guardsmen, fall back!" Zheng He, wearing a night robe of shining dark silk, strode up to the Brocades. "Will you fools attack your Admiral as well?"

By this time General Ho Fu had appeared with reinforcements. The Brocades were afraid of the one-eyed soldier, and they meekly placed their swords on the deck. The Admiral stepped through them and moved as close as he dared to the place where the boat had been. Much of the railing had been blown away, and the Admiral's eyes widened as he saw the naked ocean winking at him from below.

Chang got close enough to see that nothing remained but charred wood and little pools of fire. Remembering the cannon she had seen the other night, she was certain the landing boat had caught fire because the Brocades were loading weapons and gunpowder into it. Then, taking advantage of the confusion of the fight, they had pushed it overboard to conceal what they were doing.

But who would believe her? Especially when whatever evidence had been in the boat was sinking in bits to the ocean floor.

IN THE DIM LIGHT OF THE circus master's quarters, Lan Yi nestled his teacup in both hands, as was his habit now. It made him look like he was praying. Chang waited anxiously for his response to her theory. Finally, to her relief, he nodded.

"What you say about a gunpowder explosion last night makes sense. And it lends support to your story about seeing them offloading a cannon before. I apologize for doubting you, Fei Chang." The steam from his tea wreathed in front of his eyes. "But what worries me even more than the cannons is what you say about your brother meeting with the Confucian. What's going on between them?"

"He talks to Older Brother about being Chinese. That our country executes the will of Heaven. That we don't need the rest of the world."

Yi nodded. "Lord Yang is reciting the usual precepts. The only surprising thing is his interest in heavy weaponry. This was never a preoccupation of the great Confucius." He rubbed an eye that was still red from lack of sleep. "I suppose Lord Yang has told your brother about my criminal record."

Chang was taken aback. "Yes. But it is no concern of mine."

"Your mother and father both knew about it. Your father thought it was a miscarriage of justice. He used to say that it was far too easy for the magistrates to cast down a gentleman in our country." Yi reached inside his tunic and brought out the Panther badge. Unfolding it, he said, "Please take this to Shen. Tell him that I honor the memory of his father."

CHAPTER 21

THE SAILORS WERE STILL joking about the grotesque events surrounding the boat fire three days earlier. The Brocade who had killed an Ocean-Spanning Guard had been beheaded on the food preparation deck and his remains thrown overboard with the kitchen offal.

Shen's stomach twisted when he heard this. He was sickened by the sailors who laughed at it.

Of course the dreadful thing had been done in order to humiliate Lord Yang. It was the Admiral's revenge. That, and forcing Yang to kowtow to him in front of the crew. Yang had endured it all in dignity and silence.

Nothing but the Confucian's status as the Emperor's envoy saved him from arrest. Instead, the Admiral banned him from officers' meetings.

After the first of these meetings, Lord Yang was wild to know what had been said about him. He was reckless enough to confront Shen on the open deck. As much to get rid of him as anything, Shen hastily confided that General Ho Fu had been given permission to invade and search Lord Yang's quarters. That, said Yang, was the kind of information he needed.

"Also, the Admiral says your downfall is not far away."

"That's not information. It's mere opinion," sneered the Confucian.

Shen sat alone on the deck for some time after Lord Yang left. Often during their private meetings the Confucian had hinted that he would like to know this or that piece of information. Shen always pretended ignorance.

But now he had crossed the line. By telling Lord Yang about the planned raid on his quarters, he had betrayed the Admiral's confidence. In fact, he was a traitor.

He rolled the word around on his tongue. Traitor. Such a big step. And for such little reasons. To get a letter from Mother. Because he felt sorry for Lord Yang. Because he despised the Admiral.

Or was it because he was starting to like Lord Yang?

Later that day, when Chang brought him the Panther badge, he could not think of anything to say besides an offhand "thank you." He almost told her about the promise of a letter from Mother, but held back. He still hadn't received it. Was there a letter at all?

When he had gone to bed the previous night, it had been blindingly obvious to him that he was going to be caught visiting Lord Yang. He must seek help from Lan Yi and Temur.

But as he slipped into a dream, his friends turned into ghosts. Helpless Hungry Ghosts. They shuffled among some chairs and sat down. Shen was forced to do likewise. Then actors came onto a little stage and said, "Accept our offering, Hungry Ghosts. Let us sing and dance to take away your pain." Shen jumped up, shouting that it was a mistake. He was alive!

But the performance continued. Looking down, he saw his body becoming transparent.

He awoke in a sweat. The morning light streamed through the little porthole and warmed his skin. With relief he went and ate a hot breakfast. Now he felt potent, like a man straddling two worlds. As only a spy could do.

While he strode across the deck to the morning officers' meeting, birds of uncanny color swooped back and forth across the *China Harmony*'s broad deck. They squalled in the ship's masts, as if protesting the rising humidity of the approaching jungle shoreline.

The flagship had nosed its way across the Gulf of Siam, making for the great river that marked the home of the Thai tribe. A day's sail upriver was the golden-roofed city of Ayutthaya, their capital. It was ruled by King Ramraja.

The daily meeting began with a showdown between Grandfather Hu and Zheng He. The Admiral meant to sail the *China Harmony* straight up the vast Chao Phrya River to Ayutthaya. The old man, who held the title Guardian Engineer of the Iron-Boned Ships, reminded him that the ship's rudder ran as deep under the water as a three-story building would stand above it. "We shall stick on a sandbar like a water buffalo in the spring flood," crowed the old man. "The barbarians will laugh us to scorn."

Grandfather Hu's harsh words were affirmed by the only man in the room to have visited Ayutthaya before. Zhang Jie was a merchant who had learned to speak Thai during a long stay in King Ramraja's jail. His crime was paying for a cargo of tin with gold coins that turned out to be made mostly of tin themselves. Now everybody called him Tin Purse. Tin's scrawny frame puffed with pride when Interpreter Ma declared that Tin Purse would be the Admiral's personal interpreter to the Thai court.

The fleet's large ships lay in a long curve of the tropical shoreline where the Chao Phrya River pumped vast quantities of tea-colored water into the dazzling green expanse of the bay. A mangrove swamp along the shore, choked with flowering vines and a-churn with reptiles and fish, gave off a sickly perfumed odor that reached all the way to the vessels anchored in the bay.

As the sun rose higher in the sky, however, the fleet's merchant ships began to jostle closer and closer inshore, attracted like honeybees to the longtail boats that had glided noiselessly out of the river mouth since early that morning. The longtails were looking to do business. They were shaped like bananas, with one half sitting in the water and the other half swooping up into the air.

Tin Purse walked the deck with Chang, Shen, and Lan Yi, describing the exotic goods in the longtails. From above, their cargos looked like daubs of paint on the green water. Sampans from the merchant ships were already bobbing among them like dull brown waterbirds.

"That one is selling kingfisher feathers," said Tin Purse, pointing at a patch of blinding blue in a boat just beneath them. "Empress Xu's crown is made of kingfisher feathers."

Another boat seemed to attract more attention than the dull green of its cargo merited. Tin Purse explained that it was *dou kou*, cardamom seeds, a valuable spice.

But the merchant sampans were bashing at one another to get close to a longtail loaded with what appeared to be chunks of wood. It was steered by a young woman. "Who's going to buy firewood in this heat?" marveled Chang.

"That's aloes wood," said Tin Purse, gazing greedily at the valuables floating below them. "A fallen tree secretes a resin to stop itself from rotting. You burn a bit and the odor takes you to paradise"—his little piping voice almost sang the word *paradise*—"but it's hard to find a tree that died in a wet-enough place the right number of years ago. So it's hardly firewood! The traders will offer her a mountain of silk for those logs."

Earlier that morning Shen had requested a boat for a pleasure outing. Asking for a sampan was a privilege of working in the Admiral's office, and Shen thought a paddle through the exotic longtail boats would be a nice gift for Younger Sister and Lan Yi.

The real reason, though, was that heavily armed Marine Guards had forced their way into Lord Yang's quarters during the night. Nothing had been found.

Shen had learned this from Lan Yi, who came urgently to his room early that morning. Yi wanted to know if somebody had warned Lord Yang of the raid. When Shen remained silent, Yi had asked with brutal frankness if Shen had known about it in advance.

Shen lied. He said he knew nothing.

And because he was lying, and meant to go on doing so, he had arranged the boat trip to buy off his bad conscience.

A guard directed them to an opening near water level, where they could board the boat Shen had requested.

The four clambered into the sampan, which came equipped with two oarsmen, and within minutes were in the thick of the trading frenzy. Tin Purse had volunteered to come along as a translator, but he had his eye out to do some business on the side. The sampan stopped so he could examine a small raft of camphorwood logs towed behind a longtail.

While Tin Purse dawdled, Yi remarked on a pair of longtails rowing in unison toward the side of the flagship. They had no cargo, so it was possible they were out fishing. The way they dragged at the back suggested there might be a net slung between the two boats. Yi wondered out loud why fishing boats would come so close to the *China Harmony*.

Shen lowered his head and carefully followed the "fishing" boats with his eyes. They had stopped on either side of a port designed for the galley oars. Its watertight hatch popped open, and a cylinder the size of a man's leg wrapped in rough cotton flew out and splashed into the water, where it vanished. But it had certainly been caught in the net slung between the two boats. The hatch slammed shut and the longtails pulled for shore. The whole thing had occupied a scant few heartbeats.

Shen found Yi looking steadily at him. "Any thoughts as to what that was?" he said quietly.

Shen shook his head and bit his lip.

"Lean heavy, and overtake those boats," Yi ordered the oarsmen.

Yi flung a spare oar at Shen and then set a rapid pace, the veins on his biceps bulging. The oarsmen, including Shen, had no choice but to keep up. The sampan soon pulled close enough to the longtails that the crew could see they were being followed. They pulled harder, making for a narrow opening into the mangrove swamp.

The moment they entered, two other longtails appeared out of nowhere and blocked the opening. Grinning fishermen sat on the decks, gutting fish and waving merrily at the sampan as it came to a halt.

"Tell them to let us through," said Yi in a voice quieter than usual. A short sword had appeared in his hand. Tin Purse translated, and the fishermen said nothing. They continued to gut the fish with gleaming, razor-edged knives—and then they threw the fish back in the water. They grinned.

"Ah," said Tin Purse, "this is the Thai way of saying —"

"—we think you're fools and we don't care if you know it," completed Yi. As they bumped against the nearer boat, he leapt into it and slashed with his sword. An ugly gash appeared across the chest of the closest fisherman. His mates began to jump into the water. Yi leaped back into his own boat and directed the oarsmen to row between the mangrove trees.

Once through the mangroves, Shen saw swamp channels leading in all directions. Yi stood on tiptoe. "Oar noises that way," he said, and the boatmen directed the sampan into a wider channel.

The two longtails, hauling a load under water, could not be going very fast. But they had the aid of small sails, and they were sleek and seaworthy. The sampan was a flat-bottomed rowboat, and after a half-watch of hard rowing the oarsmen were struggling for breath. The heat was magnified by the howling of monkeys and the shrieking of birds.

Finally they emerged into a wide channel. And far down the channel, making for the sea, was a black-painted—and unmistakably Chinese—junk.

The longtails, relieved of their load and sailing separately, were quickly disappearing down another channel.

"They've completed their business," said Yi, blinking sweat from his eyes. "We won't see that black boat again."

But Chang followed her brother's gaze and saw he was still scanning the ship. So she did likewise. By the time it moved out of sight, she knew the patches on the sails and the four-clawed dragon painted on the stern.

"I KNOW I SHOULDN'T have picked it," said Chang, setting the purple lotus in a small white pottery vase. "But the channel was full of them, and I never saw one before. Do you remember when Father would mumble prayers about them in the temple?"

She and her brother were sitting in the common room outside the artists' quarters. Yi had gone to report to the Admiral what they had seen that afternoon. Shen, for his part, didn't want to talk about it. He had been humiliated when Yi took command of the sampan.

Chang tried to prop the purple lotus more securely in the vase. Instead of the customary nest of serene, light-violet petals, this one had a violently purple flower with little ragged ends on its petals. The pistils in the middle, normally a demur circle of shy yellow fronds, were also shot through with violet and pointed aggressively outward.

"Honorable Lan did what he had to do, Brother," she said, sensing the reason for his silence. "There is evil afoot, and now at least we know that Imperial property is being smuggled to other ships."

"And do we know that the smugglers are in the wrong?" replied Shen with a shrug. "Perhaps the Star Fleet is an evil thing. Think of the gold that it took to build these ships! Lord Yang says the people have been made poor because of it. And what will it bring to China that we really need? Aloes wood that smells like paradise?" He imitated Tin Purse's little soprano voice.

Then Chang remembered the black ship. "So the ship we saw has weapons on it?"

Shen shrugged. "Maybe."

"Where was it going?"

"How should I know? Maybe to Majapahit."

Her eyes lit up and her mind was intent. "You're not just guessing that. You know it. It's Lord Yang's ship, isn't it?"

"I didn't say that. I don't know."

She gave up and changed the subject. "What else does Lord Yang talk about?"

"The Grandson."

"What about him? He's dead."

"No he's not," Shen sneered. "He's alive! Even the Admiral knows that."

Chang stared at him open-mouthed. "Dear Brother, if this is so, you must tell Lan Yi. You need Lan Yi, don't you see that?"

"For what exactly? He's just one man with an illiterate Mongol and a worn-out document forger to back him up. I don't even think about him anymore."

Chang had to breathe deeply to bring her anger under control. "But he is obliged to think about you. Mistress Guo cast an oracle late last night. She said that it read your fate. It said that you are already among the ghosts."

Shen paled, remembering his own dream.

"Lan Yi is now thinking that he must take the troupe ashore in Majapahit," continued Chang. "To protect them from your recklessness. If you get into trouble, the rest of us will be punished as well."

Shen laughed. "All that because of Guo's oracle? I thought Yi was smarter. Guo plays with candles and chicken bones when she can't get to sleep."

"I wish you would leave."

"Of course, Younger Sister." He made a comical bow. "Good luck in finding Kun in Majapahit. I know that's what you're really thinking about."

The door slammed. She looked mournfully at the purple lotus. I will call it the Older Brother Flower, she thought.

CHAPTER 22

F OUR DAYS LATER the acrobats erected their
equipment on the deck. Mistress Guo had decided
the waters at the river's mouth were tranquil enough that a
practice session could be attempted. The sky was brilliantly
blue and a slight breeze dried the sweat from their foreheads.
She briskly inspected the short towers for the high-wire act
and the heavy pots the strong man would juggle.

Shen stood to one side watching Jade and Chang rehearsing their routine. It was a difficult one called the "goldfish,"
where Chang lay on her back with her legs straight up. A small
goldfish bowl sat on the soles of her feet. Jade did a handstand
on Chang's stomach, facing toward the fishbowl. Then she
bent her body at the waist so she could lower her legs and
grasp the bowl with her feet. Then she straightened up, lifting the bowl as high as her feet would stretch upward. Finally,
ever so carefully, she curled her upper body, bent her knees,
and lowered her feet toward the top of her head. Slowly the
bowl descended. Ever so gently she deposited it, and the deeply
impressed goldfish, on her own head.

Shen had seen this demanding routine many times. But

this time he was distracted by the tight outline of Jade's trousers as her legs lifted the goldfish bowl. How strange these feelings are, he thought. She is a friend of my sister and I should not think of her this way. When the routine was completed, Jade looked at him with embarrassment. Chang angrily signaled him to go away.

"If you don't learn to look at women without making them mad, you'll end up an old bachelor like me," said Lan Yi casually, coming up beside him. Shen ignored him. "And if you keep ignoring your friends, you might as well become a hermit."

Shen exhaled noisily through his nostrils. The next thing he knew his arms were pinned against the railing, with Yi's eyes just a few inches from his own. "If you know anything about the offloading of weapons, you have committed a capital offense. Think of your mother, learning you will never return. And for what?" spat Yi. Shen turned his head to one side.

"You're getting too big to wrestle with. Sit down there," said Yi, pointing at a coiled rope. Shen obeyed, while Yi himself squatted on the deck. "The Admiral's river vessel will be returning later today," he continued, suddenly amiable. "It will be preceded by King Ramraja's boat, which I understand is something to see. And of course Lord Yang will return with the Admiral. They're being very proper with each other, but don't be fooled. A number of Brocades have been questioned about the smuggling. From what I hear, it hasn't been pleasant. You'd better hope your name didn't come up."

Shen looked blankly out to sea. He was trying to imagine what torture was like.

"They won't torture you," said Yi, the annoying thought-reader. "The Admiral thinks that divine omens brought you to his service." He laughed unpleasantly, shaking his head at the Admiral's simplicity. Then he remembered something.

"The badge. Show it to me."

Shen gently removed the folded cloth from his tunic. The bit that was showing was the panther's head, raised up to look at a full moon. The moon, he knew, was the Emperor. The Panther officer's loyal gaze was always fixed on the moon.

"Men who wear this badge take their orders from the Emperor," said Yi. "Never in a thousand years have they served the Confucians."

Then Yi caught sight of a splendid boat that had just appeared at the mouth of the Chao Phrya River. He coughed a hacking cough, and a spurt of what appeared to be blood escaped his mouth. "Betel juice," he said with a red grin. "That boat bears the king of the Thai-speaking people. We've prepared a special musical performance for him. I hope you will pay particular attention."

"I wish you would wipe your chin!" complained Shen. The he flinched, expecting Yi to strike him. But the circus master just shook his head and clumped away down the deck.

———

CHANG AND JADE WERE looking out a large square porthole that gave them a view to the west. There lay the royal vessel of King Ramraja. It sat low in the water, its teak planks polished to a rich golden brown. On its deck was raised up a sort of miniature palace. It had steep roofs tiled in green with a border of yellow and orange. The gable ends were outlined in woodwork carved like long lines of flames. These met at the peak, from which rose an ornate spire covered with thin sheets of tightly fitted gold.

Chang was enchanted, but Jade was more concerned with the upcoming performance for King Ramraja.

Shen was standing well away from the performance area. His attention was focused on the Admiral and Lord Yang, who were seated uncomfortably beside each other. Next to them were King Ramraja and his ministers.

The Thai delegation was a tangle of brilliant costumes and jingling headdresses. Shen was still uncomfortable with barbarians, and found it unsettling to look at them. He turned with relief to the performance.

He was anxious for Chang as she performed the fishbowl balancing act with Jade. It was actually Chang's first public performance. He was fascinated at her coolness as she lay on her back and lifted Jade high into the air. The Thai barbarians unexpectedly stamped their feet to show appreciation, and Jade flinched as the vibration traveled across the deck. But Chang moved through the motions as calmly as if she were back in the practice room in Suzhou.

The girls were followed by the team of men who performed tricks with banners and balls and the tiny girl on the balancing pole. For Shen it had a comforting familiarity.

But where was the special novelty act that Lan Yi had mentioned?

As if in answer, Yi stepped forward. The clown's triangle

painted around his eyes and nose was a blinding white in the tropical sun. He announced that there would be a special treat for King Ramraja, a short musical play called *The Mantis and the Chariot*. Shen pricked up his ears. He noticed Tin Purse standing near the Thai delegates, translating.

There was a burst of strident string music, and the celebrated Flying Pigeon jumped out from behind a curtain, taking a deep bow. On each side of him were boy acrobats who rolled beside him like wheels. His face was painted red, with thick, graceful black eyebrows rising high on his forehead. In a high-pitched, chanting voice, accompanied by the clatter of small wooden drums, he announced that he was the King of Chi, out for a day of hunting in his chariot.

A praying mantis—this was Lan Yi, crouched down and wearing two long, green, serrated claws attached to his hands—leaped in front of the two young acrobats who played the chariot wheels and challenged the King of Chi. The mantis had a squeaking, broken voice. Sitting on its haunches, it declared that the king was a usurper and flailed with its claws.

The king jumped from the chariot, flipping in midair, and landed near the insect. "It's only a bug!" he cried. "A boy-bug with a little boy voice! What a shame. If it were a man, it would be the bravest warrior in the world."

"Kill it!" chimed the chariot wheels.

But then the King of Chi saw a white-faced man lurking to one side. Black curved lines beside his mouth looked like the whiskers of a jungle cat, and little black flares were painted under his nostrils, as if his breath were poisonous. "I, Cao

Cao, order you to strike the usurper," the sinister figure commanded the praying mantis.

The mantis looked back and forth between Cao Cao and the mighty king. He wriggled his nose, causing the white patch in the middle of his face to wobble about, and indignantly put his hands on his hips. The pincers stuck out on each side. *"Hé!* I'm just a bug. You do it!"

Then the King of Chi unsheathed a massive glue-and-paper sword, singing:

Strike not the hapless servant
Root out the evil master

With this the King of Chi killed Cao Cao with as many elaborate thrusts as he could think of, striking a pose on every drumbeat.

The Admiral and the Thai delegation were roaring with laughter. But Yang Rong sat like an upright dagger, with his eyes fixed on Shen.

CHAPTER 23

FOR THE NEXT THREE DAYS Shen's attempts to contact Lord Yang were refused.

The Confucian was angry with Shen, and it was obvious why. Every Chinese knew about Cao Cao, a prime minister of ancient times who was the emblem of treachery and cunning. A hundred stories and theater plays featured his sneering face. And his rank was roughly equal to that of Lord Yang. If anybody made the connection, then the performance had all but accused Lord Yang of plotting to overthrow the Emperor.

Shen was almost flattered that Lan Yi had gone to so much trouble to get him into trouble. Not only was Lord Yang already upset—his icy glare at the end of the performance made that clear—but it was even possible the Admiral would figure out that the "boy" praying mantis who worked for Cao Cao was Shen himself.

This last possibility was the worst. If the Admiral suspected him, it could mean interrogation and torture. He resolved to cut off his relationship with Lord Yang. But not before he had settled the business of Mother! Lord Yang still had the letter.

The more Shen thought about it, the more he had the uneasy feeling that Yang Rong was indeed a bit like Cao Cao.

Shen went back to the Brocade checkpoint, insisting once again that he had business with Lord Yang. Once again the soldier refused him.

———

THE NEXT MORNING'S STAFF meeting was endless. Shen had to copy out a lengthy list of gold and emerald gifts that King Ramraja was sending to the Admiral as a token of his loyalty. Apparently this meant the end of petty hostilities between the two countries, and it was terribly important, but he could not have cared less.

After the meeting Shen went back to his room and found a note on his bed. It described the route to a certain cabin on a certain deck, saying to come at once. When he arrived, a Thai official was just leaving. Lord Yang was alone inside the room. A soldier in sailor's whites guarded the door.

"You must be exhausted from copying all that chitchat about borders and peace agreements," said the Confucian. "Please excuse me for meeting you in this obscure place, but the eunuch's men are now posted inside my quarters. Do you drink plum brandy? If so, this is an excellent moment to enjoy a little. I have something to celebrate!"

Shen could not imagine what Lord Yang would be celebrating. But there were filled cups on the table, and Shen politely picked one up and sipped the liqueur. In spite of its sweetness, it burned his throat. It was much stronger than the wine Mother sometimes permitted him to drink at home.

"Don't you find the barbarians amusing?" said the Confucian with an eager and mischievous light in his eyes. "Did you know that in Ayutthaya the young men impress the girls by sewing bells inside the intimate parts of their bodies?"

Shen choked violently on the plum wine. His face turned bright red.

"I can see you were well brought up," said Lord Yang, pleased that Shen was embarrassed and off balance. Quickly, without missing a beat, he continued, "My good news is that today I have purchased several Thai vessels that lie at anchor in Majapahit. My people and I have business there, and it is time I told you about it."

Shen put down the cup of wine, which was stronger than he had realized. It made his head a bit foggy. It seemed to him that the Confucian was not letting him speak. "Before you tell me anything," insisted Shen, "I swear that I had nothing to do with *The Mantis and the Chariot.*"

"Of course you didn't! But now that you mention it, there was one small matter that troubled me. The performance seemed to suggest that I would plot to overthrow Emperor Zhu Di. Did you ever say that to the circus man?"

"No! Is that why you locked me out?" There was a sheen of sweat on Shen's forehead.

"Well, I *was* displeased," said Lord Yang in an insulting way. "But it's good to learn of your innocence. Wherever did Lan Yi get the idea? We Confucians do not 'plot' against Emperors. Listen to me." Lord Yang leaned back in his chair and steepled his hands under his chin. "My order of scholars has existed for eighteen hundred years. In that time, we have never attempted to overthrow an Emperor. Even a usurping Emperor. Do you know why? Because we do not care who sits on the throne. Our interest is the Rite that he embodies. The Rite is made of our beliefs and traditions, and the scholar's task is to teach it to each new ruler. We don't care if he climbed out of a sewer or floated down on a cloud. We care that he transmits the Rite."

"I understand," said Shen uncertainly.

"Do you? Because now I must reveal a larger part of my plans. If you wish to serve me, this is the point where you may not go back. Do you agree?"

Shen's head seemed to be floating just above his shoulders. "I…I want to know when Mother will be freed. For certain. And I wish to see her letter."

"Of course." Lord Yang drew a folded piece of paper from his robe and placed it on a small table. "You may take it with you when we finish our conversation."

Shen could not stop looking at the paper. He imagined Mother folding it and sealing it. "I agree. What must I do?"

Yang filled their glasses again. "Your role concerns the Grandson. When his government fell, he and his retainers correctly judged there was no safe place to hide in China. Several kingdoms refused to receive him. Finally, in desperation, he sailed south to Majapahit.

"Shortly after he arrived the local king betrayed him to the Chinese pirate, in exchange for peace for his merchant ships. The Grandson and his entourage were taken to Palembang, where they have languished ever since."

"What will the Admiral do when we get there?" asked Shen.

"Kill him, of course. The Grandson is the rightful Emperor, and so long as he is alive the throne belongs to him. From Zhu Di's point of view, death is the best medicine for this ailment. Otherwise, the Grandson might return to China and claim what is his."

Shen remembered his long-ago idea that the Grandson could not have survived without Father. "Is my father with him?"

"Your father? Captain Lee? I'm certain he is not. Were you still hoping he was alive?"

Shen felt he would look foolish if he said yes. So he shrugged and stared at his wine cup while his insides collapsed like a straw hut in the winter rain. Then he said, in a voice that sounded shrill even to him, "I don't know why you're telling me this story. I don't care about the Grandson. And you said your order doesn't interfere in these things."

"To a degree. Of course our loyalty is to Zhu Di, who occupies the throne. But we do not abandon a ruler who is unjustly overthrown. In the past we have often sheltered such men. And I particularly loved the Grandson. He was not made to be a ruler; he is too soft and affectionate. He didn't wish to rule! So why should he be butchered like a dog?" Shen could see the anger in Lord Yang's face and hear it in his voice. "My people will rescue him, and conceal him where he can live in peace."

"What do you require of me?" said Shen nervously.

Lord Yang produced that bewitching smile Shen had seen before. "Your role will be a small one. Simply put, I must know how and when the Admiral intends to seize the Grandson. He will announce his plans in one of those meetings that I am no longer allowed to attend. But *you* will be there with your little ink stone and brush. And you will tell me."

"That's all? You won't ask any more of me?"

"No. It is becoming too dangerous for us to meet. Complete this final task, and you will have earned your mother's freedom."

Shen nodded and reached for the letter. He saw Lord Yang's eyes flicker toward it. Then Shen placed the letter safely inside his tunic. "When will Mother be released?"

"I will send the order on the first ship returning to China."

Shen closed his eyes. "Thank you." In spite of all he knew about the Confucian, he needed to believe the man was telling the truth about this one thing. "Thank you," he whispered again. And meant it.

But then a troubling thought came to him. "When he arrives in Palembang, the Admiral will learn that the Grandson was taken away. Won't he suspect you?"

"He won't know I had anything to do with it. My Brocades will carry out the mission. That is why I procured ships for them in Majapahit. They have gold to bribe the pirate, and weapons to frighten him if the gold is not enough. The black ship, which your intrepid Lan Yi very nearly overtook in the swamps of Ayutthaya, is armed with Imperial cannons for that very reason. But there will be no way to connect me with any of it."

Shen sighed with relief.

"I see that this has been exhausting for you, Fei Shen." He refilled Shen's glass once more. "Have some plum wine. Let us tell each other stories."

The warmth that was generated by Lord Yang's promise to free Mother made it seem to Shen that they were friends. It was the false friendship of conspirators, but it was thrilling. And when Lord Yang admitted to him, as one friend to another, that he had made a terrible botch of the Emperor's order to oversee the Admiral, it almost seemed to Shen that they were equals.

He accepted another cup of wine as the Confucian gave a comical sigh. "Instead of me governing the eunuch, it is the eunuch who governs me! He has clipped my fingernails and toenails and trimmed my nose hairs. Really, he has trussed me up like a New Year's duck!" And they laughed and poured more wine.

"He made me unleash that yellow pennant on you!" cried Shen. It slipped out, just like that.

"No!" The Confucian's smile vanished for just an instant before he became jovial again. "What an appalling trick. And you carried it off!" And they clicked their little pottery cups together to cement their friendship.

The time came for Shen to leave. "You know, I really am at your mercy," said Lord Yang. "If you breathe a word of this conversation to the Admiral, I will end up like that poor beheaded Brocade soldier. My head and my body will be nodding to each other on the bottom of the ocean!"

And they had laughed again.

Once out on the deck, Shen sat on a capstan and let the chilly night wind clear the vapors of plum wine from his head. He thought that perhaps he shouldn't have told about the yellow pennant. Then he went unsteadily to his room to read the letter.

CHAPTER 24

THE FLEET LEFT THE Gulf of Siam and after five days of sailing crossed an invisible line into the vast South China Sea. Captain Zhou warned that they were overdue for bad weather. "We've had too much luck," he observed morosely one afternoon.

He and Zheng He stepped into the officers' quarters. "I wish you wouldn't go on like that," growled the Admiral. "Talking about storms is what brings storms."

The Admiral and Shen sat down at a table to play the ancient board game called wei-chi. Interpreter Ma and Captain Zhou looked on. Nearby several senior officers waited impatiently for the morning meeting to begin. They wanted to take action against the Brocades who were defying the Admiral's authority.

The game involved a hundred and eighty round, flat white stones and a hundred and eighty black stones, which were thought of as two armies. The object was to surround your opponent's stones, either singly or in a group. When they were blocked in and couldn't move they were considered dead, and removed from the board.

Shen was good at this game. More than once he had swept the Admiral's stones from the board. The second time this happened the Admiral glared at him silently for several moments. "From now on, boy, I'm paying attention. You won't get the better of me again."

After the game, the officers crowded close to the Admiral's table. One-eyed General Ho Fu made his report. Two hundred Brocade soldiers had been interrogated since several large bronze cannons had disappeared. None of them knew anything. But several of Lord Yang's people could not be found.

"And the captain of the munitions ship?"

"He is too ill to answer questions. I am very certain he has been poisoned." Ho Fu had the resigned tone of a man whose superior officer is not taking him seriously. "If you would give me Lord Yang for just one morning…"

"He represents the body of the Emperor," said the Admiral acidly. "Are you proposing we torture the Emperor's body?"

"Then we must find one person in his service to testify against him."

Shen's hand knocked against a jar of ink and a dark spill appeared on the silk cuff of an officer's sleeve

Shen looked up to find the Admiral doing what he had promised: paying attention. But it had nothing to do with board games. "Boy! Have you learned anything further about Lord Yang's interest in you? You have been seen with him."

The blood was pounding in Shen's head. "He has befriended me, Lord Zheng. He has given me a letter from my mother. But I can't get him to tell me anything…"

"The Confucian brought you this letter?" asked Ho Fu casually. "Was there anything of interest in it?"

"No, nothing," said Shen in a voice that was a little higher than he wished. "Just the things a mother would say."

"The boy looks ill," said Interpreter Ma. "This talk of torture is unhealthy for a young man not yet of military age. Let him go out. I'll keep the record."

Shen went out onto the observation deck, still shaking from the Admiral's challenge. His hand went to the comforting texture of Mother's letter. He had showed it to Chang several days earlier, and she examined the characters as only she could, because Mother had taught her to write. And when she declared that it was certainly Mother's writing, she had wept. It was their first proof she had survived.

My Son,
You will be aware that I may not freely write my thoughts.
But I rejoice that you are older and can certainly read this
letter with no effort. I long to see the man you have become.

   And yet I struggle to understand what it means that
you and Daughter have gone to sea with the Treasure Fleet.
It was only after a long silence that Lord Yang allowed me
to know this. He assures me that your efforts on his behalf
will secure my early release.

   What these "efforts" are I do not know. But if you wish
to put my heart at ease, do nothing that is dishonorable. If
you are in doubt, think whether you would wish to recount
it to me.

The letter went on to ask about Chang, and Father, and whether their home still stood in the city. But what did Mother mean by "dishonorable"? he wondered. Surely she wanted her freedom. And in any event, it was too late for him to back out.

It flickered across his mind that perhaps this was why Lord Yang had stopped him from seeing the letter before.

On the castle deck a droning wind sounded in the rigging. Far away, barely visible on the eastern horizon, was a bank of black clouds.

"We're in for it now," said Captain Zhou, who was standing nearby on the deck. He ordered a sailor up a short flight of stairs where a brass gong was suspended. Taking a wooden mallet in hand, the man landed three powerful blows on it.

After a short silence, the triple beating of another gong resounded from the nearest ship. Soon the sound was echoing down the line of the three hundred and seventeen vessels, as if an immense monastery in the middle of the ocean were calling the fish to prayer. Sailors on the flagship's mizzenmast were raising a black banner with the ship's name painted in white. As the forward ships slowed to allow the vessels at the back of the line to come forward, the whole fleet began to shape itself into a compact mass. Each captain would be able to spot the identity flags of the nearest ships. No vessel could founder without being seen, even in the darkest gale.

Shen heard the click of the door opening behind him. The Admiral stood on the deck, gazing at the smoky clouds. The wind pulled at the black beard he had begun to grow before the voyage began.

"A storm, sir," said Shen, gleefully looking forward to his first gale. As if it were a game.

"Well, we'll soon know about Grandfather Hu and his iron beams." The Admiral unsteadily entered his gaudily painted shrine to the goddess Tianfei. A coil of incense smoke emerged from slits in its roof.

Below on the main deck Daoist priests stood in a circle around the compass basin, preparing to ward off bad spirits. The drone of their chant rose to Shen's ears. Its final words, "Let the dark water dragons go down into the sea," coincided with the whump of a very large wave hitting the side of the ship. At the same moment, rain began to pour down.

Captain Zhou called an order through a loud hailer, and sailors below decks lowered the ship's two extra keels so the flat-bottomed vessel could hold a course as it rode into the gale. A few men, still aloft, struggled to release sails that had not yet fallen to the deck. One sailor, with an iron pry bar, tried to free a parrel-rope that had tangled a foresail against its mast. As Shen watched, the wind thumped a heavy batten against the man's back and the iron bar flew out of his hands. He lunged for the parrel-rope, which freed itself under his weight and carried him screaming into a mass of silk that plummeted toward the deck.

By now the massive square prow of the flagship was beginning to dip into the waves. The Daoist priests had scattered back to their quarters, leaving their incense burner to fizzle in the black rain.

"Get inside, boy!" cried Zheng He from the doorway to the

officers' room. But Shen heard nothing. His heart was aloft on the swaying masts. Every shudder that ran through the deck was a bolt of pleasure. "Down into the sea, Dark Water Dragons!" he intoned again and again.

Captain Zhou had seen to it that all the great sails were stowed safely. He had ordered the partial binding of the giant rudder so that it did not swing freely. Finally, he ordered all men below decks except for a select few, secured with long ropes, who would watch for damage.

Now the old man braced his feet between the pickets of the deck railing and grasped one of the grips that were built into the rail. As the ship yawed to port and starboard, and the tallest waves actually reached the impossibly high deck, the white-haired captain was tilted first one way, then the other. His face streamed with rain.

A thundering sound came from the portside of the ship. A sailor dragged his way along a storm rope to report that sheathing planks had broken loose. One of the fourteen holds was awash.

Captain Zhou assured the sailor that one wet hold was no danger to the *China Harmony*. He ordered engineers below. Shen silently mouthed the old man's commands, trying to imitate the rhythm of his voice.

Gradually the ship became steadier in the storm. Nostril-like holes had been built into its square bow so that when it dipped into a large wave, water would fill a holding tank inside. When the bow surfaced above the waves, the water ran back out again. As the waves grew tall enough to fill the holding tank, the ship ceased bobbing like a cork and assumed a stately rising and falling motion. It reminded Shen of a Mongolian pony nodding its neck as it cantered over an ocean of grass.

Merk, he thought. And tried to imagine the hellish symphony of the horses in their pitching ships.

CHAPTER 25

IT HAD BEEN A premonition. Early the next day he learned that one of the horse ships had gone down.

Shen was wildly distracted by the thought that Merk might have been on that ship. At the beginning of the morning staff meeting, he could hardly focus on the notes he was taking. But gradually he realized that the Admiral and one-eyed Ho Fu were laying out the strategy for seizing the Grandson at Palembang. This was the crucial information Lord Yang had demanded, and so Shen bent his ear and his memory to the task.

But afterward he thought of nothing but Merk, rushing to the railing and looking madly about. Through a blanket of fog he dimly made out the neighboring ships.

Then a small 110-*ch'i* warship, built low to the water, emerged from the mist. On its deck were four shivering horses, tethered to the mast. Another lay on the deck.

"Too long in the water," said Captain Zhou. "They won't find any more now."

"Merk is on one of those ships! My horse!" In his moment of fear for the chestnut pony Shen had said what he wished were true.

Shen was in such a state that Captain Zhou gave orders for him to be taken with a Marine patrol to the surviving horse ships. Shen gazed at a patch of deck planks floating past on a greasy swell. All at once his exhilaration during the storm seemed reckless and disrespectful. "Down into the sea, Dark Water Dragons. I beg you, do not come again."

One watch later, Shen and Chang were taken by the Ocean-Spanning patrol to the loading ramp of the ship *Fighting Steed*. In the general disarray, nobody asked if Chang had permission to come. Brother and sister stepped onto the horse ship's ramp, where grooms idly waited to take on rescued animals.

They moved into the echoing dark belly of the great boat. A nickering filled the air, and the pungent smell of manure settled on them like a blanket. Every so often they came to a cross-corridor. At the end of these corridors they could see square portholes.

"We couldn't close all of them," said the young groom who was guiding them over the greasy planks. "It came up like a conjuror's spell. I don't like this foreign ocean."

On the top deck the master groom scratched his head and said, "They pushed a few irregulars up here, but nothing I'd call a Mongol pony."

This was more than Shen could bear. He ran down the corridor, shouting Merk's name. Every so often a groom with a bag of grain or a muddy wooden shovel would look out sympathetically from a stall.

Chang caught up with him. "Older Brother! The master groom on this deck, I know him. He's one of the Brocade Guards from our ship."

"That's impossible. There are no soldiers on a horse ship."

"That's what he said when I asked him if we had met before. But I got a good look, and I know it's him." And she told Shen about the young Brocade with the intense, deep-set eyes who had talked with her on the foredeck that night.

"Why would he be here?" said Shen with irritation. But he remembered General Ho Fu saying that some Brocades had disappeared. This one had probably been ordered into hiding because he knew about the stolen cannons.

Chang spoke into the lengthening silence.

"Brother, you have done something you don't want me to know." She had on her little closed-mouth smile, but her face was tense. "Please tell me."

At that moment a horse whinnied gently, very close by. A young groom, perhaps twelve years old, stood before them holding a rough rope in his hand. On the other end was Merk.

Shen threw his arms around the horse's shaggy neck, his hand compulsively knotting and unknotting its mane.

The boy groom looked on with a radiant smile. "I am happy to learn his name today. Although it is a strange name. I think it is the Mongol word for fool."

Shen said stiffly, "How would you know that?"

"My uncle. He used to call me that word when I played tricks on him."

The boy placed his hands together and bowed, still smiling even though Shen was not. So this, he thought, was Temur's opinion of him. And then he remembered taking the Mongol's bow, and mocking his way of speaking, and a hundred other slights.

As the boy took Merk back to his stall, Chang talked about the day that Temur had stood on the shore, straining to hear Merk's call as the horse ship went by. This made Shen feel terrible. Yes, he thought, Temur loves the horse. And then, jealously, he thought perhaps Temur had put this terrible name on the animal as a hex. So that Shen would not love it.

And yet he did.

The master groom took them back to the boat ramp. In the bright sunshine the man avoided Chang's eye, busying himself with the longboat that was pulling alongside.

It was heavily loaded for the return to the flagship. A bundle of sail battens sprawled crossways, and thick square timbers stuck out from the stern, forcing the boat to approach the *Fighting Steed* bow first. As Chang and Shen clambered in, they had to step over buckets of square-headed iron spikes.

The benches were filled with muscular tradesmen clutching their tools in their laps. Some had circular straw hats to protect them from the midday sun. But one, under his rude hat, was wearing silk robes. He looked up, grinning.

"Such a pleasure to see both of you!" said Lord Yang. He had a set of iron hammers in his lap. Seeing the expression on their faces, he laughed. "In times of crisis, we set aside rank. I'm happy to lighten the load of our tradesmen." The carpenter beside him nodded nervously.

"Lord Yang, why is one of your Brocade Guards pretending to be a horse groom on this ship?" asked Chang.

Lord Yang didn't bat an eyelash. "I don't keep track of them. But I'd imagine it's a punishment detail. Perhaps somebody saw him speaking inappropriately with a young girl."

"What an extraordinary way to do things!" replied Chang, also not batting an eyelash. "I can't wait to share this story with my friends on the flagship. You don't mind, do you?"

"Not at all," replied Yang. His mouth smiled even as his yellow-flecked eyes registered her insolence. "But I imagine the young man would be embarrassed if you did. Oh, look, a flying fish."

There was a buzz of excitement as the tradesmen started pointing and shouting. When things calmed down, Shen was somehow sitting beside Lord Yang. Chang had been exiled several benches away where she couldn't overhear them.

"Blinky heard that you had come to the horse ship. I came here hoping to find you for a private chat. I'm sorry I had to cut your sister out of it, but this is confidential," explained Lord Yang. "Ho Fu has treated my men brutally."

"He's angry about the stolen weapons," said Shen.

"Well, what choice did I have, dear boy? We can't fight the pirate Chen Zuyi with the tassels of our hats!" He became serious. "What was discussed at this morning's meeting?"

Shen swallowed and steadied himself. "It was the meeting you were waiting for. They didn't talk much about the storm. Mostly they were setting out the plan for seizing the Grandson." His heart was beating fast. "Ho Fu thought we should go straight to Palembang and take Chen Zuyi by surprise. Deliver an ultimatum with our ships in front of his city. But the Admiral said no."

Lord Yang's eyes were glittering. "Good. And why?"

"Because the Emperor's orders say that we must first ask permission from the King of Majapahit. Palembang is in his territory."

"Excellent," breathed the Confucian. "And of course the Emperor's orders are very clear. I wrote them."

"You knew this would happen?"

"Ho Fu and the Admiral are like dogs on a leash, they always want to fight first. So I used the Emperor's orders to delay them in Majapahit while my men go to Palembang. By the time the eunuch arrives there, the Grandson will be gone."

Chang was noisily climbing over the carpenters to get to where they were. "You're sure they won't suspect you?" whispered Shen. "Yesterday the Admiral said we had been seen together. They've been watching me."

"Ah!" said Lord Yang. "That is dangerous. We must be very careful." And he smiled widely as Chang thumped down beside them.

CHAPTER 26

AFTER THEY RETURNED to the *China Harmony*, Chang berated Shen for cutting her out of the conversation. Would he have talked to Mother that way? What had Lord Yang said to him in the boat?

Shen walked off without answering. Chang seemed clever, he thought to himself. And she could outtalk a mynah bird, especially when she was with Jade. But she was, after all, just a girl. And he had been taught since childhood that women's thoughts were fuzzy and confused. Their minds were darkened by the negative *yin* energy that lives in the ground.

Shen felt fortunate to be a man. His mind was filled with admirable thoughts that grew from the *yang* energy of the sky. It was associated with men; indeed, by a happy coincidence Lord Yang's family used it as their name. Weren't his thoughts about Lord Yang crystal clear for that very reason? It was a shame that Chang and Mother couldn't see this.

Because he still had time before resuming his scribe duties, Shen spent some moments in the comforting presence of Captain Zhou on the bridge. Lately he wondered whether he might not be a ship's captain himself one day. He watched eagerly as Zhou, with a single gesture, commanded a dozen strong men on the deck below to swing the *China Harmony*'s rudder. The captain told him they would reach the Kingdom of Majapahit by sunset.

"By the way, Fei Shen," added Zhou in a tone that put Shen on his guard. "Your friend Lan Yi asked me to pass a message to you. He would like to see you in his cabin at the second watch of the night. He did not say why."

Uneasy, Shen returned to the main deck and sat in the garden. The rhubarb and squash plants were now so high that if you sat on one of the little garden benches, you disappeared from view. He stayed there until the setting sun began to ignite the water ahead of the ship.

To starboard there was a small inhabited island. Just above the village, on a steep slope, sat a temple. A squat rectangle of reddish brick with a flat protruding slab of stone that looked like a nose, it also possessed two slits that might have been eyes. And surmounting all of this was a pyramid-shaped roof made of layers of bricks worked in a pattern that both zig-zagged and undulated. As the ship drew past the island, the sun went behind it so that the temple looked like the dark heart of a blazing torch.

"Good evening, Fei Shen," said Lord Yang, whose arrival was signaled only by the swishing of robes. "Isn't the barbarian temple frightening? Majapahit is well known for that sort of thing." The Confucian sat. "A glorious sunset! We'll arrive in the kingdom's capital city, Semarang, sometime during the night. Apparently it is squalid and dirty. The king, who is named Bhre Tumapel, claims he is poor because the

Middle Kingdom will not trade with him. Ridiculous! But I am commanded to sign a treaty with him." A wrinkle of disdain appeared beside the Confucian's long nose. "Soon we'll be drowning in their smelly spices, not to mention their smelly food. Have you ever heard of durian fruit? It reeks like a long-dead animal pickled in sugar."

Shen detected fear behind the Confucian's hatefulness.

"I have sought you out for a reason," continued Lord Yang. "We are both in danger. Blinky says the Admiral suspects us and that one-eyed Ho Fu has permission to question us in any manner he sees fit." He looked meaningfully at Shen, whose face was turning pale. "To question us painfully. I am very sorry, Fei Shen. I must leave the Treasure Fleet immediately."

"But what will happen to me?" said Shen, realizing that without Lord Yang's protection he would certainly be found out.

"I will not abandon you. Listen. Tomorrow, after going ashore to sign the treaty with King Tumapel, I shall go to the black ship. You will remember it; it is the same one you and your friend Lan Yi pursued through the mangrove swamp. It sailed here ahead of the fleet, and you will find a paper in your chamber telling you where it is anchored. Join me there."

Shen was aghast. "But then they'll know!"

"Not necessarily. Tomorrow we are certain that King Tumapel will give permission for us to attack the pirate. The pirate's city, Palembang, is two days' sail from Semarang. The Admiral's plan is to leave all of the Treasure Fleet civilians here in Semarang, along with the merchant ships. Only the warships will go to Palembang.

"This is your opportunity to go ashore along with your acrobat friends. Once there, slip away and look for the black ship But come quickly, because the black ship will set sail for Palembang by tomorrow evening."

"I'll never be able to come back to the Admiral." Shen didn't know if it was the evening breeze, but he suddenly felt cold all over his body. "Or to Younger Sister."

Lord Yang smiled benevolently. "You will return to China with me. I shall secure an official position for you so that the Admiral can never touch you. Your sister—and your mother—will be lifted up to your high place in society. They will be grateful. Have you ever thought of becoming a Brocade investigator?"

"But I'm too young."

"I am their commander, Fei Shen. It will be my gift to you. Think about it tonight. If you decide to come to me, you will find a shore pass under your pillow, along with the directions to the black ship." The Confucian clasped his hands together and bowed formally. "May good fortune attend both of us, O Worthy Son of Fei Lee."

CHAPTER 27

I T SEEMED TO SHEN that his feet made a lot of noise as he reluctantly descended the steps to Lan Yi's cabin. In fact, everything seemed loud: the scraping of his fingernails over the rough wooden boards of the wall as he walked, the breath leaving his mouth, and the distant sounds of life and activity on the lower decks.

He lifted the curtain to Yi's cabin and bowed as he entered. Then he removed his shoes and sat at a low table where the circus master, Marmot, Temur, and Younger Sister were already waiting.

To his surprise, the spicy odor of a Mongolian hotpot rose from a covered bowl on the table.

"You have not eaten, Little Shen," said Temur in an unusually soft voice. "We shall all eat together. They have killed goats on the food ship today, and this portion of meat came to us. The spices, I have carried with me. It will be good!"

Shen wanted to speak to him about the matter of Merk, but it didn't seem like the right time. The others were looking at the table and remained silent. When Temur lifted the lid to begin ladling out portions of food, Yi gestured for him to wait.

"I had hoped this would be a happier gathering," said Yi. "But your sister has spoken to me today."

Shen saw the tears rising in Chang's eyes. "Forgive me, Older Brother. I couldn't carry this burden alone."

"Chang is referring to your meetings with the Confucian, Fei Shen," said Yi. "In addition, she has told me what your mother wrote in her letter to you. What are the 'efforts on his behalf' that you have made for Lord Yang? What pain I feel, learning of your duplicity! What do you have to say?"

Shen bowed his head. "I have acted so as to secure Mother's release. As for my duplicity, I have never believed in Zheng He or his 'mission.' If my father is dead, it is because the eunuch killed him. I did not wish to come on this journey! Did you think that by forcing me you would change my heart? I have never forgiven Zheng He."

Yi chewed thoughtfully. Shen dreaded the red stain of betel nut that would soon appear. Even with a careful chewer—and Yi wasn't careful—some of the thin juice would leak out of the corners of the mouth. "Earlier today," said Yi, "the Admiral asked me to help take the civilians off the ships so the fleet can fight the pirate at Palembang. This much, of course, I already knew." He gave Shen a piercing look. "But I did not know that the Grandson is alive! That he is imprisoned in Palembang! This I learned only today. But you, you traitorous filthy boy, have known it for a very long time. Haven't you?"

"Only because the eunuch told me. Long ago." Shen spoke evenly, controlling his voice. He was still shocked that Chang had broken their "secret silence" promise. But his strategy was to stay calm and bluff his way through. "I was in the eunuch's confidence before you were."

"And in Yang Rong's confidence too, I imagine!" cried Yi. "And do stop calling the Admiral 'the eunuch.' That's what the Confucians call him. Even your speech betrays you now." He spit the betel juice into a bowl on the table. "The only thing I don't understand is Lord Yang's interest in the Grandson. But in my stomach I begin to feel that this business of smuggling weapons has something to do with him. Something large is on the move."

Yi glared at Shen, who stared blankly back.

"The boy is hiding something," growled Marmot, "and he's got all of our necks on the chopping block."

"I agree with you, Marmot." Yi's voice was almost inaudible. "I can feel it. This child is full of lies. And the biggest lie he still conceals." He shook his head. "I must go to Zheng He." He began to rise.

"No!" cried Chang. "No, Lan Yi! Protector and helper! Remember what you promised Father!" She had grabbed Yi's tunic and was trying to drag him back to his seat.

Yi hesitated. Bit by bit, his customary calm returned. But Shen knew it was too late.

"This is what I will do for you, Fei Shen, the Son of Fei Lee." Yi's voice was cold. "The fleet will dock at Semarang while it is still dark. Between then and the moment the sun reaches its full height, you must flee. At midday, I will denounce you to the Admiral and his soldiers."

Chang was still crying when Shen left the room. She didn't lift her head to say good-bye.

———

IT WAS DARK IN SHEN'S ROOM where he could not sleep. He wasn't afraid of being denounced at noon, because he had already planned on leaving the ship before then. What worried him was whether he could ever repair the damage with his sister. He shouldn't have shut her out, he saw now. He should have brought her into his arrangement with Lord Yang.

He felt the impact when the *China Harmony* cast its two mighty stern anchors into the water and they bit into the harbor bottom. Moments later he heard the splash of the other two stern anchors. With a groaning of thick, plaited bamboo cables, the vessel came to a halt. There were two final splashes as the forward anchors were dropped from heavy wooden cat's-heads that projected out from each side of the bow.

At first light he stood up and dressed himself. Then he searched for the letter from Mother, which he had slipped into a crack between two wallboards. It wasn't there.

Worried about the missing letter, he climbed the inside staircase to the Admiral's quarters and stepped outside to the main deck. He was sure the guards wouldn't have let Chang into his room. But then who took it? And why?

His first sight of the port of Semarang distracted him from his worries. The rising tropical sun threw its light over hundreds of sharp-nosed fishing boats painted in colors of turquoise and tangerine, with images of strange gods on their sterns. Men and children and mothers with babies in slings on their hips looked up at the decks of the flagship towering above them.

Here and there were small trading ships with *tanjaq* sails, a wide rectangle of cloth hung at a jaunty angle on a single mast. The crewmen stood in lines on the decks, arms folded and gazing up at the alien giant ships that had appeared overnight in their harbor.

Looking down the steep side of the *China Harmony*, Shen could see a section of the ship's flank that had been lowered like a drawbridge. This was the only way to leave the vessel. Below the drawbridge were sampans that had been posted to take people ashore.

He turned away from the scene and fingered the shore pass and instructions, which had indeed been left under his pillow. Its flimsy paper was almost covered with densely printed red and black characters setting out the conditions of leaving the ship. Except for one small space where his name had been written.

It was time to go. He breathed deeply and presented himself to the detachment of Ocean-Spanning Guards posted to the wide staircase leading down to the drawbridge and freedom.

The senior guard waved dismissively at his shore pass. "Nobody leaves until the Admiral and Lord Yang have departed," he said. "The local king has sent a royal guard. Imagine if the first thing to come ashore was you!"

Looking around, Shen saw a group of men in fine dress uniforms assembling on the high deck of the castle. He made out the bulky figure and black official hat of the Admiral.

Fearfully he retreated to one side of the deck, where he concealed himself in a knot of sailors who were noisily shouting to their fellows in the little boats below.

He wasn't there long, but time seemed to crawl by. He could almost see the sun climbing in the sky. Crowds of civilians waiting to be disembarked were gathering around him. But they had to wait while the officials on the upper deck adjusted their robes and laughed as if they intended to spend the morning there. Hurry up! thought Shen.

Interpreter Ma came bustling across the deck. "Fei Shen! You look as if you haven't slept. I can't stay to talk," he said, waving his arms busily. "I must join the delegation. We're to leave immediately."

Only a short time later, though not short enough for Shen, the magnificent robes made their way down from the castle deck to the main deck and proceeded to the wide staircase. The civilian crowd opened up to let them through. Lord Yang caught Shen's eye and nodded curtly.

But then the guards blocked off the staircase again, until the official delegation boarded the sampans and headed for shore.

Shen danced anxiously from foot to foot, wondering how much time he had before Lan Yi would carry out his threat. The Admiral was gone but might well return by midday. And dangerous one-eyed Ho Fu was still here, up on the observation deck. Yes, he really had to get off the ship by noon. But then—his thoughts were racing and disorganized—it suddenly seemed more important to go to Chang and ask for one of the family mementos Mother had entrusted to her. There was a comb, and an ivory figurine of a dancer, and some notices of theater plays in which Mother had performed.

He shook his head violently. What was he thinking? Clinging to sunny memories of a vanished house and a lost life.

The crowd surged forward when the guards finally opened their book. After an eternity, it was Shen's turn. An Ocean-Spanning Guard unfolded the pass and sounded out the syllables *Fei Shen.* The other began to flip through the pages. "Certain people aren't allowed to go ashore," explained the first guard. "But if your name's not here, you're free to go."

The second guard was reading very slowly, moving his lips and touching each character with his finger. Shen felt as if his head were in a clamp.

"Only a short time longer," said the first guard, nodding confidently.

Shen felt a hand on his shoulder. He whirled around—and came face to face with Temur. "May the gods bless you with good fortune," said the giant Mongol. He reassuringly squeezed Shen's hands in his own. "You will be free!"

They were interrupted by the slow-reading guard, whose clumsy finger had finally found Shen's name on the list. "Here it is!" he cried. "You may not leave."

"Did you have pressing business on land?" came a rasping voice behind him. Shen turned to see General Ho Fu, his eyeless socket accumulating a little pool of sweat in the hot sun. Behind the general were six Ocean-Spanning Guards.

"B-but the sun is not yet at its height," stammered Shen, confused.

"I am not interested in the time of day," growled Ho Fu. "Rather more in this letter from your mother that you have mentioned. It was only last night, while you dined with your friends, that my men seized it from your room. You have some questions to answer, young Shen! On my own authority I have set you down for interrogation."

A guard stepped forward, shaking loose a short length of rope. Shen saw that he was about to be bound. So this is the end, he thought. The taste of chalk and metal in the mouth. The end of life.

And then, with blinding swiftness, a Mongol sword slashed at the rope. The guard fell backward, groping for his own sword.

"Jump!" cried Temur, sweeping the point of his sword in front of Ho Fu and his men.

Shen vaulted the railing. And then he was floating through the air, and the water far, far below was reaching out to embrace him.

The impact knocked the wind out of him and he sank fast. After a moment, the cold wetness forced his eyes open. In the green murk he saw little shafts of sunlight from the surface. Kicking his feet, he stroked toward a rippling black shadow that he guessed must be the hull of a fishing boat. His lungs ached.

Emerging on the far side of the boat, he gasped and coughed until he could breathe again. The hull hid him from the flagship deck, but he couldn't leave its shadow. The next little vessel was about sixty *ch'i* away. Filling his lungs, he pushed against the keel to force himself downward. He set a slow and deliberate underwater stroke, not wasting air, until he reached the next boat.

Boat by boat he made his way toward land. Every so often a fisherman would call out, but he couldn't understand. He prayed they would take him for a local boy out for a swim.

Not that anybody else was swimming, he noticed. And his face was light-skinned compared to Malay people. He felt terribly conspicuous. In the distance he heard voices shouting in Chinese, and fishermen answering in what must have been Malayalam. At least one boat was looking for him, but—and he perversely laughed, choking on water—nobody could understand their questions.

He wasted no time pushing past the final boats that separated him from land. Standing in the shallows just off a little sand beach, shaking from the cold harbor water, he looked behind to make sure no boats were pursuing him. There were none.

And now for the first time he thought about what he had done. He had broken all the laws of Heaven and man. Broken with his Admiral and his friends. It seemed strange to him that the air was not filled with arrows aimed at his heart. But there was silence everywhere.

The silence will not last! came an urgent thought, pushing into his mind. It was the instinct of survival taking hold again. He scuttled into the nearest patch of greenery, a swath of seagrass just tall enough to conceal him. From there he slipped into a procession of towering palm trees bordering a road that ran along the harbor toward town. He had seen it from his vantage point on the ship's high deck earlier that morning.

Though the hot sun was already drying his hair, Shen shivered from his long swim in the chill water. He felt the lack of sleep from the night before. His body cried out for rest.

But his eyes probed every ship he passed as he moved eastward along the waterfront, searching for the black junk he had glimpsed in the mangrove swamps of Ayutthaya.

There was a clop-clop of horses coming round a bend in the road behind him. Shen ran into the high grass and crouched down. But it was only a group of farmers on their way to market.

It felt comfortable in the grass. His teeth were chattering, but the sun was warm and he let his eyes close for a moment.

He had no idea how much time had passed when he awoke. But the sun, moving west in the direction of the Treasure Fleet, told him it was early afternoon. Jumping to his feet, he ran along the road, passing dozens of little boats and trading vessels. They became a blur, so much so that he was already past the Chinese junk when he realized he had seen a flash of shining black paint.

Making his way back, he stopped at the gangway of the black ship. Something about the ominous sweep of its flanks and its empty deck made his neck prickle. He remembered thinking that Lord Yang was like Cao Cao, the scheming prime minister in the play. A powerful reflex of fear drove him backward.

His thoughts racing, he remembered that Kun and Old Bao were somewhere in Majapahit. As casually as possible he walked down the road. He must find them.

Men stepped in front of him. They wore batik shirts, like the local people, but spoke Chinese. "Having second thoughts about Lord Yang's hospitality?" said one.

He was marched back to the boat with the men on all sides. Their marching rhythm told him they were Brocades.

"Shen! What a relief you have arrived safely!" cried Lord Yang, who met him at the top of the gangplank.

The heartiness of the greeting reassured him but only momentarily. As they entered the ship's cabin, Shen saw that it was full of Brocade soldiers. They sat like stone statues. "Impressive, aren't they?" said Yang. "Of course there are many more. They are billeted on the three ships in this harbor that I purchased from a Thai trader."

"But why did the Admiral let them go ashore?" asked Shen, puzzled. "Didn't he need them to fight the pirate?"

Lord Yang's laughter was surprisingly loud for so slight a man. "The eunuch didn't trust them! He thought they would go over to the pirate's side. And in a sense, he was right."

Shen said nothing. These ominous words put a chill in his blood.

"Perhaps you would be more comfortable in my private chamber?" offered Lord Yang.

The little cabin under the ship's prow was as tidy as a monk's cell. Though many Confucians were wealthy and comfortable, Yang Rong had a reputation for self-discipline. He sat in a simple wooden chair, elbows on the armrests, fingers laced together.

"You must have many questions, Fei Shen."

"My mother. Is she even alive? Where are you keeping her?"

"She is in Palembang, child. You will soon join her there. It's your father who is the real problem. We believe he is hiding in a monastery near Mount Merapi, though we can't be certain. He has been a very elusive quarry."

Shen heard these words, but they made no sense. Mother in Palembang? Father alive? His head was spinning. All that he could say was, "Father is dead. You said it yourself. Two days ago —"

The Confucian made a tut-tut sound. "I *lied*, Fei Shen. Your father is alive. He came to Majapahit with the Grandson nearly three years ago."

Shen's eyes stared at the grass cloth that covered the curving wall of the room. There was a roaring in his ears. Thoughts were falling on thoughts in his head, like trees in a forest thrown down by an earthquake. Not a single thought was left standing. Nothing made sense.

Shen tried to stand up, but a firm hand clutched his shoulder and forced him down. It must be a guard behind him, he thought. But he couldn't be bothered to look. Instead his eyes slowly found Lord Yang's face again.

"If Father is alive, please take me to him."

"I wish I could," said the Confucian with a horrible grin. "But he is hiding from me."

The roaring in Shen's ears stopped. He was breathing shallowly, and he felt his heart calming. "Father is hiding from you," repeated Shen, nodding to himself. Let's play this game, he thought. Let's pretend that's a fact. Then he would get some more facts, and see what this new forest would look like. "Why is he hiding from you?" Shen's voice echoed strangely in his head.

"A long answer, I'm afraid. Two years ago my brotherhood learned that the Grandson was alive and imprisoned in

Palembang. I decided to lead a delegation and petition the pirate Chen Zuyi for his release. We went to Palembang in this very black ship. And there I met your father again."

The Confucian chuckled maliciously, something Shen had never heard him do before. "Let me paint the picture for you. The Grandson was a prisoner, but it amused Chen Zuyi to pretend that the Grandson was still Emperor. So Grandson had a little throne room, guarded by your father with his few remaining Forest of Feathers soldiers. They were surrounded by thousands of the pirate's men, of course. But Chen would ask for an 'audience,' and the Grandson would say 'yes,' and Chen would come in clanking from all the gold and ugly jewels he was wearing. And your father had to bow down to him!"

Lord Yang told how he had come to an understanding with the pirate. He and his Confucians would restore the Grandson to the throne and take control of the government. If Chen Zuyi helped them, then he would share the power with Lord Yang.

"It was understood between us that the Grandson would have no power at all. The eunuchs would be banished and there would no Treasure Fleet bringing foreigners into our country. China would be purely Chinese once again, as it was in the stories that come to us from the time of the Yellow Emperor, when men first learned to write." Lord Yang's eyes were glazed with pleasure. Then he blinked, as if a mosquito were annoying him.

"It would have been perfect—except for your father."

"Father would never tolerate your treason," said Shen angrily.

"Do shut up, you ignorant child," cried Yang, annoyed to be

interrupted. "No, your father would not tolerate it. In fact, he went absolutely mad. Began making speeches about how he would return to Nanjing, he would expose us, and so on. The world is full of tiresome people, but your father is the god of tiresomeness. So about six months ago we brought your mother to Palembang as a hostage. That shut your father's mouth."

Lord Yang sipped tea while Shen struggled to understand. Mother was two, maybe three days' sail away.

Lord Yang stood up and paced the little cabin. "We thought your mother would talk sense to him, so we let them see each other. But she turned out to be even worse. A tigress! She knew we would kill her if your father left. So she declared that she would kill herself if he stayed there! If he didn't do the honorable thing and take a warning back to China. Your father didn't believe her." Knowing Mother, Shen had a terrible premonition of what had happened next. "Then she did try to kill herself. The pirate had to put her under restraint. But it appears that she had put some spine into your father. He took his men one night and fought his way out of Palembang."

"Heaven bless Mother! And may you never find Father!"

"Oh, I believe we will. He will soon learn that we have his son in irons. Perhaps we will have your sister as well."

Shen let the import of that sink in. He had betrayed Zheng He, and now he was bait in order to betray Father as well. Lord Yang had pretended friendship, and he had fallen for it.

The moments went by. A small water clock dripped monotonously somewhere behind him. Lord Yang, in a mockery of their old "friendship," poured him a cup of hot tea. Out of the corner of his eye Shen saw that his guard had stepped a short distance away. He could hear the gulls crying outside the black ship and the busy lap of water at its hull.

His eyes began to hunt around the table and shelves nearby. Father had taught him that there was always something at hand that could kill a man. And, once that thing was found, to do it fast.

Shen smacked Lord Yang's cup of tea back into the Confucian's face so that the hot fluid blinded him temporarily. Then he smashed the teapot against the wall and grabbed a sharp piece out of midair, driving it directly at Lord Yang's throat. But the Confucian shifted to one side, and the pottery shard opened his jaw from back to front. Then something heavy hit Shen across the back of the head.

When he came to, a long time later, he didn't know where he was. But red bolts of pain were pulsing from a wound on his head. Calling on the god of war, he whispered aloud, "Let me kill him."

"Not much chance," said a voice nearby.

With difficulty, he rolled over and focused his eyes. It was Panther Officer Chu.

"You are a most inconvenient child," said Chu.

Shen groaned. That close to killing Lord Yang and still they called him "child"! "How can you take orders from him?"

"He is a hero," replied Chu. "And, unluckily for you, he will recover. His wound is serious, but he is able to carry on. We are going to evacuate this ship and show you to your father. We leave tonight, when sufficient horses have arrived. You're going on a journey, boy, so I suggest you rest your head."

CHAPTER 28

CHANG ROSE EARLY THAT morning, hoping to persuade Lan Yi to spare her brother.

But Mistress Guo ordered the troupe to pack the costumes and props first. "We'll have to wait in this foreign city for a week at least, while the warships do their business with the pirate," she complained.

As Chang worked she could hear the elephant thumping of civilians lining up for shore transport on the deck above. One by one troupe members went up to join them, with bales of costumes lashed to their backs. As Chang moved toward the stairs, she saw a discarded acrobat's shirt on the floor. It's too pretty to leave, she thought, pulling the black shirt with its beautiful white-and-blue swirly cloud pattern over her every-day blouse. Then she joined the others.

She saw with alarm that the sun was already near its height in the sky. Lan Yi was sitting on the steps leading up to the castle, and she hurried to him.

"Don't worry about your brother," he said bitterly. "He got away, with Temur's help. And Temur is behind bars. He's been discharged from the army."

"Where did Older Brother go?" Chang's voice was urgent.

"To be united with his hero, Lord Yang," said Lan Yi, using his clown voice.

Chang wept tears of gratitude. At least Brother would not be executed, she thought. She no longer cared what dark business he had with the Confucian.

They sat on the steps until midday, when a ceremonial drum announced the return of Zheng He and his officials. Yi knelt down to speak to the Admiral, but a soldier kicked him in the side. Then both Lan Yi and Chang were hoisted to their feet and frogmarched into the Admiral's quarters.

"Ho Fu has already informed me of Shen's treason," grunted the Admiral, settling into his heavy chair. "A spy! In my quarters! And I am not forgetting, Lan Yi, that it was you who brought him to me."

Hearing himself accused, Yi threw himself flat on the floor. His voice was muffled because his mouth nearly touched the wooden planks. "I promised the boy's father I would protect him. Condemn me with him."

"I shall. Together with his sister. She must have known."

"I swear she did not!" cried Yi. "I plead for her. She comes before you filled with innocence and submission. Her brother has betrayed her."

Chang knew she was not so innocent as that. But she pressed her lips together and watched a charcoal brazier as it swung slowly on a chain suspended from the ceiling. It squeaked with every arc, lighting the Admiral from behind. The shadows made his eyes seem like dark pockets. His interlaced fingers moved as if they were the visible messengers of his agitated thoughts.

"I also have been foolish," he said unexpectedly. "I thought the gods had brought this boy to me. But it was nothing, except perhaps feelings natural to a man who has no children. An attachment forbidden to me, because of what I am." He lowered his head and, separating his hands, placed them resolutely on his knees. Then he looked up. A haunted expression, Chang thought. "I will not punish the girl. But you have failed to master the boy. You must bring him to me."

"On my oath I will," said Lan Yi, "but only if you agree to hear him before he is condemned. There may be matters here that neither of us know."

"How astonishing that you set conditions," said the Admiral. "And what is your oath? Who are you to give an oath?"

"It is the oath of a Leopard officer in the Forest of Feathers Guard," said Yi. Chang's mouth fell open. A Leopard was a third-ranking officer, just below a general—and three ranks above Father.

The Admiral considered. "I always knew you were not what you pretended to be. But this... surprises me. You're in disgrace, I take it."

"According to our laws, I failed in my duty."

"And yet you offer your oath."

"'The guiltless soul will pass untroubled into the next life.'"

More silence. Chang thought the squeaking of the brazier would drive her mad. She was relieved when one of the guards standing behind the Admiral reached out a hand to steady it.

"I do not like this exchange, circus man," rumbled the Admiral. "This is my offer. Bring Shen to me. If he has acted for evil reasons, you shall both die. If something can be said to lessen his guilt, he will be punished accordingly. I alone decide."

As Chang and Yi stood up, the Admiral added: "And the girl stays on board to ensure your return."

———

AS THEY WERE ESCORTED from the castle deck, Chang looked out over the harbor. Then she bowed to say good-bye to Yi, who was going below decks to free Temur. The Admiral had agreed that they were likelier to find her brother if they worked together.

A single guard led her down many stairs to an unlighted and isolated room in the ship's brig. As the door was closed on her, she put her face against the worn straw mattress. Tears leaked from her eyes and slowly dampened it.

Less than a watch later she was awakened by a rising tide of noise and commotion. The guard opened the door. "We are to move to a merchant ship, girl. Come quickly. They're already placing cannons on the parade deck. All civilians off the *China Harmony.*"

Chang shielded her eyes from the setting sun as they walked down the gangplank to the wharf. She and her guard were pushed together with people from other boats. Everybody on the Semarang wharf had a paper token to say which ship they were going to, and the harried soldiers struggled to get them into the correct longboats and sampans.

"Suzhou Acrobat Troupe! Prepare to move to the second wharf for transportation!" cried an Ocean-Spanning officer.

Chang looked around and in the distance saw Jade and the others marching away across the sandy beach in their light cotton shoes. Jade kept hopping on one foot while emptying sand from her other shoe.

The long wooden wharf on which she stood began to echo with heavy footfalls. Looking toward the harbor end, she saw that a horse ship had pulled in. Powerful cavalry mounts, which had spent long weeks in confinement, were led toward her. The pirate would be fought at sea, not on land, so of course there was no need for cavalry.

The officials on the dock squeezed to one side. They were complaining about the horse ship, which in the confusion had apparently come to the wrong wharf. Her own guard was shouting as loudly as the rest.

Chang looked down the procession of animals as they clumped toward her. Not too far away, led by the young groom she had seen before, Merk was approaching. She saw that her own guard was arguing with an official. She waved to the boy.

"Greetings, Sister," he said. "I remember you and your brother from the ship."

"Where are you taking Merk?"

The boy pointed south, where a hill rose, and indicated that the horses were being gathered in a field on the other side.

"Could I ride him to the top of the hill?" said Chang.

"Oh, miss, I don't know!" said the boy.

"Come, I'll ride slowly. You can walk alongside."

"Very slowly," he cautioned her.

She nodded brightly, leaped on Merk's bare back, and pulled the reins tight. Her guard began to shout at her. "Goodbye," she called to the boy.

And then she kicked Merk's flanks and galloped him not up the hill, but straight through the line of guards and toward the eastern road that followed the harbor.

She was looking for the black ship.

CHAPTER 29

IT WAS ALMOST EVENING by the time Chang found the black ship.

Shortly after she started out, an approaching patrol of Ocean-Spanning Guards had forced her to hide in a strip of trees on the side of the road away from the harbor. Here, as a light-skinned girl with a horse, she attracted the attention of picnicking families. The women, seeing that she could not understand them and had nothing to eat, clucked in a worried way and forced her to accept a ragged cloth bag filled with bread and fruit. In exchange, she hoisted children onto Merk's back, and he accepted them with indifference. Bowing and smiling, she found it strangely agreeable to be among barbarians for the first time.

But soon she had to approach the road again. And there, through the trees, she saw the ship. Even in the dimming evening light it glittered black, with two square patches on the mainsail and a four-clawed dragon painted on the stern. Merk peaceably cropped the grass nearby while she debated what to do.

It was impossible to get closer. The boat was moored just on the other side of the road, with its long side against the wharf. Men in merchant robes—Confucians in disguise, she guessed—were sitting on the forward deck, their faces bright in the light of their lamps. Camped on the pier was a group of young men in yellow and brown batik shirts. Poorly concealed weapons glinted from under a nearby canvas cloth.

How long could they stay there? she wondered. The enraged Admiral would surely find them soon. Or else they might sail away with Older Brother! She cursed him because he had told her so little.

Two watches later, shivering in the night chill, she studied the moon as it began to ascend from the wobbling, teasing image of itself in the warm ocean. Fishing boats knocked gently against one another in the swell. From behind she heard Merk's restless nickering.

Without realizing it, she fell asleep. The sound of new horses and men arriving awakened her. The moon had moved to the other side of the sky, and the howling of birds signaled that dawn was near.

The deckhouse door swung open, and several men with lanterns walked down the gangplank. The face of one was swathed in bandages. From his Crane badge, she knew it was Lord Yang. Behind him was a young man, his arms tied to his sides. She mouthed the word *Shen* and began to untie Merk.

Then things happened fast. The party of riders crashed into the woods where she was, and she scrambled to mount Merk and catch up. By the time she emerged from the woods she was bleeding from the branches that had struck her face.

About twenty horsemen were cantering far ahead, on a

road that led into a flat plain. Within a short time the first pumpkin-colored rays of the sun were picking out the slopes of steep mountains in the distance. She realized with dismay that a long journey lay ahead.

By midmorning it was clear that the road was streaming toward a cleft between two black mountains. One was topped with a slender plume of gray smoke that occasionally thickened to a black, fist-shaped ball. She shivered at the thought of the volcano god it must house.

Riding bareback was agony. Sharp pains in her thighs warned her that she could not maintain the pace. She cried with relief when the horsemen stopped to rest. But she hardly had time to drink from a ditch before they moved on.

About midafternoon the men left the main road and began to climb toward a monastery. They vanished through a bizarre gateway that looked like a pagoda sliced in half, with smooth interior walls.

There she could not follow. Instead she allowed black thoughts about her brother to invade her mind. Had he been so vain as to think he could outwit these men? Didn't he see how it would end? Hadn't she warned him?

She was sitting under a tree by the road, rubbing her stiff legs. She calmed down a little and tried to think clearly. Obviously she needed to go back to Semarang and get help. But who would help? Lan Yi was sworn to seize Shen, so she didn't dare ask him. And there was nobody else. Tears of rage, strangely tasteless and saltless, welled up. Older Brother had brought this on himself.

Running her fingers over the scratches and crusted blood on her cheeks and forehead, she made a cruel decision. She was done with Older Brother. She was leaving.

You will never find his body, whispered a voice in her head.

"I don't care," she muttered.

A young voice from nearby replied in a language she didn't understand. She rose and limped toward it.

There was a boy squatting in front of Merk, feeding him fistfuls of grass. On the ground was his knitted pillbox cap, with a banana leaf folded inside to hold water. Seeing her, he smiled, displaying brilliant white teeth. He bowed his head, murmuring a greeting.

Out of habit she placed her hands together and bowed from the waist. A stabbing pain went up her back, forcing her to sit down and support herself against a tree. She closed her eyes, and her mouth fell open from fatigue.

A few moments later there was a gentle tugging on her right sleeve. Lolling her head to that side, she saw that the boy was offering a hatful of water. She drank greedily and fell back against the tree trunk. Blinking her eyes, she released several more tears that rolled down her cheeks.

The boy sat next to her. The last light was disappearing, and with it the last of her reserves of strength. She desperately needed to sleep. The boy, seeming to understand, reached forward and gently closed her eyes with the tips of his fingers. Fatigue overwhelmed her.

After a time—she had no idea how much time—there was a jingling in the distance. Merk began to whinny, and answering huffs and chuffs came from the darkness. Opening her eyes, Chang saw the orange smoke of oil lamps swaying lazily from side to side. It outlined the figures of many people, and of some kind of wagon pulled by horses.

Exhausted, she couldn't summon the will to run away.

The boy ran out into the road. There was rapid talk, and then several women came into the trees with a wooden bowl filled with soup. The flavors were strange, and Chang couldn't decide if it was meat or fish, but she gulped down the cold fluid anyway.

A man approached with a lantern, and the women began to fuss over her dust-caked face, with its little streaks of dried tears. But one of them also tugged at the fabric of her patterned blouse with frank curiosity. Then they lifted her to her feet and helped her climb onto the wagon. She fretted about Merk, but the boy made hand signals to say that he would be safe tethered where he was. Then he climbed into the wagon beside Chang.

Within moments the little caravan left the road and began to climb the hill to the monastery. Chang sat up, alarmed, but the calming presence of the boy as he whispered to her relaxed her and she leaned back again. She said a short prayer, placing her fate in the hands of the immortals. She felt the strength returning to her legs and added a brief thanks for that as well.

The wagon lurched over a rock beside the trail, and the driver began to jabber. A man jogged up and held a lamp so the driver could see the road's edge. The lamp also illuminated what was beside Chang in the wagon, and she sat up with a jerk.

Monstrous faces leered at her, their curling noses and spotted eyes alive with orange light. Tiny, cruel black pupils peered at her, and long, skinny arms were poised to grab. One, with huge blocky teeth, seemed to have fire in his mouth and looked as if he were about to speak.

The boy was smiling. He reached past her and pulled one of the figures out of the piece of wood in which it was resting. Chang felt its leathery surface and realized it was a kind of doll or puppet supported on a stick. Her heartbeat returned to normal.

Ahead she could see the towering ceremonial gateway that was split in half, and felt a little thrill about going through it at last. Then she thought of her brother, and her stomach was turbulent. It was like being sick in the dusty season back home.

During the uphill climb, the woman who had fingered her blouse tried to barter a batik tunic for it. The boy set himself up as Chang's protector and refused several tunics in succession. Chang watched this with amusement, until it occurred to her that her cloud blouse was the most Chinese thing she could be wearing. Her brother's captors would spot it right away. She signaled to the boy to accept the latest tunic on offer—a batik of interlocking circles, each containing a tiny flower. He held a piece of cotton fabric around her in the cramped back seat of the wagon as she changed into it. She was thankful for the privacy afforded by the darkness.

The wagons halted abruptly inside the courtyard. Monks in orange-yellow robes waved them into a large hall, brilliantly lit by torches.

Men from the caravan busied themselves setting up a

puppet theater on a raised platform. They erected a white cotton screen and hung a coconut-shell oil lamp behind it.

The boy pulled Chang into a group of monks sitting on the floor. She was comforted by their saffron robes, so similar to the monks at home. She guessed that a performance was about to begin.

Soon, a man carrying one of the leather puppets went behind the screen and lit the lamp. The puppet threw a gigantic black silhouette on the screen, and all the little holes cut in it were outlined by the orange flame. They turned into eyes, nostrils, and teeth of a strange and magical creature. When the man was satisfied with the lighting, he went to bring in the other puppets.

Just at that moment Chang caught sight of Brocade soldiers moving to block all the exits from the hall. Noticing the fear in her eyes, the boy tapped her arm. He pointed at the soldiers and then at Chang. She nodded, signaled with hands and grimaces that she was afraid of them. The boy watched her carefully.

Several tall men in black robes entered. Chang saw that one of them was Lord Yang, with his freshly bandaged jaw. He looked pale, and his thin lips were tight with pain. Behind him, heavily guarded, came Shen. His feet were tied together.

Then something happened that left her stupefied. A Forest of Feathers soldier entered the hall. His tunic was dirty and torn, but there could be no doubt. Father's brigade—here!

The soldier spoke briefly to Shen and then left the hall.

The boy beside Chang wagged his finger back and forth between Chang and Shen to ask if there was a connection.

Chang nodded and made an awkward gesture of embracing Shen. Had she come so close to abandoning him? Her tears returned, and the boy nodded, wide-eyed as a wise monkey.

The torches were extinguished as the puppet master began the show. A tok-tok-tok sound emerged, and one of the puppets dashed into the playing area, speaking in a melodious, high-pitched voice. The thousand punctured holes sparkled with orange light. Chang was momentarily hypnotized by the spectacle.

The boy beside her suddenly scampered away, returning a few moments later with a yellow-robed monk. He bowed and sat close by, his penetrating black eyes studying her.

On the screen, a gap-toothed giant appeared. "Raksasa," murmured the boy. A young warrior emerged to fight him—here a gong was beating furiously—but the giant easily swept his sword away. Gathering the warrior under his arm, he lurched out of the circle of light and vanished.

A princess then appeared, turning her head left and right, crying out. With a graceful pirouette she inclined her head toward the ground. Then she reached down with her hands— how delicate they are, thought Chang—and seemed to search about. She picked up the sword and followed the trail where the giant had fled.

Chang realized with a start that this story mimicked her own. It was surely a coincidence, but maybe one she could use.

Glancing at the monk, she found that he was still watching her closely. He could tell she had come here for a purpose. Could she make him understand what it was?

The black silhouette of the giant reappeared, and Chang threw caution to the wind. She touched the monk's arm, and he leaned closer. She pointed at the giant, and then she pointed across the room at Lord Yang. The monk nodded.

Then the giant threw the young warrior to the ground. She pointed at the warrior puppet, injured and flailing about, and then she pointed at Shen. The monk nodded again.

Suddenly the flute began to blow piercing, urgent tones. The princess stepped into the light, her slender body moving in rhythm with the notes of the flute. The giant swung a great paw at her, but she leaped into the air as if she were a bird. The flute trilled. Then she settled back to earth and began her remorseless advance once again, the flute matching her tread, the little sword tracing a graceful arc. Then—a shrill dying note—the sword impaled the giant. The gong echoed a single mighty tone through the hall.

Chang was so absorbed that she had almost forgotten the monk and the boy. But now the monk was nudging her. He pointed at the princess. And then he pointed at her.

She nodded vigorously, and the monk bowed his head quickly to show he had understood. Then he rose to his feet, signaling for Chang to follow. They crept out of the hall, leaving the boy behind.

Outside the hall was an open courtyard leading to a low-slung building a short distance away. In the black night Chang spotted an angry halo of red at the crest of the volcano. A group of monks around a circular stone basin was burning offerings and lifting their arms toward the mountain. The monk bowed briefly and whispered to them. Several rose, with stout walking sticks, and followed the monk and Chang into the low-slung building.

They entered a long corridor with many doors. Chang guessed they hid the tiny cells where the monks lived and meditated. In front of one door stood a young Chinese man with a sword on his hip who glowered unpleasantly at the monks. They bowed and spoke pleasantly. But as they straightened up from their bow, one of them rammed his walking stick into the guard's throat. The others muffled his mouth and struck a single blow to render him unconscious.

The lead monk stepped around the fallen soldier and fumbled nervously with a ring of keys. As the door swung open, the monk's lantern lit up the skull-like face of a fellow cowering in the corner.

"Tin Purse!" exclaimed Chang.

Tin squinted at the bright light and crawled forward. "Girl? Are you the girl from the boat?"

"Yes, it's me. What are you doing here?"

"Paying for my sins. I was in the marketplace alone, and Lord Yang's people picked me off my feet and put me on a horse. Said they needed a translator. Now here I am."

The monk spoke quickly and urgently.

"The abbot says we haven't got much time," said Tin Purse. "He and his people are very upset because they had to hit the guard. They're pacifists, you know. Oh, gods! Did they hit the guard?" He glanced outside the door. "Ancestors preserve us! Now we're dead for sure."

"Ask them why they're doing this," whispered Chang urgently. Tin Purse spoke to the abbot.

"He says that the Confucians intend a great evil. He knows about them. A Chinese officer warned him."

"What Chinese officer?"

"A man who came here with soldiers two months ago. He wore a steel helmet with tall green feathers."

"That's a Forest of Feathers —"

Tin Purse cut her off. "The holy man insists that I take the sword. He doesn't seem to understand that I'm a coward, though I've explained it several times!"

The abbot spoke again.

"He says that the Chinese officer is hiding on the mountain. Lord Yang wanted to talk to the officer, but the soldier came instead. And the soldier secretly warned the monks that there would be an attack on the Confucians tonight. It will be a diversion, to free the boy." Tin Purse's face lit up, as if he had just understood something. "The boy is your brother, isn't he?"

"Yes!" moaned Chang.

The abbot spoke again. Tin Purse looked woeful.

"The puppet show is almost finished, and a signal has been sent to the Chinese soldiers. When the Confucians leave the hall and come into the courtyard with your brother, that will be the moment. To free him."

"How?" asked Chang, fearing the answer.

The young abbot began speaking rapidly, and Tin Purse translated as well as he could. "He says you should take the sword and cut your brother's thongs. When you see him, it's *snip-snip* and we all run like madmen out of the monastery."

"But my brother is surrounded by soldiers!" protested Chang.

"The abbot says the holy men will deal with that. Be a good girl, take the sword, cut the ropes."

There was no time to argue. She accepted a short, light sword from the abbot, and a tiny lantern. She crept into the corridor and looked around. It seemed they had come from the right, so she retraced her steps in that direction. The lantern threw huge shadows up the wall.

Soon, directly ahead, she saw the rough ironwork of the door leading into the courtyard where the monks were praying around the stone basin.

The abbot had said she should not open the door until she heard a commotion in the courtyard outside. The noise would mean that the Confucian's party had come out of the main hall and reached the stone basin. The monks had a surprise ready for them.

Who needs any more surprises? she thought to herself. Time crawled by. She hefted the sword and tested its upper edge near the tip. Wet drops of blood promptly ran down her finger. She bit her tongue to make no sound. And waited some more. The little lantern guttered out, and she was in complete darkness.

A rhythmic murmuring from outside in the courtyard came faintly through the door. Finally she couldn't wait any more and pushed it open a crack, peeping around carefully to make sure nobody was looking in her direction. Then she focused on the circle of monks who were still omm-ing around the stone basin. Every so often they bowed and chanted together.

As they straightened up, a square of light appeared in the distant wall of the great hall. A door had been opened. Soldiers and Confucians began to spill into the courtyard. She made out Lord Yang, who was leaning on an official and looked very tired. Behind him shuffled Shen, closely guarded.

One of the monks detached himself from the worshipping group and indicated that the foreign visitors should arrange themselves around the stone basin.

"I'm in no mood for this nonsense," grumbled Lord Yang, his voice muffled by the bandage. "Where is our translator?"

"Locked in his room," came the voice of Panther Officer Chu. "Lord Yang, this is a ritual to placate the volcano god. If we cooperate with it, we will gain face with the monks. And we need their goodwill. They are very upset that we have brought violence into their monastery. They may even believe we are further angering the volcano god. It is a very good idea for us to show some reverence toward this god, whatever it is."

"Didn't we attend that barbarian puppet show to placate their god? How much placating must we do?"

"Only a few moments, my Lord."

With a groan and some assistance from the official he was leaning on, the Confucian was lowered to a kneeling position by the stone basin. The others circled it and did likewise. Chang saw that Shen was positioned directly in front of her, his wrists tied together. Soldiers clenched him by each arm.

The monks began to chant once again, lifting their candles in unison and holding them up in a circle of light. One of the monks made a signal to the others. They dropped the candles into the basin.

There was a crackling sound, like fireworks, and a cloud of black smoke erupted. Everybody began coughing and hacking and spitting. Some of the soldiers staggered away, gasping for air. At the same moment shouts and clamor came from the hall, and a number of soldiers ran inside to see what it was.

That was the diversion, Chang thought. Now was the time. Holding her breath, she pushed the door open and rushed forward. As she grabbed the leather thong that attached Shen's feet, he fell down, rubbing his eyes and cursing. He couldn't see who she was, and she didn't dare speak with his guards nearby. Instead she pulled the thong tight with one hand and hooked the sharp, curved end of the blade under it. Then she sawed back and forth till she felt the strands snapping apart. With a final tug of the blade, the thong separated.

"It's me, keep quiet," she whispered, trying to keep the black smoke out of her lungs. Shen stopped kicking and let her lift him to his feet.

They ran quickly back to the dormitory door, pushing it shut behind them. Darkness enveloped them. They slowly felt their way along the wall.

Ahead was an outside door, a little shaft of starlight leaking in where the abbot had propped it open. But behind them there was the sudden crash of the dormitory door being flung wide. Lantern light and angry voices flooded in.

"We have to run," said Chang.

"I can't see," said Shen, still rubbing his eyes.

"Hang on to me and run where I'm running."

They pushed through the little exterior door and two monks braced it shut behind them. In front of them stood the abbot and Tin Purse. The abbot pointed urgently to a rough path up the mountain slope.

"The abbot's frightened now," said Tin Purse. "We'd better hurry."

———

THEY CLAMBERED UP THE path till they came to the lower edge of the evergreen forest that covered the mountain. The abbot ordered them to halt.

"The abbot says his name is Surya," said Tin Purse, panting heavily from the exertion. "We're to wait here. A Chinese soldier will come for us."

Below, the various gates in the monastery wall were flung open. Monks spilled out, running in all directions. At one door some Brocades appeared. They ignored the fleeing monks, spreading out to search the monastery grounds.

"Surya says they're looking for the boy. But when they don't find him, they may kill the monks," said Tin Purse. "Or burn the library, which is worse."

Chang tried to see the abbot's face, but it was lost in the shadows of the trees.

After a moment, an urgent voiced called to them in Chinese. A Forest of Feathers soldier was waving to them from a small clearing. They followed him.

He led them on a winding path across the mountain face and down the far side of the monastery. There, hidden from view, was a small group of men and horses.

And striding out to meet them was an officer wearing a green-plumed helmet. It was Father.

CHAPTER 30

SHEN ALWAYS REMEMBERED that moment as if it had just happened. As soon as he threw his arms around Father's waist, the family he had believed lost became real again. But he also wept. And from his tears he learned that he had not been so certain of Father's survival as he had noisily told everybody.

He awkwardly stepped back from Father and wiped his face on his sleeve. He saw that Chang was standing quietly. The only thing that betrayed her feelings was the quivering of her lower lip. She bowed deeply, and he remembered that he had forgotten his bow. He bent from his waist, so that his head descended nearly to his knees.

Then the three stood silently for some moments. Shen had smelled the dirt and decay of Father's uniform, and felt the bony, underfed leanness of his chest and arms when they embraced. He noticed the empty patch on his chest where the Panther badge had been.

"Approach, Daughter," said Father hoarsely.

Chang knelt and placed her hands on her lap. Her eyes were clear, and she spoke softly but distinctly. "I am overjoyed that you are well. We have often prayed for your safety."

"So I am... well," said Father, his voice filled with wonder. "But how is it that my children have found me? How will I protect you in this terrible place?"

A soldier came running up the path to say that yet more Brocades were approaching the monastery. Father cursed and ordered his men to horse.

It wasn't until then that Shen saw the state of things. Father had only five men. They were all that was left of the proud regiment of guards who had saved their Emperor. None looked well fed.

One of the soldiers was sent to fetch Merk from the main road where Chang had tethered him. The others prudently followed a twisted track to stay out of sight of their enemies. When the soldier rejoined them, with the chestnut pony cantering alongside his own horse, there was an awkward moment. Shen immediately claimed Merk for himself, though he looked guiltily at Chang, who had ridden so magnificently. So it must be between brother and sister, thought Chang sadly. She mounted behind one of the soldiers.

They followed the track until it rejoined the road to Semarang. Father signaled a halt, and a scout went ahead.

He returned hastily with the news that a large number of mounted Brocades, along with the Confucian with the bandage on his face, were returning to Semarang at a gallop.

"Amitofo," said Father, uttering the short Buddhist prayer of thanks. "May they have left the monks in peace."

He motioned the little detachment to move carefully out onto the road. Once they were certain that all of Lord Yang's riders were ahead of them, Father ordered his men to follow the Confucian at a gallop.

The horses' hooves thudded softly on the sandy road. A soldier was sent ahead to bring a warning if they started to get too close to the Brocades. There was no question of fighting them. The handful of Feathers could only stay out of sight.

They rode for a very long time. The moon shed little light, but Shen could tell that two, almost three watches had passed. The road began to curve to the left and descend from the highlands. Finally he could make out the wink of distant lights where Semarang folded itself against the ocean.

But the horses were bathed in sweat, and several could not keep up the pace. Father called a halt.

As the men stretched their legs, Father walked among them, whispering words of encouragement, promising an end to their long ordeal. Every so often he glanced at his children, and Shen considered how awkward it was for him that they were there. An officer should never be distracted by soft feelings when he was on the field of war. And Shen had understood that Father and his men were at war with the terrible Brocades.

And yet—they had been apart so long! As if in answer, Father came and put his arms around them, taking them to one side.

He kissed them both, very formally, on the top of the head. To Shen he said, "I thank Kuan Yin, the Heavenly Guardian of Children, that you have survived the night. The Confucian wanted to exchange you for me, to prevent me from carrying a warning to your Admiral. By doing what I did, I placed your life in danger. I beg your forgiveness." And he bowed to his son, something which had never happened before.

He turned to Chang. "Daughter, were you also a captive?"

Chang lowered her eyes. "I came here alone, Respected Father. It was improper. I —"

"Alone! For what reason?"

"So that Older Brother would not be lost."

"Ho!" said Father with the slightest puff of breath. "And where did you find your horse?"

"I seized it from the Ocean-Spanning Guards," said Chang, lowering her eyes.

Father took off his helmet, pulled one of the ragged green feathers from it, and replaced the helmet on his head. "Raise your eyes, Daughter."

She looked up, and Father slipped the feather into her hair. Then he placed his hands on her shoulders and said, "When we are safe, I shall have a silver ornament made in the shape of this feather. You will always wear it in your hair, so that your foolish father does not forget that there is another warrior in our house."

Chang bowed and removed the feather because she was afraid it would blow away when they were riding again. "I want to show it to Mother, when she is free."

A shadow passed over Father's face. "Do you know your mother is at Palembang?"

Chang gasped.

"Younger Sister did not know of this," said Shen. "Is Mother well?"

"I had to leave that place," said Father. "I don't know… I don't know how she is now. Come, we must find your Star Fleet. Then we shall know… Is the fleet still at Semarang?"

"I don't know, Father," replied Shen. "Yesterday it was being fitted out for battle."

"To attack Palembang?"

"Yes, Father."

"It's a trap. The pirate will lure the Admiral into narrow waters where the big ships can't turn about. He has shore batteries, and fast warships hiding in coves. Even worse, there are traitors on the fleet itself."

"But why?" cried Shen. "Why destroy it?"

"To stop the world from turning," said Father. "To make it go back to what was."

Captain Fei Lee barked a short order to his men. Within moments the little detachment was moving down the road. Now Chang was riding with Father. In the glimmer of false dawn they saw that the descending road was empty for many *li*. "Force the horses!" cried Father, and he and Chang galloped ahead of the others.

The animals tumbled down a curving incline that scalloped around the edge of a rice paddy, and suddenly the town seemed much closer. There was an empty stretch of harbor where the flagships and warships had been. Only the merchant ships remained.

Father ordered a halt. "The ships have gone." He dismounted, his arm wearily draped across his horse's neck.

"Can't we find a boat to overtake them?" asked Shen.

Father lifted his head. "You mean go into the town?" He was thinking hard. "King Tumapel's men have a standing order to kill us. But with the fleet gone, why would they care?"

"We'd be safer in the Chinese quarter," said a nervous

horseman who had seen Tumapel's soldiers kill many of his comrades.

Father nodded. "An excellent idea. And a better chance of finding a boat. Horsemen, weapons at ready and keep the main road. We are going to Pecinan."

As they briskly made their way into Pecinan, the neighborhood at the far eastern end of the city where the Chinese lived, Father explained that he and his men had been hiding in the jungle for two months.

"I was loyal to the Grandson, Little Shen. For a time I even agreed with Lord Yang's plan for a second civil war. But then I thought of what the first one had done to our family. To millions of families. How could I wish such a thing on our country again? When I learned about the preparations to destroy the Star Fleet—and believe me, they weren't hard to miss, we could see the pirate's forges burning day and night making new cannons—that's when we decided to escape."

Father at that time had nearly forty men. The pirate, he explained, had not wanted to lose men in the bloodshed that was certain if he tried to disarm them by force. "Instead he stole our horses to prevent us from fleeing. And then they brought Wife, to take away my courage."

Father fell silent, idly wrapping and unwrapping the reins around the saddle pommel. He seemed not to notice the morning throngs filling up the streets.

One of his soldiers cantered alongside. "The merchants' hall is just ahead, sir."

He pointed to a squat, mud-brick building with a palm thatch roof.

A tall, shifty-eyed man who spoke southern Chinese introduced himself as the Prefect—a high title usually given to the governor of a province, not to the head of a little band of refugees far from the homeland.

But Father humored him by bowing and offering his services as an officer of the Emperor's bodyguard. The Prefect was flattered, until he learned that Father's mission was to carry a warning to the Star Fleet. "We have no business with this Star Fleet. The Confucians have warned us—"

"The Confucians do not obey the will of Zhu Di, the new Emperor who rules over all Chinese people," said Father, calmly interrupting. "It is Zhu Di's will that we protect the Star Fleet. You'll be rewarded." At this point he removed his helmet, like a farmer removing his straw hat at the end of a hard day's work. "Prefect, I know we don't look very impressive. But fifty thousand men wear this helmet with the green feathers. As a rule they keep the feathers cleaner than this. Let us work together."

Father spoke in a soft voice that Shen had rarely heard. The old pomposity was gone, replaced by quiet will. The Prefect bowed. "So many men, however fine their green feathers, I would not wish to see in my country." He promised to summon the traders and secure a boat and men. Meanwhile, the captain and his men could rest briefly in a guesthouse adjacent to the hall.

Less than a watch later the group assembled. That was when Shen noticed a boy skulking at the back. His every gesture was familiar, including the way he swung his arms as he dashed from the room.

Shen ran out a different door and almost collided with him.

"Kun!"

They stared at each other. Kun cleared his throat.

"I was going to get my *ba*! Seems like a meeting. Seems like your *ba*'s in trouble." He spoke too quickly, with a jittery grin.

"Just like last time. And I suppose you have the same kind of 'help' in mind—running like a rabbit!"

Kun took a swing at him, but Shen grabbed his fist and twisted it behind his back. Then he tripped the larger boy and fell on top of him. Kun's arms were pinned, but he thrust with all his strength, pushing Shen away.

Shen punched him on the jaw, once, very soundly. Kun's head hit the pavement, and he stared up disbelievingly. "You got strong!" Then they both began to laugh.

Chang had followed them outside. "Touching reunion," she said.

Kun wriggled out, trying to wipe the blood from his mouth. He was blushing.

"Greetings, Fei Chang." He managed a bow. "It's… a surprise seeing you here. What's a girl doing on the Treasure Fleet?"

"And what is our servant doing in the Kingdom of Majapahit? Did you get lost on the way to the Nanjing market?"

"Ha! You sound like your mother. Ha!" But Kun's heart wasn't really in it. He hung his head, and his long hair draped each side of his neck. The two little knots of hair that denoted a servant were long gone, and Shen could see that he hated to be reminded of his former status.

"What did you do with our money?" demanded Shen.

"My *ba* has a boat. We're traders."

Old Bao came running up to them. "You bad-tempered

child! Why are you brawling in the street? You make me lose face. Who is this boy?"

And then a look of recognition spread over his wrinkled face. "Ah, Fei Shen. Such an unexpected honor."

SHEN AND CHANG WATCHED Old Bao kowtowing to Father, under the watchful eyes of the Prefect. Father's eyes were bulging, whether with rage or astonishment Shen couldn't really tell. Long ago, before the battle, Father feared that Bao might steal his money. Now he learned that it had indeed been stolen.

"Look on it as good fortune," said Bao, who was still on his knees. He was smiling, but he was talking fast. Robbing one's master was punishable by death. "What you need right now is a fast boat, and a good navigator to sail it. Ask anyone here, I'm the fastest smuggler on the coast."

The Prefect stepped between the two. "It seems to me you should accept Bao's offer, Captain Fei. The boat was bought with your money, after all. And it's quick. It will serve you well."

"Dear Father," said Chang, "even as we talk, the fleet is moving away!"

Father saw that she was right. This was no time to pursue personal quarrels. "Will your vessel accommodate five soldiers and my children, as well as its own crew?" he asked Bao.

"Without difficulty," replied Bao. "And I understand we must also take on board your friends."

Father frowned. "Friends?"

"Three men on horseback appeared here yesterday in the early morning," said the Prefect. "They claimed a boy had been kidnapped, and his sister had gone after him on a horse."

Father looked puzzled.

"It's Lan Yi," whispered Chang to Father, who raised his massive eyebrow.

"Yi! I had forgotten him. Where is he?"

"I believe he is in an eating-place, with a Mongol and a man with a mustache," replied the Prefect. "Since there is no time to lose, I will have them sent directly to the boat."

———

TIN PURSE TOOK HIS LEAVE of the group before it set out toward the harbor. "I wish you well in your battles, Captain Fei. In this I'm sure I speak for my brother merchants, whom I hope to find safely lodged in a good drinking house." And he bowed and left.

Father and his soldiers, in their ragged uniforms, walked beside their exhausted horses. Their spears stood high, fixed in leather sockets, except for one that drooped backward because the stitching on the socket was torn. One man, who had lost his sword and acquired a replacement, had lashed it to his scabbard because it didn't fit inside. Two had lost bows and quivers, while another had only the bow. That left two men who could serve as archers.

Chang, Shen, and Kun walked behind, talking. Kun was impressed to hear about Chang's lonely journey on horseback to find her brother.

"To Gunung Merapi? The volcano mountain?" He spoke breathlessly. "Fei Chang, all blessings on you. You've done a mighty thing."

Chang cocked her head forward, wrinkling her brow. "Why are you talking like a book?"

Kun blushed. "Well, it's not every day a girl gallops away after a regiment of traitors. It's … I don't know … it's like Mulan, the girl in the story who went to kill the Mongols."

"You should stop blushing so much," said Chang with a mocking smile.

This made Kun blush brighter. "Not that girls on horseback are so hard to find around here," he added snippily. "You see them in packs, like hunting dogs."

Shen's attention was distracted by Father, who was walking faster now that he had caught sight of the water. Old Bao was dancing beside him like a mange-afflicted dog looking for affection. "You see her there? The little *tanjaq* trader?"

Father did. And he saw Lan Yi waving at him from the deck.

Father began to run down the hill.

CHAPTER 31

THE TRADING BOAT SPREAD its great *tanjaq* sail almost from stem to stern. But it was also equipped with a mizzen mast, to which its crew was busily rigging a smaller second sail, covered with patches.

Father ran up the gangplank, with Old Bao and Kun scuttling after him. He and Yi collided on the deck with whoops of joy. Temur and Marmot stood to one side as the two of them grasped each other's arms at the elbow and repeated broken phrases like "dear friend" and "gods spared" in explosive bursts while bobbing their heads.

Then they did something very rare, almost improper: they hugged each other.

Shen stiffened. Father was doing altogether too much forgiving of thieving servants and Panther-badge-concealing old friends. It wasn't proper.

At that moment he caught Chang smiling at him. It was her don't-be-a-donkey smile. Then she lifted her eyebrows and nodded her head, very slightly, as if to say: "Well, at least one of us didn't lose faith in Lan Yi." As for the revelation of Lan Yi's military past, she thought she would save the pleasure of that for a moment alone with Older Brother.

As the sailors were casting off, Lan Yi took Shen aside. "Your father and I have renewed our friendship. May you and I do likewise!"

Shen frowned, his fingers idly unthreading the loose end of a rope. "Possibly. After all, you didn't get a chance to denounce me. Who knows, maybe you wouldn't have done it."

"I would have done it."

"Well, then," said Shen, his voice husky, "I just don't know."

Yi bowed. "We will speak about it again."

A LIGHT BREEZE PULLED the boat out of the harbor at the beginning of the second watch of the day, as the sun was even with the tallest roofs in the town. Lan Yi, who by now had been told of the trap into which the Treasure Fleet was sailing, was glum.

"The fleet left this morning when it was still dark," he told Fei Lee. "There are many *li* of ocean between them and us, and the wind isn't strong."

"We'll catch them," said Kun, who was standing beside Shen on the sloped cabin roof. "Whatever the wind, we're doing twice the speed of those fat boxes." He looked with satisfaction at the mizzen sail, which was standing stoutly in the breeze.

Then his expression changed to alarm. "What is that boat?" he shouted to the watch on the mast.

"*Perahu lambo!*" cried the man, and the clutch of Bao's sailors on deck began running around and throwing ropes and ballast overboard. Shen glanced at the distant boat, still just a patch of sail in the distance, before his ears were drawn to the sound of axes thudding on the deck. He watched open-mouthed as sailors chopped the anchor rope and pushed the heavy thing into the sea, where it vanished with finality.

"*Perahu lambo* is the fastest kind of local boat," said Kun as he and Shen hopped down to the deck. "This one has set a course to cross our bow."

"Can we make it back to the harbor?" asked Shen.

"We will not turn about," declared Father. "Lan Yi, what do we have?"

"Good swords for the crewmen. Throwing spears. Even a couple of bows. All from the Confucian's black ship, after he fled."

"Bao! Is that a cannon under the shroud?"

"Just a little one," said Bao, shivering in the breeze. "I keep it for when my trading partners have trouble remembering what we've agreed to. But it's no use against pirates."

"Keep it hidden for the moment."

———

BAO'S FOUR SAILORS WERE still hauling ballast out of the hold and throwing it overboard. The boat had picked up speed. But its lightness made it unsteady as it leaped over the wavetops. Father examined the crew with a squinting eye.

"Who are these men, Bao?"

"Good Chinese settlers like me," said Bao with a gap-toothed smile.

"What do they trade?"

"This and that."

"They're smugglers, aren't they?" said Father with distaste.

"Well, if you want to start peeling words apart like onions —"

"Lee," said Lan Yi. "Today we need the onions in the pot. You know me for an outlaw, and Marmot was a pirate"—he tossed his head in Marmot's direction—"until he realized he doesn't like boats."

Father stared at Marmot, who was crouching behind a windlass.

"He's looking for the safest place from arrows," added Yi. "But if we're boarded, he'll fight."

"I see," said Father doubtfully. "And the Mongol?"

"His father was of the Imperial Bodyguard."

Father hesitated, struggling with this. "Those were *pardoned* Mongols. But I suppose this one will do."

Temur had silently approached as they spoke. Now he bowed and pointed: "Look. The *perahu* is falling back."

Bao's little trading boat, being farther out to sea than the *perahu,* had stepped into a strong wind. The sailors were pulling so hard on the ropes they were almost flat on the deck. The *tanjaq* rig skipped from one wave crest to the next. Each impact sent a shudder along the hull.

The *perahu* was diminishing visibly, caught as it was behind a headland and deprived of the ocean breeze. Perhaps hoping to frighten the *tanjaq* into surrender, its captain ordered a volley. Three cannonballs flew over the water and landed very close to Bao's boat. One of them struck a floating ballast barrel, sending a dirty plume of water and smashed wood into the air.

The party on the boat stood gaping. "How can it throw an iron ball so far?" asked Yi.

"It's a new cannon," said Shen. "A stolen Imperial weapon."

"That you knew about," said Yi accusingly.

Shen hung his head.

"What shameful thing have you done, First Son?" said Fei Lee.

Luckily for Shen, the watchman shouted that the *perahu* had emerged from behind the headland and was picking up speed. With a last reproachful look at Shen, Father turned his attention to the threat. Old Bao guessed that that the pursuing vessel would reach them shortly after midday.

Shen watched as Father and Yi squatted on the deck, deep in animated conversation. He saw Father counting Bao's crewmen—there were only four—and Yi pointing at the roof of the deck cabin. The humming of the ocean breeze prevented him from hearing them, so his attention strayed to the western horizon. He eyes searched hungrily for a touch of red that would be a sail of the Treasure Fleet. But the ocean was empty.

Cat-footed Yi was suddenly beside him. "Your father and I believe that Lord Yang is on that *perahu*. I command on this vessel. You will take orders from me."

"Why isn't Father commanding?"

"They don't know he's here. If they spot him, they'll destroy us with cannons from a distance. We must make them come aboard and search. Then we can fight them properly." He looked at Shen appraisingly. "You aren't strong enough to cross swords with Brocades. For you it's the bow and arrow, shooting from concealment."

Yi moved on to other duties, and Shen stood awhile watching Kun waving about a curious piece of wood in his hand. Sharply bent and smoothly sanded, it looked like the wings of a bird in flight. "What is that thing?"

"A boomerang. In the southern islands, people use them for war."

"It looks like something you'd hang a water bucket from."

"You'll see."

Meanwhile Father was pacing about the boat, looking for places where archers and spear throwers might conceal themselves. Arriving at the bow, where Chang was facing into the ocean breeze, he examined the little cannon.

"Daughter, Lord Yang must not see you. Please go below. And the sailors need this place in order to fire the cannon."

She stood up and made a slight shoulder bow. "I will hide myself in the cabin, as Father requests."

But as she moved away, Father touched her lightly on the shoulder. "I have not forgotten your courage, Daughter. But one of us must stay alive, to tell Mother what happened here."

She flinched as she understood his meaning. It was possible that Father and Lan Yi might lose this fight. "May the gods strengthen your arm," she said quietly. "And whatever happens today, I shall always wear the silver feather."

She bowed and went below.

"Will we see Mother alive?" asked Shen, stepping forward. "Or will they kill the prisoners when the Star Fleet attacks?"

"It won't be that simple," said Father, considering. "Palembang is far from the ocean, where the battle will be fought. If we win, the garrison in the city may flee. If we are lucky, they will forget their captives."

"If we are unlucky?" said Shen.

"It is best not to think of bad luck," said Father.

───────

BY NOW THE *PERAHU* WAS leaping toward them. Lan Yi had issued Bao's four sailors army sabers and spears, which seemed to delight them. They in turn produced some rough armor of plaited straw and leather, which they called the "smuggler's friend." The first mate, who was also the gunner, took his place near the cannon.

It was Father who handed Shen a bow and a quiver of arrows. "You and I are two bowmen. Our third will be Temur. Since Lord Yang's boat fired three balls at once, we guess they have three cannonneers." He gave Shen a searching look. "My Son, don't hesitate. All three must fall before they fire a single round."

"I've never killed anyone."

"And it may be that you never will again. But today you must intend your enemy's death."

The *perahu* hull was colored a light turquoise. As it drew closer Shen made out featherlike white and red ornaments painted just below the gunwales. The boat's masts were daubed in alternating bands of dark blue and white, and its sails were as yellow as spring flowers. It was like a forest bird, thought Shen. Snared and put to base use.

Shen saw Old Bao take up a loud hailer. But before the old

man could speak, a powerful yet oddly cheerful voice rolled across the waves.

"Greetings to the *tanjaq* trader!" said the voice, booming through its own loud hailer.

"Greetings to the Semarang *perahu*," cried Bao. "What is your business?"

"We wish to come aboard."

His bow and quiver slung over his shoulder, Shen was holding the ladder poles that he, Father, and Temur would use to leap up on low side of the cabin roof. Once there, the slope of the roof would be just steep enough to protect them from enemy fire.

Now Father joined him behind the deckhouse, speaking in hushed tones. "It's the Confucian—with his face bandaged, just as you said!" Shen couldn't tell whether Father was impressed. "He has fifteen men on deck," continued Father. "Some are bowmen, so fire your arrow quickly and then flatten yourself on the roof slope. Be careful, too, when you expose yourself to make your next shot. Pull quickly and duck down. Don't wait to see where the arrow goes."

They heard the thump of grappling irons landing on Bao's deck, followed by the voice of Lord Yang.

"Your sailors are armored. Do you intend to fight?"

"State your reason for boarding," cried Bao.

"We are looking for deserters from the Chinese fleet. You will not be harmed."

Lan Yi could see that the Brocades were about to board. Now was the moment to strike. He signaled, and the five concealed

Feather soldiers hurled spears at the legs of the Brocades, which were protected only by felt padding. Two of them went down, which drew the attention of the bowmen behind them. A volley of arrows raked the deck of Bao's boat, doing little harm.

"Archers!" cried Yi, taking advantage of the few moments the Brocade bowmen would need to set new arrows. Father, Shen, and Temur sprang onto the cabin roof, loosing arrows rapidly. Two of the *perahu*'s cannoneers went down immediately, but Shen's arrow was wide of the third. The man grabbed the red-hot wire used to ignite the gunpowder and tried to plunge it into the firing hole. Shen's second arrow took him down.

Shen flattened himself on the cabin roof as a ragged volley of Brocade arrows sang over his head. Then he leaped up for a quick look. The dead eyes of his victim were peering heavenward. He also saw a second Brocade push the body aside and make for the cannon.

Father's arrow raced over Shen's head and buried itself in the Brocade's shoulder, disabling him. "Get down!" cried Father as a new volley of Brocade arrows came at them. He and Shen were now face to face, their hair tangled in the grit of the cabin roof. Father glared proudly at him. "Well done. But now—keep shooting."

Shen struggled to raise his bow and aim again. He felt the bitter taste of stomach acid rising in his throat, and swallowed repeatedly until it was forced back down. He unleashed an arrow, then another

Where the boats were closest, Shen saw a Brocade take a running leap across the gap. A boomerang collided with his head and he fell like a stone into the ocean. But a return volley of spears and arrows killed a sailor on Bao's boat and one of Father's soldiers.

Under cover of this heavy fire, several Brocades threw wide hooked boards across the gap, locking them to the gunwale of Bao's boat. Others, wielding swords, raced across the newly made bridge. Father's four remaining men, and two brave sailors, tried to repel them.

Shen saw Yi signal the men who were concealing the cannon. They jumped aside, the first mate touched the firing pin, and the iron ball raced toward the base of the *perahu*'s mainmast.

For a long moment Lord Yang stared at the mast, as if he were willing it to stand erect. Then, very slowly, it toppled backward, dipping its tip and much of the sail into the ocean. Only the ropes kept it connected to the *perahu* at all.

But part of the falling sail had hooked onto Bao's boat and dragged the two vessels together again. The Brocades came leaping across in numbers. Marmot scythed at them with a short sword while Yi bore down on one and plunged his sword behind the breastplate and between the man's ribs. Others fell to the remaining Feather soldiers, who crouched low and stabbed upward as the Brocades leaped over the boat's railing.

Temur, kneeling on the cabin roof, was able to force several Brocade archers to take cover. Father concentrated his fire on the soldiers trying to get to the cannons.

But Shen could not go on. His arms shook from exhaustion as he tried to pull each arrow into tension. One of his shots went wild, spiraling out over the blue water.

As tears of frustration filled his eyes, he heard Yi cry, "Turn us about!" Looking down, Shen saw Bao straining at the tiller. Kun and Chang—who had come back on deck when she saw how desperate things were—had grabbed a ladder pole that had fallen on the deck and were trying to push the boats apart.

Remembering all the days he had spent skylarking in the high sails of the *China Harmony*, Shen saw at once that the big sail had to be trimmed before Bao's boat could turn about. But two of his sailors were down, and the other two were fighting.

Abandoning his bow, Shen leaped from the roof to a halyard rope and from there slid to the deck, where he loosened the halyard on its windlass. Then he ran to the windlass on the other side of the mast, which he tried to tighten in order to pull the sail about. But his whole strength could not budge the windlass handle. To make things worse, one of the Brocade archers saw what he was doing: the arrow that thudded into the deck at his feet contained a good deal of disapproval.

Kun materialized beside Shen and threw his weight into the task. In tiny increments they forced the flapping sail past the midpoint and a few degrees into the wind, so that it swung around at last and bellied out in the other direction. The prow of Bao's boat separated from the *perahu*. A Brocade, caught unawares, went into the sea, his arms windmilling uselessly.

And then there was a general silence, as the boats swung about so that they were end to end, separated by only a short stretch of water. The *perahu*'s three fixed cannons were now pointed uselessly out to sea, and with one of its masts in the water it could not turn about to menace the *tanjaq* again.

But the *tanjaq* was drifting, and it lacked sailors. Kun had to run back to help his father hold the rudder while Lan Yi had staggered under cover, his chest and left arm bleeding severely. Father and Temur had been forced by arrow fire to drop back to the deck and return fire from behind the deckhouse. The first mate had reloaded the cannon, but could not get a clear shot at the *perahu*.

Lord Yang was the first to find his voice. "An indecisive engagement, Captain Fei!" came the familiar lilting, faintly mocking tones.

Before stepping out to face the Confucian, Father first looked over his shoulder to the far west. This time the ocean was not empty. Several faint smudges of red could be seen on the horizon. "I do not think you can stop us from joining the Treasure Fleet," replied Father as he stepped out in plain view on the deck.

But Lord Yang held aloft a small copper pigeon cage. "The bird's home is the citadel at Palembang," he said, stretching each syllable to be sure that his voice was audible. "The message is attached."

"He means Mother, doesn't he?" said Shen, coming to Father's side. Fei Lee nodded. Chang stood to one side, a hand over her mouth.

Kun's face was intensely tight and thoughtful as he pieced it together. "Let me see if I understand this. The bird is carrying a message to kill your mother?" Kun's voice carried a trace of admiration at the sheer malice of the trick.

"It's terribly hot out here," continued Lord Yang. "Let's lash the boats together, lay down your weapons, and I'll send my doctor to tend your wounded. You can't ask for better. I'll be neglecting my own men."

Father touched Temur's bow and pointed at the birdcage. Temur shook his head. "It is impossible."

"I have a better idea," said Kun, leaning down to rummage in a bag at his feet. "Let's put the boat between him and Palembang. Where the bird has to fly."

He extracted one of the wing-shaped wooden objects and waved it so his father could see. Bao nodded and leaned on the tiller. The *tanjaq* began to move off in the direction of the Treasure Fleet.

"You can't mean it, Fei Lee!" screamed Lord Yang, for once losing his composure. "You will kill her."

"I think I can do it!" said Kun.

Father looked blankly at him.

"Please, Captain Fei, let me try!" said Kun, balancing a small boomerang on the tips of his fingers.

"Is it possible?" said Father, studying the wooden arc. It shivered in the wind, as if anxious for flight.

Kun licked his lips. "I've seen it done! I've done it! But ... you know, I can't promise."

"Then do it."

Lord Yang had opened the gate of the cage, and the pigeon had hopped onto the projecting peg. It was crouching to launch itself.

And as the gray-feathered ball leaped into the air, Kun arced in a slow pirouette like a dancer. His boomerang rose in a lazy curve, there was a quiet explosion of feathers, and then there was nothing but sunlight.

CHAPTER 32

KUN HAD BEEN WRONG about one thing. The galleons of the Treasure Fleet moved faster than he thought, and it was not until late afternoon of the following day that their boat was hailed by an outlying warship. They had sailed several hundred *li*, and the shoreline of the island of Pulau Bangka, which guarded the eastern coast of Sumatra and sheltered the city of Palembang, was already visible in the distance.

For Kun the delay was entirely good news, since it gave him many hours to spin tales for Chang in the little quiet spot on the *tanjaq* deck behind the deckhouse. More than once he told the story of how he and his father had been blown off course the previous winter. They had been forced to lay over on the Great Southern Island.

Old Bao had thought at first they were wasting their time. The black-skinned men seemed to have nothing to trade but boomerangs, bird feathers, and long, hollow tubes that made a booming sound to no particular effect.

Then one day they produced some perfect opals, and a small quantity of raw gold. After that there was no question of leaving. Kun had spent "the dullest months of my life" practicing the boomerang with boys his age. Meanwhile his father produced cases of *pisang*, an abominable Javanese liquor made from green bananas and cinnamon. The local men produced more opals.

"I swear it was the *pisang* that taught me the principle of the thing," enthused Kun, who grew expansive due to Chang's wide-eyed attention. "I drank just enough to be extremely relaxed. And that's when I noticed that the boomerang hits the bird because it flies like a bird. What I mean is, if you throw at the right moment it rises on the same air current."

"Well, you're the man who knows about hot air," interjected Shen, who had approached without being noticed.

Kun waggled his finger in disapproval. "This is a private conversation with your sister."

"So leave," laughed Chang, waving Shen away. "I'll call you when I need rescuing."

"I wouldn't do anything improper!" huffed Kun.

"I mean from boredom," replied Chang.

It was a strange interlude, thought Shen. When Lord Yang's deadly carrier pigeon had been struck down, a feeling of relief and even elation settled over the company on Bao's boat. The wind had borne them steadily away from the broken-masted *perahu*, leaving the Confucian and his soldiers staring at them across the glassy sea as if they were a mirage.

As their little boat drew alongside the *China Harmony*, Father decreed that Chang would remain with Old Bao and Kun. The servant-turned-smuggler would set his own course toward the city of Palembang with a particular mission to gather intelligence about Mother. Father and Shen, meanwhile, would go aboard the flagship and warn the Star Fleet of the trap that had been laid for it in the Strait of Pulau Bangka.

Chang was still nervous about the treason charge outstanding against her brother, but Father assured her that it would be set aside. After all, weren't he and Shen about to save the entire fleet from destruction?

When it came time to part, Shen could tell from the desperate way Chang embraced him that she wasn't convinced. "We'll meet again," he said reassuringly.

"Perhaps so." She forced a smile. "When that happens, you must tell me everything."

———

SHEN THOUGHT THAT WOULD be easy, starting with his pardon. But his return to the Admiral wasn't as simple as he had hoped. Zheng He greeted Shen in such a black mood, and thundered against his insolence and treachery with such force, that Captain Zhou couldn't get a word in edgewise about the trap they were sailing into. It wasn't until the old captain had shouted that he could count the trees on the shore of Pulau Bangka that the Admiral roused himself to the danger. Fortunately the strait was still just wide enough for the fleet to turn about and return to the open sea. Shen imagined the pirate's lookouts on the headland plunging back into the jungle to carry the news to Chen Zuyi that the trap had failed.

But this merely postponed the battle—and Shen's fate, which the Admiral decreed would be settled after Chen Zuyi was dealt with.

For Shen, time crawled like a tortoise in a mud swale. First there was the slow overnight sea voyage the long way around the island of Pulau Bangka, with the pirates presumably beating back down the strait to meet them on the open ocean near Palembang. The tedium was broken by a terrifying interview with Blinky, who had got it into his head that Shen should stand trial. Father came to him and assured him that no such thing would happen.

———

BUT SHEN WAS CONFINED to quarters, and it was through the narrow porthole that he saw what he could of the fight that would be remembered as The Battle of Palembang. He felt the timbers shudder when the massed cannons on the *China Harmony*'s deck fired a broadside. As steel bolts shot from crossbows hissed past his porthole on their way to tear the sails, and the bodies, of Chen Zuyi's sailors, he thought of Father, who had volunteered to fight as a crossbowman.

Down below—because the *China Harmony*'s deck stood so far above the warships of both armies—the battle looked like a child's game. But Shen no longer had a child's eyes. When one of Chen Zuyi's pirate ships lobbed a cannonball from an impossible distance, and it crushed the ribs of an Imperial ship close by, Shen knew that there was blood on his hands. He had helped the pirate to build that weapon.

Mercifully, a pall of smoke began to cover Shen's narrow field of vision. The last thing he saw clearly was one of the fleet's savage little oar-boats being rowed at high speed into a group of Zuyi's vessels, armed with its single peculiar weapon: a fire-throwing cannon powered by the liquid naphtha that could be found in tar pits. It belched flame through the mouth of a bronze dragon, causing the enemy's sails to burst into flames. They reminded Shen of poppies blossoming on a hillside.

He replaced the wooden hatch of the porthole to keep the smoke out. And waited. A long time later his door was unbolted. It was Father, unharmed.

"Come, First Son. It is time we found your mother."

SHEN'S FOOT SLIPPED ON the blood-streaked deck. He saw with a shock that part of the *China Harmony*'s castle had been burnt. But the other flagships stood proud. As the red and blue pennants atop their nine masts snapped gaily in the wind, Shen realized that the civil war had been averted. Lord Yang's great plan was broken.

Father talked their way aboard one of the oar-boats that would pursue the pirate's shattered fleet upriver to Palembang. It made good time on the wide and placid green water. The only obstacle was a massive iron chain that came into view around a bend in the river. It was suspended from one riverbank to the other. "The ancient kings of this place built it to keep pirates out," explained Father.

The pirates themselves had abandoned their boats and fled into the jungle. The young officer in charge of the oar-boats sent engineers to break the chain. As their own boat slid up against a small sandy clearing on the shore, Father shook his head. "Heaven only knows how long wc will wait here."

Shen noticed people looking out from the tangled mangroves of the riverbank. They seemed to be standing on reeds floating in the water, but then he saw that there were heavy planks underneath and a little house built atop. It was a raft.

A boy about Shen's age ventured into the riverbank clearing. Shen left the boat and walked over to him, smiling and making polite shoulder bows. The boy raised one eyebrow skeptically. "Captives," he said distinctly in Chinese and pointed toward the forest.

At the sound of that word, Father came running up the riverbank, shouting at the boy in broken Malayalam. Then he grabbed Shen's hand and pulled him toward a barely visible trail. "The boy says the pirate soldiers fled Palembang even before the sea battle ended. The local people have freed Chen Zuyi's captives. A few are in the bush. Others are in raft-houses farther up the river."

And with no further thought they were running down a faint jungle trail, tripping over vines while Father darted glances at the branches above ("Snakes," he muttered when Shen asked) and the local boy pulled steadily ahead.

Finally the boy stopped by a small clump of rafts gathered in a tributary stream just out of sight of the big river. Squatting on the deck of one of them, noisily engaged in a game that involved scooping handfuls of nuts from one wooden cup and throwing them into another, was a group of locals and Chinese. The most exuberant nut-thrower, and easily the noisiest in predicting her imminent victory, was Mother.

At the sight of Father she stood up, frowning as if looking at an uninvited guest, but her eyes bright and inquiring. She gathered around herself the frayed and torn remnants of a brown cotton gown. "So! Husband! You return with an army of one?"

Shen bowed. "Is my estimable mother well?"

"Ha?" And then, through the dirt and the mustache and the extra three years and the shaggy hair that had not been knotted properly for many days, she recognized her son. And she leaped off the boat and grasped his hands while tears rolled down her bony cheeks. Learning that Younger Sister was nearby, rather than far away in China, made her almost frantic with happiness.

Father, however, was subjected to something resembling a police inquisition. What had he done since she had driven him out? Got to Majapahit, good, good. Driven into the mountains by Tumapel's army, very bad. "Fat little Tumapel, he wobbles when he walks. How can his soldiers frighten you?"

"His soldiers are not fat, Ting," said Father, making a great show of protesting while his eyes danced. "But they are not as skinny as you either."

"Well," she replied, bending her head forward so her eyes looked up at him, "perhaps I will eat when I see this wonderful fleet you say you have summoned." And then, "The Grandson! They still have him."

———

PALEMBANG WAS AN OLD city surrounded by a low wall of red bricks. Its massive wooden gate was thrown open, and the defenders had fled. The Fei family walked unopposed through streets of empty houses with woven-bamboo walls. The houses stood on wooden posts that had been driven into the swampy ground, and their steep thatched roofs were adorned with a wooden god carved in the shape of a bull.

Here and there a few tribespeople who lived in the town were still hoisting bedrolls and baskets on their backs, anxious for the jungle where they would find neither pirates nor foreigners with giant ships. They barely glanced at Father and Mother and Shen making their way to the Royal Pavilion.

There Shen was surprised to find two Confucian officials, each dressed in a full formal black gown. They bowed to Father and one, named Heng, addressed him by name. The Grandson's attendants had fled when news of the pirate's defeat arrived. Heng and his companion had stayed to protect him from the local people.

"We beg you, Honorable Fei Lee. Do nothing to dishonor the Grandson Hui Di. He never forgot that you brought us here safely. We do not know why you abandoned us. The Grandson always asked for you."

Shen took Mother aside. "Why do they speak of the Grandson as if he were dead?"

Mother looked searchingly at the red brick wall of the pavilion, as if she could see through it. She silenced Shen by brushing his lips with her fingertips. "These two good men are protecting his ghost."

HENG PUSHED OPEN a wooden door that had been polished to a golden red color like cinnamon.

Though gloomy and ill-lit, the room was richly appointed with woven rattan settees and thick rugs. But its only window was closed with a wooden shutter. Little dusty shafts of light came from ventilation holes punched in the bricks near the ceiling.

"I can't see him," said Mother from the doorway. She was not inclined to come into the room.

"He is here," replied Father, who had walked several paces ahead. Shen followed. In front of them on the floor was a dark heap of clothing. Father squatted down and pulled aside a thick flap of yellow silk. Beneath it was Hui Di, lying in a spreading pool of blood. In his hand was a short dagger with an odd curling blade.

Farther off in a corner were two female attendants, also dead.

Shen had never seen Hui Di. Now, looking on him, he was moved by how young he was. Though in his mid-twenties, he had the unlined face of a boy who had wished to be left alone with his books of poetry and philosophy. Whatever the laws of inheritance, Shen was sure that this unwilling teenager should not have been made to rule. Had the Grandson finally understood that Chen Zuyi and Lord Yang were using him? Was this his answer?

But then Shen's pulse began to race. He remembered that the ghost of a suicide stayed close by, filled with rage against the living. He saw that only Father had entered with him.

"Take my arm," said Father, clutching Shen so he could not move.

Then Father began to recite, very quickly, a prayer that he was making up as he went along. You will not be abandoned, he told the ghost. You must not pass into the stone and wood of this room, for the body to which you belong will be carried to China and properly buried. You will be fed, sustained, and honored by your family.

He sympathized with the ghost's pain and anger, and begged it to do no evil to any living creature. Then he hastily guided Shen from the room.

PRIESTS CAME TO PERFORM the needed rituals and bring the Grandson back to the *China Harmony*.

About midmorning the following day, Bao's little *tanjaq*, with Chang aboard, pulled alongside the flagship. It had spent two nights at a tiny village on Pulau Bangka, which the old trader knew. He wouldn't move until a runner came overland to say that the great sea battle was finished. He apologized for failing to reach Mother before they did.

Chang was shocked at Mother's thinness, but had to admit that she looked regal in a tangerine-colored silk gown with two tiny red chrysanthemums embroidered just above the hem. "Do you like it, Daughter? One of the flower girls gave it to me as a present. Apparently this is the only kind of women's clothing on the ship."

Chang smiled. "I see you are better already."

Mother became thoughtful. "I am told it is nearly three years, Daughter, since we sat together in the village of Xinfeng. For long periods I was not permitted to know the day or the month. But you are grown up now." She sighed with a little laugh. "Soon we shall have to seek a husband for you."

Somebody at the doorway cleared his throat.

"Kun?" said Father. "It's too soon for you to come here."

"Is it Kun?" said Mother. "Come to me, Boy Kun. Kneel down."

Kun readily played along with Mother's belief that he was still their servant. He kowtowed and begged forgiveness for the day when his father's rough men had threatened her. "Mistress Fei, I can't find an excuse for the terrible thing my *ba* did to you. But we—um—our boat, I mean your boat—um—I'm sure Captain Fei will explain everything. I just wanted to say that we took especially good care of your daughter. I wouldn't see her hurt for anything."

"Ah!" said Mother, the light of understanding dawning in her eyes. "Well, we shall talk about that later." Then she recalled something. "I seem to remember my daughter struck you a good blow with a pump handle. You can take that as a mark of her character."

"Mother!" said Chang.

———

MOTHER RESTED IN THE afternoon. Then, as evening drew on, Father and Shen led her and Chang to the deck garden.

Attendants were pulling back gauzy cotton cloths that protected the plants from the tropical sun. A hush had fallen over the ship. Chang stood looking out to sea, while Mother sat on a bench and leaned down to pick a flower. Father intervened and picked it for her.

It was only now Shen was able to accept that his family was reunited. And yet there was a mystery to it, because none of them were as they had been before. Especially Mother and Father. She had put a knife to her throat and humbled him.

And yet—Father plucked a stalk of rhubarb and began to tickle Mother's neck. She laughed foolishly and broke off one of her own. They dueled with rhubarb, and then she stood up and ran, and he ran after her. For a few moments they were like puppies, until Mother tired. Then Father sat against a mast, and she sprawled across him like a doll.

Lan Yi had approached like a ghost, leaning on a walking stick.

"Are your wounds better, Honorable Yi?" asked Chang.

"Very much," replied Yi. "But my message is for your brother. My dear Fei Shen, I have been asked to bring you to the quarters of the Ocean Lord."

Shen's heart sank. Father, noticing the solemn mood around the two, came over. "What is this about? They have not decided to —"

"I do not know," said Yi. And he took Shen by the arm to lead him away.

He left Shen at the door to the familiar chamber, which had survived the fire that had consumed much of the castle. Only Interpreter Ma was inside. The sharp odor of smoke and blackened wood was still in the air.

Ma rose and bowed, strangely solemn. "Lord Zheng wishes you to know that you acted correctly in returning to us. Moreover he honors your father, who has averted a catastrophe." Ma explained that the navigators and captains who had advocated the short route through the strait had been severely questioned. It was found that several were in the pay of Lord Yang.

Then Ma was silent. Shen knew that his fate rested on a delicate balance. He felt he should not say anything. After a time, the interpreter continued.

"You have seen that Lord Zheng is not here. Since you have betrayed him, he does not wish to be in your presence." Shen marked the beating of his heart in the silence that followed. "However, in his graciousness, the Ocean Lord has pardoned your crime."

Shen sank to his knees with relief. "I thank him, I —"

"It is not yet time for you to speak," said Interpreter Ma uncomfortably. He clearly did not enjoy the role of judge and sentence-giver that had been thrust on him. "You may no longer serve the Admiral."

"But why?" cried Shen.

Ma bowed his head and cleared his throat. He avoided Shen's eyes. "Dear Fei Shen, you deceived him. You have shamed him in front of his officers. Even worse, some will say the Ocean Lord was shamed by a boy, for you barely stand on the threshold of manhood. It is possible you will never be admitted to this chamber again."

Ma looked thoughtfully out to sea through the room's generous porthole.

"Of course," he continued, "when you came to the fleet, all you desired was safety for yourself and your sister. Then Lord Yang offered your mother's freedom as well. Having achieved these things, you will surely wish to return to Nanjing with your family."

Shen heard the dismissal behind these soft words. He was to leave the fleet.

"I thank you for your counsel," said Shen. "I shall think about what you have said."

He was permitted to spend some time alone in the little room that had once been his. Then he went below to visit Lan Yi. The circus master had asked for him.

From his chair he leaned forward and clenched Shen's arm in an iron grip. Then he shook the arm playfully. "Now it's your turn. Poor Fei Shen! They will send you home without face. But at least you go home! Lord Yang's agents will go home without their heads."

"Master Yi, you, too, were once condemned. Lord Yang told me you betrayed the Emperor."

Yi's eyes flashed. "There is treason and treason, Fei Shen. I commanded soldiers sent to carry New Year's presents to the eldest son of Taizu, the first Emperor. I let them visit a tavern when it was too cold to stay outside. They got liqored up by a gang of thieves who fell on us later in the night. What was the point of getting them killed when they weren't fit to fight? So I surrendered immediately. Handed over the presents in exchange for our lives. I never thought much of fighting over boxes of silver plates. He leaned back in his chair. "Then we continued to our destination, Yan's court. His father had dressed us in Yan's court livery, to do him honor. So we arrived empty-handed, every one of us in green trousers."

When Shen stopped laughing, he said, "And now that you're a pardoned man, will you get some new pants?"

"I might."

"And give up the —"

"Betel nut? Too late for that. I am as I am." He laughed a wheezing laugh. "But lucky you. You shall go home with your family. Be grateful. Burn incense."

Shen nodded. But when he climbed back to the main deck, he realized that he did not wish to go home.

He looked up at the observation deck, where Captain Zhou gave orders to the midshipmen. He saw the polished gong that communicated with the other ships. The immensity of the ocean flooded into him, with its restless swells and hidden dragons. He tried to think of being home again, in a little street in Nanjing, but nothing came into his mind. He was only there, on the ocean. Beneath the "blue transparency."

These were words that the Admiral had dictated one day for him to write down. Interpreter Ma had copied them into the ship's log.

> We have beheld in the ocean huge waves like mountains rising sky-high, and we have set eyes on barbarian regions far away, hidden in a blue transparency of light vapors. Our sails, loftily unfurled like clouds, day and night continued their course, rapid like that of a star.

The words had caught in his mind. The Admiral wasn't usually a man for poetry, and he had hated the ocean. But now he was harnessed to it. He was caught in the stars. And so, thought Shen, am I.

He peered past the bow of the *China Harmony* to see if the mountains of Majapahit were visible. There was a faint purple trace on the horizon but too distant to be certain. Never mind. He would see Semarang soon enough.

"Hello, Brother."

Chang was beside him.

"Are Mother and Father well?" asked Shen.

"Mother was tired. Father put her back to bed. They are well." Several moments passed. Then: "We'll be together on the vessel returning to China. This is a great blessing, Brother. Please don't be sad."

"I can't help it."

"We can perhaps come back this way in two years' time. That is when I will be permitted to join the household of Father Bao. If Kun is anywhere to be found, as Mother puts it!"

Shen stuck out his lips like a seahorse. "You're not obliged to accept his suit, you know. It wasn't arranged by the parents. It seems you two came up with it yourselves. What if back in Nanjing hordes of rich young men hurl themselves at you? Like June bugs."

"And then fall dead at my feet, you mean?"

They both gazed at the horizon, uncertain what to say next.

"You know," said Chang, "travelling isn't as special as you believe. Think about it. You travel through somebody else's country, and you sleep at an inn, and you go away without leaving a trace. Nobody will remember you. It's as if you were never there."

He shrugged, so she tried a different tack.

"Suppose you had gone with the Star Fleet. Wouldn't you be afraid of sailing off the edge?"

"There isn't one. It's round, like Interpreter Ma says."

"That's silly."

"I'm not so sure. Have you noticed when we're approaching land, how you see the tops of the trees before you see the bottoms? It's because the ocean is curved."

"Water is curved? How can that be?"

"I'll prove it. One day I'll captain a ship that will sail away to the west and come back from the east."

Something in Shen's voice alerted Chang. She let a long silence stretch out between them. Then she said, "If you really mean to do that, then you mustn't come home. You must stay here." She tapped her foot on the deck.

He shrugged.

"Don't be so beaten," she said. "It's true you can't see Lord Zheng again. But scribes don't turn into ship's captains anyway. Sailors do. Go to Captain Zhou."

"And tell him what?"

"That you want to scrub decks. You want to apprentice. There are three hundred ships, Older Brother! I'm sure one of them will be sailing far enough from this one!"

IT TOOK SOME TIME to convince Father and Mother. If Shen wasn't coming home to take care of them when they got old, they might have to keep Chang with them. Did he want his sister to be an old maid?

"And you all the while scattering children around the edge of the ocean that I will never see!" moaned Mother.

Shen maintained a filial silence while he processed this bizarre thought. He also knew he would do as they commanded.

But he was secretly certain of success. He remembered that Father never made little Chang come down when she climbed into the rafters of their old house. No more would he stop her from marrying Kun. Or himself from voyaging.

Finally, though, there was the Panther badge. This was most difficult for Father. He reminded Shen that the badge was his to inherit, if he accepted a military career. If not, it would leave the family forever. He spoke of Shen's bravery when Lord Yang attacked them. Then he waited.

Shen was careful and respectful. But all the while he remembered the dead eyes of the cannoneer he had killed.

"I can't be a soldier, Father."

"Then what can you do in life?

Shen pointed at the command deck looming above them. "Up there, Father. That's where I want to be."

———

WHEN THE TREASURE FLEET arrived in Semarang, it was learned that Lord Yang had fled. Protected by his Brocade regiment, he was beyond the reach of Bhre Tumapel's little army.

The Confucians and the Brocades had boarded their three ships and sailed back to China. The mast of the black ship, which Lan Yi had thoughtfully sunk after stripping it of weapons, would be a landmark in Semarang harbor for years to come.

"We will hear from him again, I'm afraid," said Yi.

That afternoon Shen and his family gathered respectfully in Captain Zhou's cabin. Their mission was to obtain an appointment for Shen on a different ship. Father reminded Zhou that both of them had once supported the Grandson. He pointed to Grandfather Hu, at one time a foreigner and an enemy. Now he was the fleet's chief engineer.

"Many have changed one lord for another. Many have lost face and gained it again. If it were not so, how could the world continue?" said Father. "My son is not an assassin. He is a child who acted foolishly. Had I been there, I could have prevented it. Let him not suffer for my absence." The captain started pulling at one of his muttonchops. He didn't look comfortable.

"I shall have to speak to the Admiral. May I say to him that Fei Shen is willing to accept the lowest job in the meanest ship? May I say that he will labor there without knowing when his labor will end? And should Lord Zheng refuse, will you accept the shame of his refusal?"

Shen held his breath. Finally, as one, Mother and Father inclined their heads.

Captain Zhou inhaled noisily through his nostrils. "Well, then."

THREE DAYS LATER FATHER, Mother, and Chang took passage on one of the merchant ships. Its captain had done well in Majapahit and wanted to return home. With them was Temur, who together with Marmot had been pardoned by the Admiral. Temur had decided to live in northern China, where Mongols were now permitted to marry. Father said that he would get Temur a post with a regiment in Beijing.

Shen's farewell with Mother was sad because they had been together so little. But for Chang he had a gift that made him gleeful. In a merchant's stall he had seen a huge heap of perfect copies of her cloud blouse. It seemed the lady from Mount Merapi had sold the design to a batik house. Women all over Semarang were wearing it. Handing the copy to her, he mimicked her voice and posture. "'Nobody remembers a traveler! It'll be like I was never here!'"

He stood on the wharf as the heavy merchant ship made its way out of the harbor. His heart was pushing against his ribs, but beside the sadness there was also a wild exhilaration. Even as he gazed at the departing ship, his eyes kept straying to the west.

"Eyes front and center, Fei Shen," said the Admiral's deep voice, just behind him. "You won't see them again for two years."

"My Lord Zheng," said Shen, dropping to his knees.

"Don't do that just now. It attracts attention. And I don't wish to be seen speaking with you."

As far as Shen could tell, there did not seem to be anyone else on the wharf, except for two of the Admiral's personal assistants. These were dutifully looking the other way, so as to be able to say that the encounter never took place.

"I understand you will be cleaning up chicken guts and lambs' blood on the provisions ship. An excellent position."

"Far better than I deserve, my Lord."

"The kitchen master will flog you for sneezing."

"I shall request extra flogging."

"Don't be witty. It is a great failing. Work hard, and in a year's time you may be invited aboard the *China Harmony*. To be tested in celestial navigation."

"I know nothing of it."

"You will find that the provisions ship has surprising resources. Now, you can still see the boat that carries your parents. Follow it with your eyes until you can see it no longer."

This is what Shen did. The evening shadows had grown long by the time the final dot of white sails had vanished into the great blue transparency.

He blinked and rubbed his eyes.

And then he looked out to the western horizon, and the whole wide world, and the setting sun lit him like a torch.

ACKNOWLEDGMENTS

I WOULD LIKE TO thank the scholars who have translated the stories and explored the daily life of early Ming China. Without them, this kind of novel could not be written.

And I am particularly grateful to my editors, Barbara Pulling and Heather Sangster, for their patience through many drafts of a first novel.

AUTHOR BIOGRAPHY

RAY CONLOGUE is an award-winning arts journalist, theater critic, and magazine writer who has also worked as a political speechwriter. He has written a nonfiction book for adults and worked as a literary translator. This is his first novel for young readers. He lives in Toronto.